Harry C. Thomson

Rhodesia

and its government

Harry C. Thomson

Rhodesia
and its government

ISBN/EAN: 9783337378912

Printed in Europe, USA, Canada, Australia, Japan

Cover: Foto ©Andreas Hilbeck / pixelio.de

More available books at **www.hansebooks.com**

RHODESIA

AND ITS GOVERNMENT

BY

H. C. THOMSON

AUTHOR OF "THE CHITRAL CAMPAIGN," AND OF
"THE OUTGOING TURK."

"Restrain those engrossings of the rich that are as bad almost as monopolies."— UTOPIA.

"Reverence for the rights and freedom of every nation is what we should earnestly cherish if we would be true defenders of our own."—FREDERICK DENISON MAURICE.

WITH ILLUSTRATIONS

LONDON

SMITH, ELDER, & CO., 15 WATERLOO PLACE

1898

Printed by BALLANTYNE, HANSON & Co.
At the Ballantyne Press

PREFACE

During my first few months in South Africa I was tossed about in a kind of mental whirlpool. Every man seemed to me to be in the right until I came to listen to the next. But gradually certain principles and ideas began to crystallise into definite shape; and these I have tried to make clear, not merely from what I myself heard and saw, but from the declarations made from time to time by various South African politicians and writers.

I have to thank most gratefully the many friends, both English and Dutch, who have helped me in my work. What there may be of value in it is due to my having made myself in great measure the mouthpiece of their strongly felt and conflicting opinions.

H. C. T.

September 1898.

CONTENTS

CHAPTER V

CHAPTER VI

CHAPTER VII

CHAPTER VIII

CHAPTER IX

CHAPTER X

CHAPTER XI

CHAPTER XII

CHAPTER XIII

CHAPTER XIV

CHAPTER XV

CHAPTER XVI

CHAPTER XVII

CHAPTER XVIII

CHAPTER XIX

CHAPTER XX

CHAPTER XXI

CHAPTER XXII

CHAPTER XXIII

CHAPTER XXIV

LIST OF ILLUSTRATIONS

MASHONALAND & MATABELELAND.
MASHONALAND
MATABELELAND
GERMAN
SOUTH WEST
AFRICA
Tropic of Capricorn
BECHUANA
LAND
(Protectorate)
Bechuana Land
(To Cape Colony)
Griqualand
West
BRITISH CENTRAL AFRICA
RHODESIA
PORTUGUESE
TRANSVAL
ORANGE FREE STATE
CAPE COLONY
GERMAN EAST AFRICA
Lake Tanganyika
Lake Nyasa
KHAMAS
COUNTRY
SOUTH AFRICA.
Boundary of British Territory shown thus
Railways
Longitude East 30° of Greenwich

RHODESIA

AND ITS GOVERNMENT

INTRODUCTION

An impression seems to prevail both in England and in South Africa that the climate of Mashonaland is peculiarly unhealthy: I cannot say I found it so, and I put it to a sufficiently severe test. I wished to see as much of the country as I could, so instead of going by coach, I walked up last autumn from Massi-Kessi to Salisbury, straying off the road to visit various farmers and prospectors. It was at the hottest time of a year of exceptional heat and drought, but I found I could walk all through the day without difficulty, for, although Mashonaland is near the tropics, the heat is nothing like so great as it is in India. In the valleys it is sometimes oppressive, but on the crest of the hills there is nearly always a breeze. Undoubtedly a good deal of fever occurs in the rainy season, in the low-lying districts, or where the soil has been turned up for the first time—that is invariably the case with virgin soil in every new country—but the fever is not of a virulent type, and drink, and bad, insufficient food are as a rule more responsible for sickness than the climate.

I was weak and easily fatigued when I started, as I was suffering from the effects of a bad attack of influenza, but by the time I reached Salisbury I felt fairly strong and well. The walk was a delightful one, through scenery of a strangely beautiful and unusual type, and it enabled me to see a good deal both of the settlers and of the natives.

The former I found smarting under the vehement invectives with which they had lately. been assailed—invectives which, as a community, they feel they have not deserved. One of the leading men in Salisbury said to me, "If you are going to describe us at all, do try and describe us as we really are. We are tired alike of undiscriminating eulogy, and of undiscriminating abuse. We have had a hard and bitter struggle, and have made many and grievous mistakes which we unfeignedly regret. We are doing our best now to retrieve them, and we feel most keenly the readiness of people at home to accept whatever tells against us, and to ignore what is in our favour. All we want is fair play. It is quite true that regrettable, that indeed even terrible things have been done: but if the circumstances are stated fairly, and allowance made for the difficulties we have had to contend with, I think even our opponents will view our conduct in a different light."

And if in trying to draw this true picture I have sometimes expressed myself strongly, it is not because

I think the settlers in Rhodesia have behaved in a harsher or more cruel way than those in any other newly-acquired country. On the contrary, taken as a whole, I think they have been less cruel. The subjugation of an inferior race, in whatever part of the world it has been effected, by whichever of the European nations, has invariably been attended, in the first instance, by oppression on the one side and reprisals on the other. Look at the conquests of the two Americas, of Mexico, and more lately of the other portions of South Africa and of Australia.

Moreover, in Rhodesia allowance must be made for men who have had the terrible provocation of the murder of white women under circumstances of peculiar atrocity. In all savage warfare brutalities are invariably perpetrated by both the combatants; but the greater publicity given to them now leads to greater censure. People who have lived in Europe in perfect security all their lives, feel very differently from their great-great-grandfathers, but the feelings of those who have to guard a hostile frontier alter but little from generation to generation; the basis of human nature remains the same—it is always violent and forceful; if it were not so, the world would never be opened up.

The Afghan graves this legend on his blade, " In the time of necessity, when no hope remains, the hand grasps the hilt of a sharp sword." At home we have been swathed in security so long that we have almost forgotten the feeling that the sword, after all, is our ultimate and strongest argument; but amongst those who have to make their lives on the fringes of barbarism, it is a feeling that exists as strongly as ever. Men who live, as it were, with the sword-hilt in their fingers, must not be judged by a European standard; they cannot reason out quietly abstract principles of right and wrong: their peril, and too often their grief, is too great and too near them for that—they do things in the heat of conflict that afterwards they bitterly regret; but those who sit peacefully at home are unable to comprehend the stormy passions that have swayed them. Infinite allowance must be made for men placed in circumstances of such peculiar trial.

We must remember, too, that we in England are directly responsible for all that has been done. We shrank from the task of civilising these regions ourselves, and delegated the work we should have undertaken as a nation to a community not powerful enough to perform it effectually, and these excesses have been the direct result. Earl Grey, in a despatch to Sir George Cathcart dated 2nd February 1852, uses words which might well have been used by his nephew, the present Earl Grey, in defence of the Rhodesian settlers. "In like manner," he says, "there are other considerations affecting the native races which ought not to be lost sight of. If colonists of European descent are to be left unsupported by the power of the mother-country, to rely solely on themselves for protection from fierce barbarians, with whom they are placed in immediate contact, they must also be left to the unchecked exercise of those severe measures of self-defence, which a position of so much danger will naturally dictate. Experience shows that, in such circumstances, measures of self-defence will degenerate into indiscriminate vengeance, and will lead to the gradual extermination of the less civilised race."

Happily, things have not been as bad as that in Rhodesia, nor are they likely to be. The Home Government has awakened to the necessity of enforcing a more direct imperial control, and the people of Rhodesia themselves seem determined that what has happened in the past shall not happen again—that the good name of the many shall no longer be besmirched by the misdeeds of the few.

Mr. Duncan, the late Surveyor-General, who during the most critical part of the rebellion was acting as administrator in Matabililand, at the luncheon given in Salisbury last November to Sir Alfred Milner, made a speech which accurately represents the feelings of the responsible portion of the community. After a few words of welcome to the High Commissioner, he continued thus: "The completion of the railway to Bulawayo, and the anticipated extension of the railway from Beira, tend to dispel the dark clouds which have hovered over us for so long, and we may feel sure, now that the day is breaking, that our countrymen in South Africa and beyond the seas, who have watched with interest, perhaps even with amazement, the extension of the

British Dominion during the past twelve years from Griqualand West to the shores of Tanganyika—we may feel sure that they, whether they may belong to the one great political party or the other, will wish us at this season God-speed. But we must remember that these good wishes are conditional upon our respect for the obligations imposed upon us as the representatives in this land of an imperial and of a civilising race. The nineteenth century has witnessed a softening of manners, a gentler consideration for those who are opposed to us, and for those who are beneath us, and when our methods and our actions during the past six years have been criticised, can we feel that we are free from blame? In my opinion the people who have prepared these charges against us have not sufficiently investigated the facts, but if outrages have been committed they have been perpetrated by those whom you and I contemn. Moreover, personally I am of opinion —I believe—that the proportion of cases of cruelty here, even in time of war, has been in terms of the population less than in England. But of this I am sure—the people of this country condone no cruelty and sanction no crime. They wish to live at peace themselves, and to follow their occupations undisturbed. They wish to live in amity with the native tribes, and to feel that the lot of the natives, under the rule of Great Britain, is a happier one than before. This will give us prosperity. This is the prosperity we desire."

No one who has been in Rhodesia, and has made himself acquainted with the hardships, the dangers, and the privations which the people there have to undergo, but will utter from his heart the God-speed for which Mr. Duncan hoped. One thing, too, must not be lost sight of; in redressing a committed injustice it is easy to be carried to too great a length, and to be led into the committal of an injustice equally great. Whatever excesses the settlers may have been guilty of—and no one who is conversant with the facts will deny that some detestable things have been done—the fact remains that almost unaided, and at little cost to England, they have won for her what will eventually prove to be a fair and beautiful country; a heritage of untold value for generations yet to come, when the pressure of population in the mother-land shall have become almost unendurable.

In any change, therefore, that may be effected in the Government of Rhodesia, a liberal measure of justice should be meted out to those who have staked their all in the country, and have lost—many of them—not only money but health, in their endeavour to develop its resources. "*Qui sentit commodum debet sentire et onus,*" is a maxim that applies with even greater force to nations than to individuals: if England is to reap the fruit, she must first pay for the tillage. But when I say that Rhodesia will eventually prove a valuable country, I do not mean for a moment to assert that it will pay a dividend to its present shareholders, as to that I am not capable of judging—it requires a mining and an agricultural expert to give an opinion; but of this I feel sure, that with thrift and patience it will become in time a country peopled by a fairly well-to-do population. If gold should be found in payable quantities, and found speedily, it will be spared the financial difficulties and vicissitudes which have beset the upward progress of most of our other colonies; but even if gold should not be found, it will, in course of years, become like them the home of a frugal people who will develop its resources to the utmost, because their lives will be bound up with it. And should emigration from England for any reason be checked, the Afrikanders, as they are called, will gradually convert it into a habitable land, as the Dutch have the Orange Free State, where the droughts are far worse, and where, in many other ways, the conditions are less favourable.

But though the settlers deserve generous treatment, the Chartered Company itself, as a government, has no claim whatever to indulgence. It has caused terrible bloodshed; it has brought unrest into the whole of South Africa (for the Bechuanaland rising seems to have derived its stimulus from the rising in Rhodesia); it has given cause for just suspicion to the Boers, to the Portuguese, and to the neighbouring native states; and it has cruelly wronged and oppressed those natives who have been placed under its control. It is due to ourselves as a governing nation that it should be deprived of its powers, and that we should take over charge of the territories and peoples it has misgoverned, just as we took over charge of India.

For whatever allowance we may feel disposed to make for the Rhodesian settlers, our duty to the native tribes is clear. No one has asserted this more plainly than Mr. Chamberlain. "But the British Empire is not confined to the self-governing colonies and the United Kingdom. It includes a much greater area, a much more numerous population in tropical climes, where no considerable European settlement is possible, and where the native population must always vastly out-number the white inhabitants; and in these cases also the same change has come over the Imperial idea.

"Here also the sense of possession has given place to a different sentiment—the sense of obligation. We feel now that our rule over these territories can only be justified if we can show that it adds to the happiness and prosperity of the people, and I maintain that our rule does, and has, brought security and peace and comparative prosperity to countries that never knew these blessings before."

It may possibly bring all these things to the natives of Rhodesia in time, but up to the present, through the neglect of the British Government to look into the doings of those to whom they have delegated their imperial authority, it has brought them neither security nor peace, nor even comparative prosperity, but only intensified misery, rebellion, and death. For these things Mr. Rhodes is directly responsible. It was he who destroyed Lobengula; it was he who evolved the idea of a charter, and induced the British Government to grant it ; and it was he who, as managing director of the Company he had created, neglected to prevent or to punish the oppression which has brought such discredit upon the English name.

He has laid down the doctrine of equal rights for every white man south of the Zambesi, but he has purposely omitted all mention of the blacks. Rhodesia has shown what his rule of them is like, and a heavy responsibility will rest upon Mr. Chamberlain if he assists him back into power, as he seems inclined to do. Fine sentiments weigh nothing in the scale against committed deeds. Mr. Rhodes' record in Rhodesia has been written in blood, and cannot be obliterated by the assertion, however emphatic, of his adherents and himself that his motives have been disinterested and patriotic.

I have gone with some detail into the nature of the influence exercised by Mr. Rhodes in South Africa, because the coming struggle there will be one, not, as so many people in England believe, between the English and the Dutch, but between Mr. Rhodes, as the representative of monopoly and capital, and his opponents, as representing individual effort; between violence and legality — between company serfage and freedom. It will be a bitter struggle, and on its outcome depends the direction in which South Africa will develop. The difference in policy of the parties is clear. In Natal Mr. Escombe has been turned out of power for being too much in favour of the Dutch. "England's might throughout the world," he asserted, "could not be sustained by arms alone, but is founded on truth, and faith, and justice."

There, for the moment, the Rhodes party is triumphing, and one of its most prominent leaders told his constituents that "it was absolutely essential to the welfare of South Africa that South Africa, from the Zambesi to Cape Point, should be under British supremacy. The thing to aim at was the carrying out on broad lines of the policy of Cecil Rhodes. Whether the methods of Rhodes were right or not was beside the issue."

Mr. Rhodes himself, time after time, has illustrated the same doctrine in his policy—that the end justifies the means—a doctrine that until the Jameson raid he managed to make both the English and the Dutch accept. Now there are many, and a gradually increasing number, who agree with Mr. Schreiner in the statement he made to the electors of Barkly West: "Convinced as I am of the gravity of the evils experienced and threatened, flowing from the continued influence of Mr. Rhodes upon the institutions and politics of the colony, I could not but oppose, with what power I have, his candidature, or that of any one who would support him politically in future."

What I have actually seen myself I have described, but I have tried not so much to give my own views as to marshal the facts that have led to the formation of those views, so that the reader may judge for himself whether they are justified or not. I have only touched upon Transvaal politics so far as they are concerned with the Jameson raid, of which I have given a brief account extracted from the notes taken by a friend who was in a position to know all its details. He has kindly allowed me to use them just as they stand, and I prefer to give his own words, as they show how cruelly the Johannesburg people—the Judasburgers as they are often called—were misunderstood in England; how, instead of sacrificing Dr. Jameson, it was Dr. Jameson who sacrificed them; and how, rather than prejudice him and his officers at their trial, they kept silence whilst they themselves were being tried, although by speaking out they could in great measure have justified themselves in the eyes of Europe, and have strengthened their legal position enormously.

The Rev. T. Darragh, speaking on the 17th May 1896, at the funeral of Mr. Gray, one of the Reform Committee (and he expressed truly the feelings of all who knew the inner history of the Raid), said: "Outsiders have not hesitated to call us curs and cowards, not recking of that nobler heroism which consists of self-control under provocation. I tell you I am proud of this town for its self-restraint through this terrible crisis, a self-restraint only equalled by the endurance of the sixty-three hostages—now alas only sixty-two—and their reticence as to the secrets of the prison-house, and the rest of this sad business."

This reticence, at a moment so critical to themselves, has been ill repaid by the sustained reticence of Dr. Jameson and his officers, when a frank statement of what really took place would do them no harm; and the insinuations of perfidy and cowardice contained in the report of Sir John Willoughby to the War Office have naturally aroused in Johannesburg an exceedingly bitter resentment. These insinuations have been in part rebutted by Mr. Lionel Phillips in the famous article in the *Nineteenth Century*, which led to his being exiled from the Transvaal, but an intelligible delicacy, with which one cannot but sympathise, has prevented him from stating fully what actually occurred. These notes supply what Mr. Phillips left unsaid, and show with what moderation he has stated the case for his associates and himself. They show, too, that though the Johannesburg people had just grievances for the repeal of which they were entitled to agitate, the Raid was not undertaken to procure reforms, but for altogether other motives.

Unfortunately President Kruger has thrown away the advantage he then gained. By allowing himself to be swayed by vindictive feelings, by a continued denial of the just demands of the Uitlanders, by his treatment of Chief Justice Kotze, and his tampering with the administration of justice, he has forfeited the sympathy of many who originally sided entirely with him, but who, whilst recognising to the full the wickedness of the raid, are quite as fully convinced of the inherent strength of the Johannesburg cause.

Should he persist in the unwise course he has lately been pursuing, nothing can prevent a revolt of English

and Dutch combined, for the more enlightened of the
Boers are becoming as restive as the Uitlanders under
the misgovernment which is impoverishing a land so
teeming with natural advantages that it might be made
one of the most prosperous on the face of the earth. If
any one is in doubt about this let him read the open
letter recently addressed to President Steyn by Advocate
Papenfus, a Free State burgher who has lived several
years in the Transvaal.

President Kruger will listen to no advice that comes
from an English source, but he would do well to
hearken to the warnings uttered by those of his own
blood. The *Natal Afrikander*, a Dutch paper published in Pieter-Maritzburg, on the first of January 1896,
immediately before the raid, spoke out very plainly :
" We therefore trust that the Transvaal authorities will,
in the interests of the Republic in the present complica-
tions, set to work most cautiously. A single wrong step
may have fatal results to the State. The Transvaal
Government cannot with any show of right expect that
the persons who own seventy-five per cent. of the landed
property of the Republic, and contribute nine-tenths of
the whole State revenue, will allow themselves to be
treated like Kaffirs. They are quite right in demanding
burgher rights, although such rights cannot be granted
to all Uitlanders. Those who own landed property
there should get them." This was written more than
two years ago, and the condition and prospects of the
Uitlanders are worse now than they were then.

What the Uitlanders have done to make the Transvaal prosperous is shown by the following table, which I have taken from the annual report of the Durban Chamber of Commerce :—

A.—Direct imports into the Transvaal from abroad.

	vià Cape Colony.	*vià* Natal.	*vià* Delagoa Bay.
1895 . .	5,255,406	265,192	759,029
1896 .	6,035,920	1,554,427	1,674,031

B.—Imports from Coast stocks and South African produce and manufacture.

	From Cape Colony.	From Natal.	From Delagoa Bay.	From Orange Free State.
1895 .	1,652,740	717,204	204,102	926,631
1896 .	1,981,309	1,446,606	451,512	944,325

C.—Imports from and vià the places named.

	Cape Colony.	*vià* Natal.	Delagoa Bay.	Orange Free State.
1895 .	6,908,146	982,396	999,131	926,631
1896 .	8,017,229	3,001,033	2,125,543	944,325
Increase per cent.	15	205	113	2

These figures show that the good government of the Transvaal is vital to the whole of South Africa, and that the other South African States have a perfect right to bring combined action to bear if its present state of misgovernment should continue. Mr. Findlay, the chairman at the annual meeting of the Durban Chamber on the 22d March 1897, made use in his speech of these words: "As regards the future prospects of our trade, I must say I find it most difficult to give an opinion. Johannesburg is the centre of South African trade, and therefore Transvaal politics are the principal factor with which we are concerned. At the present moment commercial confidence is destroyed, and it is impossible for us to see unmoved the perilous position into which the Transvaal government are bringing their country. The danger now probably arises from foes within rather than from foes without. The shrinkage in trade is only now beginning to be felt, but doubtless the shrinkage will rapidly increase. I feel sure we need not fear the ultimate consequences. No government can permanently stop the development of its country's natural resources, and we know that in the Transvaal those resources are practically unlimited. Although for a time we may have to pass through some depression, the future prosperity of South Africa is beyond a doubt, and in that prosperity Natal will participate."

That Mr. Rhodes' action was altogether unwarrantable does not absolve President Kruger from his duty to the suffering people who have made the Transvaal what it is. Moreover, his refusal to remedy their grievances is a distinct breach of faith, for the people of Johannesburg laid down their arms on the express understanding that this should be done. So far, however, from it being done, their condition has been made immeasurably worse, and until reasonable reforms are granted the root cause of the trouble will remain; argue as one may about the rights and wrongs of the matter, there is no getting away from that.

Nevertheless, the position is one of extreme difficulty, for any interference from outside on the part of England is sure to produce a sympathetic action amongst the Dutch all over South Africa. A Free State burgher explained their feelings to me in this way: "If my brother gets drunk, is he not still my brother? I may put him under restraint myself, but I will not permit any one else to do so." Besides, we have put ourselves so hopelessly in the wrong by the attitude we have adopted ever since the Raid, that it is difficult to see how we can interfere until we have at any rate made some honest effort to prove to the Republics that we have no sinister design underlying our solicitude.

Like President Kruger, Mr. Chamberlain has thrown away a magnificent opportunity. The prompt action he took at the time of the Raid disarmed the suspicion which was at first felt of the complicity of the Home Government, and had he afterwards employed a different tone to that which he has unhappily thought fit to adopt, he might have obtained substantial and lasting concessions; but the language in which his despatches have been couched, and still more his ostentatious championship of Mr. Rhodes, have led them to believe that, though he was not privy to Mr. Rhodes' designs, he has since practically condoned them; and that it is hopeless to look to him for fair treatment. The feeling against him is as strong in the Free State and in Cape Colony as it is in Pretoria. Indeed he has done as much, if not more, than Mr. Rhodes to accentuate the cleavage between the races: a truly regrettable result, for before the Raid they were rapidly coalescing—President Steyn's wife is Scotch; Chief-Justice de Villiers' wife is Irish; Mrs. Merriman belongs to one of the great Dutch families of the Cape—all through South Africa a quiet and unnoticed fusion was going on which the Raid has almost stopped.

The continual rumours of war, and the jibes against the Boers with which the English papers have been filled, have done the greatest possible harm. The Dutch feel that they have been cruelly and wantonly maligned, and held up to obloquy and ridicule before the eyes of the whole civilised world, by people who have reaped the benefit of the privations they have endured in making the interior of South Africa inhabitable, privations which have prevented them from attaining to the same degree of education and refinement as the newer emigrants from Europe.

They assert—and many Englishmen will be found to agree with them—that they gave up Dr. Jameson and his officers under a promise that a fair and impartial inquiry should be held into all the circumstances of the Raid, and that so far from that promise being kept, the inquiry was converted into what was practically an arraignment of the Transvaal Government, with Mr. Chamberlain as counsel for the prosecution. A distrust has thereby been aroused which it will take years to allay. That is the impression I gathered from all the Dutchmen to whom I spoke. They were unanimous in their opinion about the unfairness of the inquiry.

It is not too late even yet to remove that distrust, but it will be no easy task, for we must prove our sincerity by deeds and not by words, however smooth and fair. It is of no avail for Sir Alfred Milner to assert that England has no hostility to the Transvaal, whilst at the same moment Mr. Chamberlain is ardently befriending Mr. Rhodes, and thereby throwing all the weight of the English Government into his favour during the coming Cape election.

But if that distrust were once removed, there would be no difficulty in bringing the joint action of all the South African States to bear upon the Transvaal for the enforcement of better government, for the Cape Colony, Natal, the Free State, and the Transvaal itself, have all at different times affirmed the doctrine that South Africa as a whole is entitled to interfere if any State should be pursuing a policy inimical to the combined interests of the others.

What Sir Michael Hicks Beach wrote in his despatch of November 20, 1879, to Sir Garnet Wolseley, states accurately the position that England has always held, and still holds towards the Transvaal; it has been repeatedly acknowledged, and rests on a truer basis than the doubtful suzerainty about which there has been so much pedantic wrangling: "The power and authority of England have for many years been paramount there, and neither by the Sand River Convention of 1852, nor at any other time, did Her Majesty's Government surrender the right and duty of requiring that the Transvaal should be governed with a view to the common safety of the various European communities."

Nothing that has occurred since then has altered England's position in this regard, but to enable her to intervene with any pretence of right she must first repair the wrongdoing which she has permitted. She must pay, or must cause the Chartered Company to pay, a reasonable indemnity for the damage done by the Raid, and must make it clear that her motives for intervention are disinterested and not felonious; that she does not desire to obtain the country for herself, but only to procure better government. If she can succeed in making the Dutch believe that her professions are sincere, her task will be comparatively easy, for she will have in it their support as well as that of the English colonists.

CHAPTER I

Durban is a charmingly pretty town, semi-tropical in appearance, but with distinctly English ways. It is a remarkable instance of what energy and courage can make out of the most unpromising material. There are men still living who can remember when it was a mere handful of houses, scattered along the sea-shore, when the site of the present public gardens and of the town-hall was ankle-deep in sand, and when elephants roamed over the Berea, the hill that rises immediately behind. Its progress would have been more rapid had it not been for the difficulty of making a satisfactory harbour. At the first glance it seems an ideal position for a seaport, with a deep land-locked bay or lagoon four miles in length and two in width, connected with the sea by a narrow channel, and sheltered effectually from the heavy gales which blow at certain seasons. Unfortunately the mouth of the channel is blocked by a shifting sand-bar, the depth of which varied originally from eight to seventeen feet. At great expense, by dredging and other methods, the accumulation of sand has been prevented, and the water over the bar has been permanently deepened, and now, except in bad weather, all but very large vessels are able to pass in and out. Mr. Escombe, the late Prime Minister, in spite of his other multifarious occupations, has devoted the greater part of his life to this indispensable and difficult work.

He is a firm believer in the necessity of a cordial understanding between the English and the Dutch. They are, he says, like oxen in one yoke: they cannot get away from each other, and the sooner they learn to pull together the better for both. At the same time I found him an ardent imperialist in the truest and fullest sense of the word. He believes, too, in a generous though firm treatment of the natives, and has done much to make them the happy people that in Natal they certainly are.

But in spite of all that has been done to deepen the bar, it is still a serious hindrance to the trade of Durban. I was detained for several days longer than I intended, on account of a heavy gale which had silted up the sand so much that ships were unable either to come in or to go out. Finally, I left in the *Pongola*, a small but comfortable boat going to Madras to bring over coolies for the Natal tea-gardens and sugar plantations. It it is only a twenty-four hours' run to Delagoa Bay, and from there to Beira I was fortunate enough to have as my cabin passenger Don Egas Moniz Coelho, the Portuguese *intendente*, who represents the Portuguese Government in the Mozambique Company's territories, holding a position analogous to that held by Sir Richard Martin in Rhodesia.

Delagoa Bay is not a cheerful place to live in—it is hot and exceedingly unhealthy; but the fever is not worse than it was in Durban in its early days, and every year it is diminishing and growing less dangerous in character. There is no bar, but deep water right up to the town, and in time it cannot fail to become one of the most important of the South African harbours, being, as it is, the natural port for the Transvaal. Between it and Durban we passed Kosi Bay in Amatongaland, of which President Kruger is so anxious to obtain possession. The lagoon is shallow throughout, and there is not more than two feet of water on the bar. If it has been so long and so difficult a task to make a harbour of Durban with its minimum of eight feet, it would take years of labour, and an enormous outlay, to make anything at all of Kosi Bay. In all probability, when the practical difficulties came to be considered, the project of turning it into the port of Johannesburg would be abandoned in favour of Delagoa Bay, which is already connected with the Transvaal by a railroad.

The Portuguese territory stretches all the way from Delagoa Bay to Beira, a distance of 488 miles. It is a run of two days, along a monotonous coast of low hills covered with scanty scrub, fringed in places with a belt of sand. Beira is not the native name, but is the name of a province in Portugal, and the hereditary title of the heir to the throne, like the Prince of Wales. The native name is Arangúa, and before 1891 what is now known as Beira was a desolate, uninhabited sandspit at

the mouth of the Pungwe River, which is joined a mile
or two below the town by the Busi; the two rivers
together forming an estuary three and a half miles
broad. Most of it is shoal water, but there is a channel
to the open sea half a mile in breadth, and seventeen
miles in length, which is well marked out by buoys, and
easily followed, for sailing vessels constantly come in.
There are no pilots as yet, but the Portuguese Government is having a naval survey made, and a proper pilot
department is being organised. When ships have once
reached the port they are in absolute safety, protected
as they are by the horse-shoe banks of the estuary.
The disadvantage of Beira as a port is that during
neap-tides lighters cannot be brought under the crane
because they cannot approach sufficiently close to the
wharf, and the town lies so low, that in equinoctial
spring-tides the main streets are not infrequently under
water; but a French company has been granted a concession to fill up and drain the creek which runs behind
it, and to make a proper channel from which boats can
be discharged. I should mention that the Pungwe is a
tidal river navigable as far as Fontesvilla, about forty
miles from Beira, and that the Busi is also navigable
for a short distance.

As a town Beira has several advantages. It is almost
separated from the mainland by a narrow creek, and is,
for East Africa, exceptionally healthy. There is nearly
always a cool breeze from the sea, which blows back the
miasma from the swamps that lie behind. Being on

sand, there is an entire absence of the irritating dust so prevalent in South Africa; and as the sand absorbs any rain that may fall, the ground is dry again within a very short time. But this said, there is nothing else to be said in favour of Beira, and it is wonderful that so comparatively flourishing a place should have been created in so arid and forbidding a spot. The sand on which it is built is so loose that a tidal wave would wash it away altogether, so the Mozambique Company are having a sea-wall built at great expense to prevent the possibility of such a disaster. Another serious drawback is the scarcity of water, sea-water having to be used for washing purposes, but I was told that steps are being taken to construct proper water-works which will give a supply large enough for all the needs of the town.

Beira, of course, owes it existence to Rhodesia, and its future development depends largely upon the future of that country, but up to the present it has been remarkable.

In 1895 only 16,772 tons of merchandise came into the port, whilst in 1896 there were 30,388 tons. The same increase is observable in everything. In 1895 the imports amounted to £157,048 as against £205,006, the transit duties rising in those years from £142,959 to £192,042; and the number of ships entering the port from 115, carrying 2046 passengers, to 178, carrying 6593 passengers—the port dues increasing in proportion from £1195 to £2644.

These figures are interesting, because they show what

has been done whilst the Mozambique Company's territory is still in a practically undeveloped state, and in spite of the terrible delay caused by the rinderpest. When the Beira railway has been completed to the Manica gold-fields, and from there on to Salisbury, and when the projected line has been made from Fontesvilla to Tête, Beira bids fair to become one of the most important of the East African ports; for just as Delagoa Bay is the natural port for the Transvaal, so Beira is the natural port, not only for Mashonaland, but for the whole of Rhodesia. That it is confidently anticipated it will become so is shown by the rapid increase in the value of land, and by the fact that most of the principal steamship lines now call there regularly. I should add that the population, which in 1893 consisted of only 319 Europeans and 722 natives, in 1896 amounted to 692 Europeans and 1929 natives.

The country is fertile, and will grow maize, rice, sugar-cane, fruit, spices, and tobacco in abundance. On the high lands in the Gorongoza district, north of the Pungwe, coffee will probably thrive, and cotton also. Tea has been suggested, but it will be next to impossible to make it pay owing to the difficulty of obtaining skilled labour. The same difficulty is experienced in Assam, where labour has to be imported from Bengal; here it would be almost insurmountable. On the Busi, and in Portuguese Gazaland, india-rubber is said to be plentiful, but at present it is only brought in by the natives in a crude state, and no effort has been made to cultivate it, though it is reported to be of exceptionally good quality; it is also said to be plentiful in the Zambesi district. Nevertheless, rapid development must not be looked for; the difficulties in the way are too great, the chief being that of labour.

The native labour as yet is unreliable, and farms could only be worked profitably by coolies. They, unfortunately, are not obtainable, as the Government of India very properly refuses to allow them to be exported to any but the British colonies. Not long ago some contractors wished to import a thousand, and took steps to have them brought over, but their agent in India was met with this refusal. In Johannesburg it is constantly asserted that any amount of labour could be obtained if the Portuguese Government did not place unnecessary obstacles in the way; and from what I was able to gather, I believe that an unlimited supply might be obtained from the thickly inhabited district of Gazaland. But the Mozambique Company's territory is sparsely populated, and does not yield sufficient labour for the Company's own requirements; they will probably have to procure it either from Gazaland or from the Zambesi.

The railway, and the forwarding trade to Mashonaland, must for some time to come be the backbone of Beira, but there is every reason to hope that before long the town will also derive a substantial revenue from its local trade. Both the Portuguese Government and the Mozambique Company are doing all they can to assist

the railway, and to encourage enterprise, and it is pleasant to find English and Portuguese working amicably
together, as in the main they do. When its sudden rise
is considered, as well as that of Delagoa Bay, which in
1882, like it, was an uninhabited lagoon, it is evident
that the Portuguese have not wholly lost the colonising
instinct which at one time made them the foremost
maritime power in the world. They are lethargic, and
crippled by poverty, but the East African seaboard is
the fruit of their early enterprise, and they have the
good sense to allow it to be developed for them by the
introduction of foreign capital.

Delagoa Bay has been retained under the direct
control of the Home Government, but Beira forms part
of the district granted by Royal Charter to the Mozambique Company, who have been given full commercial
control of the territory entrusted to them. The Portuguese Government controller—the *intendente*, as he is
called—the judges, and indeed the whole of the legal
officials, including the Attorney-General, are, however,
appointed by the Government in Lisbon, and foreigners
residing in the country have the right of appeal from
any decision of the Company to the Court in Mozambique, the capital of the Portuguese possessions in East
Africa. In every other respect, the entire control of the
country has been left in the Company's hands.

What the Company now requires to do is to form
subsidiary companies for the development of the country
in detail. These companies might easily be converted

into a means of defence, and would save the mother company the necessity of maintaining an armed force. M. Xavier Hoffer, a retired officer of the French navy, who was asked to report upon the subject, suggested that the farms should be linked together by a battery of guns, worked by an artillery corps furnished by the colonists themselves, and the suggestion is an excellent one. It would be an easy matter to raise enough food for an increasing black population, as rice, maize, and millet all grow in abundance. But the natives would have to be carefully watched, for they are an improvident race, and care would have to be taken to compel them to cultivate for themselves each year a certain portion of the land. Most vegetables will grow well, but for a time there will be difficulty in obtaining sufficient meat on account of the rinderpest, and transport, because of the tetzé-fly. The rinderpest, however, is a temporary calamity, and when it has been stamped out may not occur again for years, and the country can easily be re-stocked from Madagascar. The fly will disappear before civilisation, as it has in other parts of South Africa. In Khama's country it no longer exists, although Baines and the earlier travellers mention it as a terrible scourge.

In the Zambesi district M. Hoffer told me gum-arabic is plentiful, as well as india-rubber, and he said that both in soil and in climate the Gorongoza district greatly resembles parts of Brazil, so that coffee ought also to do well.

Subsidiary companies might well be formed to work all these products, for the extent of territory is too extensive for the mother company to deal with them efficiently.

Gorongoza, and the Mozambique Company's portion of the Inyanga mountains, are capable of supporting a limited white population, but it would be advisable to give colonists a free passage and free grants of land, and to supply them for a time with everything they might require in the way of seed and agricultural implements. Without help of that kind they would be sure to fail. Mr. Hoffer does not think it advisable to attempt European colonisation in the Zambesi district, as it is too feverish for white people to live in, and from what I saw of the coast district of Manicaland I do not think it would be advisable there either. These districts will have to be opened up entirely by native or coolie labour under the direction of Europeans.

I started from Beira on the 20th September by the mail train which leaves every Wednesday morning at five o'clock, sharing a carriage with three missionaries, who were on their way to found a mission station in Mashonaland, and a colonial lawyer who had heard such good accounts of Umtali that he was thinking of settling there, but was going up to have a look at it before deciding. The carriage, though dirty, was comfortable enough, but I found that carriages are only put on for the weekly mail; on other days passengers have to sit in open trucks exposed to the rain and intense heat, and worse still, to such showers of sparks from the engine (which chiefly burns wood) that they are not only an annoyance but a positive danger. The distance to Chimoio, the terminus of the line, is only 153 miles, but the fare is heavy, and better accommodation might certainly be provided for the passengers by the ordinary trains. As it is, they have to travel in the same way as the natives, who are only charged 15s., and yet have to pay the same fare—£4—as by the mail train.

Between Beira and Fontesvilla, we passed through a long stretch of flat, swampy country, for the most part thickly wooded, but in places with open glades and little clusters of trees like an English park. It is said to be full of game, but the animals have become shy of the train, and all we saw was a herd of zebras and quaggas. Lions are plentiful, as they always are where big game is abundant. The young grass comes up in the lowlands before it does in the hilly country of the interior, so the buffalo come down to the lagoons that lie between Beira and the Busi, and where there are buffalo there are sure to be lions. One was killed on the other side of the creek, quite close to the town, whilst I was there, and farther up the line they are still uncomfortably bold. Not long before one of them sprang into a kraal, seized a Kaffir who was lying asleep, dragged him out and ate him, meeting his death soon after at the hands of some of the railway men. Captain Ewing, who was then harbour-master, told me that at Mapandas four lions were shot from the windows of a house around which they were prowling, a feat which rivals the four lions tackled by Lord Randolph Churchill in Mashonaland.

Last year some natives who were bringing a boat down from Fontesvilla came upon a lion stuck fast in the mud. It was discovered afterwards that he had been wounded by a hunter, and had taken refuge in the river, sinking so deep in the soft mud that he had been unable to extricate himself. The boys (all natives are called boys; it does not matter how old they are) had no assegais with them, but they beat him to death with their oars. They brought the skin down to Beira, and obtained the Government reward of £2, and Colonel Machado, who was then Governor, gave them another £5 for their bravery.

At Fontesvilla, a dismal, malaria-stricken railway settlement, the line crosses the Pungwe, and twenty miles farther on begins the ascent of the Manicaland mountains. The scenery is pretty, though not in any way striking, the train winding for hours up the Chiruvu hills in an open semi-tropical bush, through gaps in which we got an occasional glimpse of the blue line of hills beyond. Coming suddenly round a curve we ran full tilt into a tree which had fallen across the line, and the engine became firmly fixed in the branches —the white ants had eaten the trunk away close to the ground. Luckily we were on the up-grade, and the driver saw it in time to slow down, otherwise we might have had a nasty accident. As it was, it formed an amusing break in the monotony of the journey. We had to get out and help to disentangle the engine, and to lift the tree off the track. The line has only a two-foot gauge, but it struck me as well maintained, for there was not nearly so much oscillation as might be expected with heavy carriages running on so narrow a gauge with steep gradients and incessant curves. There are occasional accidents, it is true, but they have not been frequent nor of any consequence. It has not been an expensive line to build, costing only— so Mr. Lawley, the contractor, told me—£2800 a mile, but the loss of life has been terrible. Fontesvilla still has an evil repute among the railway employés, and in the early days of the line the climate was deadly. Of thirteen carpenters employed on the bridge, eleven died before it was finished. Another bridge over the Revué River, not far from Massi-Kessi, although the country there is 2145 feet in height, has an even more sorrowful record; of eighty-three white men at work upon it, eighty died or became permanently incapacitated. Beira itself at certain times of the year is bad enough. When I passed through it in February twenty-nine men had died in four days of fever and heat-apoplexy out of a population of 780. It was the rainy season, and the moist heat was exceedingly trying; but the people do not give themselves a fair chance, the climate induces a craving for drink and there are not many who resist it.

CHAPTER II

At Massi-Kessi I said good-bye to my travelling-companions, the missionaries, who were going by coach to Umtali. They were all interesting men, who had taken to missionary work from conviction. They believed that the proper way to convert the natives is through the influence of conduct, and not by bringing political pressure to bear upon them. That is to say, they did not believe in large mission stations, and native locations, or in the acquisition of political power over the chiefs. They said it is liable to be abused, and that missionaries are tempted to make use of the power so acquired to obtain concessions and other advantages for themselves, and to go into trade.

None of my friends were in holy orders; one of them was the secretary of the mission (the South Africa General Mission), another had been a mining manager in Johannesburg, and the third was a mason. They hoped to obtain a small piece of land somewhere in the Melsetter district of Rhodesia, as far away as possible from the white settlers; and the two last proposed to build a house there, and to live among the natives in the hope of converting them by example, and by an endeavour to live themselves according to the precepts of their Master. They were enthusiasts, all of them, and such ardent believers in the power of faith and of prayer, that they intended to trust to them alone, and not to quinine and other medicines against fever and dysentery, and the numberless other maladies they were going out so light-heartedly to encounter. I thought them mad, as Festus thought St. Paul, but I could not but admire their courage and respect their transparent sincerity. They told me that one of the rules of their society forbade any of them to engage in trade. It is a society that does much good work all over South Africa, and its influence is due largely, I think, to the strict enforcement of this rule. Most of the missionary societies impose a similar restriction on their members; but it would be well if they were all to do so, for certain missionaries in Rhodesia have virtually become traders, and have thereby done more harm than good. The Jesuits, I should mention, are strictly forbidden by the law of their order to do anything that has even the semblance of trading, any *species commercii.*

Everywhere in Rhodesia, and in fact all over South Africa, I heard complaints against the missionaries, that they ruined the natives, and converted an originally decent folk into thieves and profligates. But when the reason of the dislike to them is probed, it will be found to be mainly due to the fact that they stand up for the natives, and insist that justice shall be done to them. That there have been bad missionaries, untrue to their holy calling, is undeniable. Amongst so large a number of men there are sure to be a few bad ones; but, taken as a body, the South African missionaries have done, and are doing, a great and self-denying work. The rule prohibiting trade, and any intermeddling with politics or concessions, should, however, be rigidly enforced by all the societies. And I think that when missionaries penetrate into savage and unexplored lands, they should do so at their own risk; that if they are murdered, no steps should be taken to avenge them. That is what the missionaries themselves desire. St. Paul, they say, had no dynamite or maxims behind him; he went forth armed only with his staff and his scrip, and for that very reason preached mightily. Governments have been too apt to clutch at the unavoidable tragedies of missionary life as opportunities for acquisition of territory. They have used the Bible as a stalking-horse for temporal aggrand-isement—an undesirable thing, to say the least of it.

The matured colonial feeling about missionary work is set out very clearly in the report of the Commission appointed by the Cape Government in 1881 to inquire into native laws and customs: "While confining ourselves generally, in terms of the instructions given to us, to the consideration of the improvement of the condition of the natives by means of legislative action, we consider we would fail in our duty to the

Government and people of the colony, if we proposed to hold that only by means of such legislative action can the natives be caused to advance, or their condition be ameliorated. There are happily other beneficent forces at work gradually remoulding their nature and character, by guiding them to superior knowledge and higher hopes, as well as training them in civilised arts and habits, and the social order of a well-regulated community.

"Among the most powerful of those operating at present are the various Christian missions, which at great expense and untiring devotedness, and in spite of heavy losses and manifold discouragements, have established their agencies throughout the native territories. The influence of these agencies, in raising the natives both morally and industrially in their standing as men, can hardly be over-estimated. The printed records of the Commission contain ample evidence of the success which has attended and continues to attend such labours. A few adverse criticisms with regard to the results of their work have come to our notice, but these have not been substantiated, notwithstanding that even the best friends of missions admit and deplore the fact that what is accomplished falls far short of the objects aimed at and wished for. It is a sincere gratification, therefore, to the Commission to be able to bear its unanimous testimony to the high opinion formed, both from hearsay and from personal observation and experience, of the good which is being effected, morally, educationally, and industrially, by Christian missionaries among the native population, and we recommend that all the countenance, protection, and support which may be possible should be extended to them by the Government."

On my return to Johannesburg I happened to meet Mr. Kidd, one of my missionary companions, and was grieved to hear from him that they had all been ill, and that one of them, poor Coupland the mason, had died.

The Melsetter district is healthy enough, but they had to go through terrible exposure and fatigue to reach it, and Coupland must have contracted the fever on the journey. Mr. Kidd told me he was glad he had gone up to Gazaland, as it had enabled him to understand, in a manner he could not otherwise have done, the terrible hardships and loneliness of a prospector's life; how many of them die out on the veldt alone, without a soul at hand to cheer or to help them, and with everything to aggravate the discomforts of illness. Many allowances, he said, must be made for the shortcomings of men who have to lead the rough and lonely lives of pioneers in these inhospitable regions.

Massi-Kessi is a well-laid-out little town, and the scenery around it is exquisite; but lying as it does in a valley, encircled by hills on every side, it is hot and feverish. Various attempts have been made to farm in the neighbourhood, but so far without success, and the town must depend for its prosperity entirely upon its forwarding trade to Mashonaland, and prospectively upon the mines in the adjacent Revué valley. Most of the local trade is in the hands of Hindu traders, called *banians*, who come over from Bombay and rapidly acquire great wealth. I was amused to find that gaudy parasols form one of their principal articles of sale. They are bought by the natives, not to protect their complexion from the sun, but because they like to strut about with anything brightly coloured. I bought one for two shillings, and was surprised to find marked inside it, "Made in Japan." It is a proof of the rapidity with which that country is going ahead, and how dangerous a competitor she will be to European nations in the near future, that she should have already secured a footing in the East African trade.

These banians are an objectionable, insolent set of people, and a determined opposition has been made to their coming into Rhodesia. They sell spirits to the natives, and have a demoralising influence in many other ways. But if they were admitted they would do one good thing, they would rapidly bring down the price of goods, which is maintained at an unnecessarily high rate by the clique of storekeepers who at present have the control of the market. I bought a tin of biscuits at one of the banian stores, and paid half the price that I had to pay for a similar tin in Umtali, only sixteen miles away.[1] I took this photograph outside a

---

[1] Since this was written the High Commissioner has ordered the magistrate in Umtali not to refuse them trading licences, as they are British subjects, and consequently entitled to them.

store at Andrada, of a Mashona man and woman who had come to make purchases. They chiefly buy brass wire to work into bangles, and cast-off uniforms, which they like because of their bright colours, and because they are warm. They can get a good uniform coat for four shillings which will last them for years. They say they never noticed the cold before we came, but now that we have taught them the pleasure of warmth, they feel it intensely, and buy both clothes and blankets.

The wooden instrument lying at the man's feet is a Kaffir piano. It consists of pieces of wood of different lengths strung together, which are generally placed on a rude sounding-board, and tapped with another piece of wood to produce the different notes. I have one almost exactly like it, made of bamboo, which came from Burmah. The Mashonas also use a stringed instrument played with the fingers, which consists of hard wood, strung with gut, to the bottom of which a calabash, cut in half, is attached to increase the sound.

From Massi-Kessi I walked over to the Penhalonga valley, crossing the mountains by a Kaffir footpath which passed first through the Revué valley. On the hills on the far side I could see Pardy's mine, and the place where the fort stood which was attacked on May 11, 1891, by Captain Heyman, when he invaded the Portuguese territory. It was a Jameson raid on a small scale. That he had no justification for what he did is proved by the fact that the arbitrator, the Italian senator, Vigliani, has fixed the border several miles

MASHONAS AT ANDRADA, IN PORTUGUESE TERRITORY. KAFIR PIANO LYING ON THE GROUND
TO THE LEFT.

farther into the interior than the place where the fort stood.

Immediately after Mashonaland was occupied, Major Forbes was asked by Mtassa, a Manicaland chief, to protect him against Baron Rezende. He thereupon came down to Umtali, and took Baron Rezende, Colonel Andrada, Señor Paiva, and a Frenchman called Llamby, prisoners. Andrada and Llamby he took through Salisbury to Cape Town, where they were released. In the following year came Heyman's fight at Massi-Kessi. At that time the country was directly under the Portuguese Government, but in 1894 a charter was granted to the Mozambique Company, which was made completely international in character, the shares being held in France, England, Germany, and Portugal, and no group being allowed to acquire controlling power. But according to the terms of the charter, the majority of the board must be Portuguese: so, too, must the governor and officials of the company. For some time after there was much friction between the Mozambique Company and the British South Africa Company's officials, who acted in an extremely arbitrary manner, and made both the Mozambique Company and the Portuguese Government justly suspicious of their intentions. They felt that the B.S.A. Company would never relax its efforts to secure possession of Beira as a port for Mashonaland. That this was not a chimera is proved by an interesting article in the *Financial Record*, dated Oct. 7, 1893, which shows that even then the people of

Johannesburg fully realised the danger to South Africa of a company of imperfectly controlled merchant adventurers. "The only trouble which the Company (the Mozambique Company) has now to encounter," says the *Financial Record*, "is the silent and constant pressure on its border by the B.S.A. Company in the neighbourhood of the Sabi River. There is little doubt that Mr. Rhodes accepted with very ill grace the refusal of Lord Salisbury in 1891 to sanction the Chartered Company's steady progress towards the coast; and the Anglo-Portuguese Convention which arrested the Company's march and reserved a fair margin of country to Portugal, together with all the sea-board, has been a source of unacknowledged irritation to it ever since. No one can wish aught else but success to the Chartered Company in its impending struggle with the Matabili, but what guarantee is there that, when it has broken up the savage hordes on its western frontier, it will not cast longing and covetous eyes on the Mozambique Company's territory? It might, indeed, prove a very useful and convenient thing for the Chartered Company, seeing that Delagoa Bay is likely to be the centre of high politics during the course of the next two or three years, to seek to embroil the Portuguese with the British in every possible way, so as to imperil the present strong maritime position as a whole. It would ill become the agents of a company professedly devoted to the exploitation and release from barbarism of the country south of the Zambesi, if it should thus seek to interfere with its peaceful and friendly neighbour, who by its able management and steady devotion to the improvement of its harbours, navigation, commerce, and mining industries, hopes to realise the objects for which it was founded. It would be a matter of little wonder if the Mozambique Company took advantage of the fact that the B.S.A. Company has its hands very full just now, and firmly demanded substantial guarantees that the present encroachments should cease."

Recently things have been on a more friendly footing, and the settlers in Mashonaland cannot but feel grateful to the Portuguese authorities for permitting the English troops, in spite of all that had previously occurred, to pass freely through their country for the suppression of the Mashona rebellion.

At Andrada we got some tea from a banian, who was very pleased when he found I could talk Hindustani. He said he did not care for Africa and would be glad to go back to Bombay, his birthplace, though there is plenty of money to be made in Africa. Like most others in Massi-Kessi, Europeans as well as natives, he was suffering from an insect called a jigger, which bores under the toe-nail. If not cut out at once it produces violent inflammation, which may go on for months, and sometimes becomes really serious. Half the people in Massi-Kessi were hobbling about with their feet in carpet slippers. This insect—the *Pulex penetrans*—is a new comer in Manicaland, and there is a theory that it has been brought down in coffee from Nyassaland and the Lake District.

After crossing the Revué River I ascended the Penhalonga range, reaching the highest point, the Crow's Nest, 5500 feet in height, just before sunset. The view was magnificent; more from the marvellous colouring than from the height of the mountains. In the fading light the distant tints assumed the loveliest shades of grey and blue and purple, deepening gradually into black, whilst above them the sky glowed like a cooling furnace.

I reached the mining camp about nine o'clock and received a hospitable welcome. It is twenty-three miles from Massi-Kessi, and a stiffish climb to the Crow's Nest, but at that elevation one does not feel the same fatigue as on the plains.[1]

---

[1] The question of licences to Hindu traders has again been brought forward. The Chartered Company still refuses to grant them ; and the Colonial Office has declined to interfere with the discretion of the local authorities.

CHAPTER III

The Christmas Pass — New Umtali — The Penhalonga
Mines—General Mining Prospects in Rhodesia.

THE main obstacles to the development of Mashonaland
are the want of transport and the want of labour. The
first is being remedied by the extension of the line to
Salisbury, and by the introduction of cattle from Madagascar to take the place of those killed off by the rinderpest. But until the rinderpest has been thoroughly
stamped out, it is not safe to introduce fresh animals;
they only keep the disease going. It was believed to
have been got under last summer, but just before I left
Salisbury it broke out again amongst some newly-im-
ported cattle.

The labour difficulty is far more serious. At present
it is nearly impossible to obtain boys, those who are
willing to work being engaged at once by the railway and
other contractors. My own experience will show how
hard it is for a private person to obtain even one boy.
I was unable to get any one to take my things on from
the Penhalonga valley, so I was obliged to leave them
and walk on to Old Umtali to try and get a couple
of boys there. I found it in a deserted condition, most
of the people having shifted to the new township,

to which I had therefore to make my way. It is ten miles distant, on the other side of the Christmas Pass, which is 4450 feet in height, with a superb view; range after range of hills of gradually decreasing height stretching away to the lowlands of Manicaland, until the eye loses itself in an empurpled haze. On the right is the rugged range of granite that intervenes between Umtali and Gazaland, and looking back over the narrow spur I had just crossed, I could see the broad valley of the Umtali River and the corrugated iron roofs of the old township gleaming white in the brilliant sunshine.

It was deemed necessary to shift the site of the township to avoid the necessity of making zig-zags for the railway across the Christmas Pass, but it is a pity that it should have had to be done; the old town, from a sanitary point of view, being excellently situated on the side of a plain sloping gently down to the Umtali River, so that a perfect system of natural drainage was secured. The surroundings of the new town are infinitely more beautiful, but it is likely to prove unhealthy, a brook running through it which even in the hot weather is not dry, and in the rains becomes a regular morass. It is being drained, but for some time to come cannot fail to be a source of ill-health. Captain Scott-Turner, the magistrate, lives on the crest of the hill looking down the valley up which the railway is to come from Massi-Kessi. His house is so close to the Portuguese frontier, that his kitchen is actually on the other side of the boundary.

This proximity will inevitably lead to friction, because the Hindu traders, when the town grows in importance, are sure to erect stores within a few yards of the border, but inside the Mozambique Company's territory, where the Rhodesia liquor law is not in force, and it will be impossible to prevent the natives from crossing over to buy drink.

In new Umtali I found the labour question in the same acute form. I wasted a couple of days in trying to get boys, and was finally indebted to the kindness of a friend, who said that as it was Sunday I could take two of his. To the Penhalonga valley and back was twenty-two miles, but I saw no other chance of getting my things, and though the sun was hot I had an enjoyable walk, the country being exceedingly beautiful.

A few days later, I walked over once more to look at the mines. If gold should eventually be found in payable quantities, there are various circumstances which are greatly in their favour. The fact that the reef dips vertically from the top of the hills will obviate the necessity of haulage, and will enable the exploitation to be done by gravitation, and there is a waterfall 300 feet in height formed by the Umtali River which can easily be dammed for storage purposes, and will give sufficient electric power to work such of them as are in the immediate neighbourhood. But against these advantages must be placed the exceedingly refractory nature of the ore, and the difficulties of transport and labour.

Up to the present only rough extraction of gold by amalgam has been possible. There has been no treatment of the tailings or concentrates. Some of the mines have been worked now for many years, and as yet have not paid, but it is quite possible that, when the conditions are more favourable, and they can be worked on a large scale, they will yet do so. If they should ultimately prove payable, the Penhalonga valley will have the further advantage over the other gold districts of Rhodesia of being a great deal nearer the coast. There is every reason to hope that they will turn out to be of value, but it will be wise to allow the existing companies to *prove* that their properties are payable, now that the initial difficulties have been overcome and the railway is within easy reach. There is no reason for undue despondency—the want of development so far has been due to perfectly explicable causes; but neither is there anything to warrant extravagant expectations. Several of the companies have done solid work, whatever the result may be, and have expended large sums of money, in spite of everything having been against them, in the development of their properties. A good many others have done nothing, and it is a general belief in the district that they have not developed because they know that development will lay bare the poverty of their claims. " You must remember," a man said to me significantly " that when output begins speculation ceases."

While I am on the subject, I will sum up briefly,

what I gathered of the gold prospects all over Rhodesia. The early explorers used such extravagant language that they have discredited the country altogether. Mauch said of Matabililand, "There the extent and beauty of the gold-fields are such that I stood as it were transfixed, and for a few minutes was unable to use the hammer. . . . Thousands of persons might work on these extensive gold-fields without interfering with one another," and Baines' language was almost equally enthusiastic.

Still there is no reason why gold should not yet be found, and in large quantities, for Rhodesia is an enormous tract of country, and there is no telling what it may not contain. The people who assert that there is no gold there are as little to be relied upon as the enthusiasts. When the first discoveries of gold were made in South Africa they were received with the utmost incredulity. "The stories about gold," wrote Sir George Cathcart, "are, if not entirely false, monstrously exaggerated. There is gold in Scotland and Ireland; so there may be a little in minute particles to be found in certain places in South Africa."

Lord Randolph Churchill's is by far the fairest estimate both of the agricultural and of the mining prospects of the country that I have seen: so far almost everything he has said has come true. Anything like a boom would be most hurtful to its ultimate welfare, and if not maintained might be followed by a collapse as great as that of the Panama Canal.

I have talked to a great many prospectors, and they all agreed that the country is full of gold-bearing quartz reefs, and that it might be made a payable field for men working on a small scale, but that as a rule the gold is too patchy, and the reefs too distant from each other to give much of a return to over-capitalised companies. Certain mines are said to give promise of turning out very rich; and if only a few do so the ultimate prosperity of the country will be assured. I should add that there is a strong feeling in Rhodesia that the B.S.A. Company ought to make a drastic change in its gold laws, and to foster private enterprise by reducing the existing tax of fifty per cent. of the vendor's scrip on all gold flotations. But, in fact, it has never exacted more than thirty-three per cent., and I do not think that amount can really be excessive, because in the future the Mozambique Company propose to enforce a similar contribution. What is more serious, is, that the B.S.A. Company, instead of developing the territory it already has, is always gambling in more. When Mashonaland proved to be a disappointment it was said that the reefs in Matabililand were of phenomenal richness. Now Mr. Rhodes assures us that the richest portions of Rhodesia are north of the Zambesi. The tribes will have first to be subdued, though they have done us no harm. Do we intend that they shall be dealt with humanely? It is a more important question than the possible effect of fresh annexations upon the share market.

CHAPTER IV

WHEN I returned from the Rezende valley I was told I
ought to go to Melsetter, a fertile upland 4000 feet in
height, about seventy miles from Umtali, which is said
to contain the best farming land in Rhodesia, but I
tried in vain to get boys to carry my baggage. There
were very few waggons on the road, and no stores where
I could sleep or obtain food, so I was reluctantly obliged
to give up my visit. It is said to be well watered, and
an excellent grazing ground, but the colony, numbering
in all about 300 souls, chiefly Dutch, were in such straits
in 1896 for want of food that the Government had to
send them supplies. There is but little communication
with the outside world, the rate of transport being too
high. When I was in Umtali it was £4, 10s. for 100 lbs.
(£45 per ton), so that up to the present there has been
scarcely any market for the farmers' produce. This has
dispirited them, and as, after the manner of Dutchmen,
they only grew enough grain for their immediate needs,
when the rinderpest came, and their crops were destroyed
by the locusts, they were reduced to terrible straits.

In Umtali I was told precisely the same thing; that

it is of no use to grow vegetables, the market being so limited that a few bags of potatoes will flood it. But the real cause of this apathy is want of energy, for vegetables of all kinds fetch high prices, and the Hindus who have market gardens on the outskirts of the town, and the few Englishmen who have taken to gardening, have all made large profits.

New Umtali had only been in existence a couple of months, and was still in a chrysalis state. Mr. Creech, an enterprising American, was draining it, and had also taken a contract for the erection of the trans-continental telegraph poles as far as Tête. He said he hoped to put them up all the way to Cairo. He had no difficulty in getting boys, for he paid them well, most of them being Shangaans from Gazaland, but it was difficult for any one else to get boys at all. They are, in fact, masters of the situation, and they know it, and are very independent in consequence, and to any one accustomed to the servility of the Hindu servant class, they often seem most insolent in manner. Whatever else their faults may be, there is nothing cringing in any branch of the Bantu race. However ill-used they may be, they are very rarely abject, and they have such an inexhaustible buoyancy that the least prosperity will make them objectionably uppish. The Jesuit fathers told me they are always trying to suppress what they call the horrible Kaffir pride, but find it an almost hopeless task. Put a Kaffir in however small a position of authority over his fellows, and he will fancy himself a great man at once, and presume accordingly. That is why the native police have been such a failure. Above all things familiarity with a Kaffir should be avoided; he cannot understand it, and regards it as a sign of weakness. It is a mistake Englishmen, especially when freshly out from home, frequently make, but a Dutchman never.

In Umtali, in spite of the high wages, the boys are utterly spoiled as servants; they will leave without the slightest warning, and they will do nothing outside the strict routine of their work unless they are paid for it. I came in one afternoon about tea-time (in South African hotels afternoon tea is supplied as a matter of course), and a man whose room was next mine told his servant to fetch me a cup. He did so, and at once asked what tip he was to get. The same boy heated some water for my bath, and when I gave him sixpence looked at it superciliously as though it should have been a shilling. Most of them are poor servants; even when trained they cannot adapt themselves to service like the Hindus, and the wages they are paid are so excessive that most people do with as few of them as possible, while the discomforts of life are proportionately great. A house-boy gets £2, 10s. a month and his food and clothing, more than many housemaids get in England.

The natives in and near Umtali are certainly not badly treated. However irritating they may be—and no one can be so irritating as a Kaffir—people are too anxious to retain their services to ill-use them. No doubt the original pioneers knocked them about a good deal, but now they are, if anything, over-pampered, and, from fear lest they should decamp, are generally allowed to have pretty much their own way.

This scarcity of labour is a serious matter for private people, but it will be a vital question when the mines begin to be developed: until there is a regular supply of cheap and abundant labour, it will be impossible to work them at a profit, unless they should prove to be of unusual richness. When the railway is completed, they will no doubt depend mainly upon Shangaans and Zambesi boys, but if, under a firm administration, the Mashonas should regain confidence, and believe that they will be fairly treated, there is no reason why they should not become proficient miners. They have always been skilled ironworkers, and if they begin when quite young they take kindly to the work in the mines. At first they dislike the idea of going underground, but after a time they prefer it to overground work. In the Penhalonga district they are paid 30s. a month and their food, which is equivalent to another 30s., and their hours are from sunrise to sundown, with a midday break for food. I was shown a Mashona who had remained at his work for six years without a break. This boy, however, was an exception. As a rule, they will work for a year, and will then go home for three months, coming back to the same employer if they have been well treated.

Rather than wait in Umtali whilst trying to arrange for boys, I preferred to walk down the coach-road

to Massi-Kessi. The first night I slept at Hawes &
Taylor's store, about eight miles away. Mr. Hawes told
me he had started a market garden, and had as many
as 5000 cabbages: he also told me that pigs do well,
and grow remarkably fat, and he thought Mashonaland
might be made a great pig-producing country, as the
pig is not liable to any disease peculiar to the country,
as almost every other animal is. On the following
day I walked on to Massi-Kessi, where I met Captain
Serejo, of the Portuguese navy, to whom Don Egas had
kindly given me a letter. He represents, under Don
Egas, the Portuguese Government in Manicaland. He
kindly asked me to stay the night with him at Andrada,
where he lives, and the next day showed me some
extensive ancient alluvial workings along the course of
the Revué River. They may possibly be the work of
the Phœnicians in olden times, but were more probably
made by the Portuguese when they took possession of
the country in the sixteenth century, for the records in
Lisbon show that a great deal of gold was sent to Portugal at that time from Eastern Africa. They have been
so thoroughly exploited that little gold is to be found
in them now. There are similar excavations in the
Penhalonga valley, and an attempt has recently been
made to work them anew, but not, I believe, with a
satisfactory result.

Captain Serejo had been making a number of agricultural experiments, and had formed a high opinion of
the fertility of the country; the one thing needful is

improved transport, and cheapened goods. An iron bedstead which in England cost 14s. 9d. in Umtali then cost 105s., a 4d. bottle of stout cost 6s.; everything was in the same proportion. It is impossible that any serious attempt can be made to develop the country until the cost of living is lowered.

Captain Serejo sent a boy with me to show me the road, so instead of going back to Massi-Kessi I followed a Kaffir footpath to the head of the Revué valley, and from there crossed the intervening range of hills to one of the stores on the Umtali coach-road. The scenery everywhere was exquisite, and the view from the crest of the hill, looking both ways into the Massi-Kessi and Revué valleys, was singularly beautiful; what struck me most being the softness of the tints, and the delicacy of their gradations. During my walk I came upon the only snake I saw in Mashonaland. The boy, who was walking in front of me, suddenly called out "Nyoka" (snake), and jumped to one side, and I just caught sight of something wriggling through the grass, but could not tell what kind of snake it was. There are many varieties in Mashonaland, both of venomous snakes and constrictors, but they are not often seen except by prospectors and people whose work takes them constantly into the bush. They are not common as they are in India. One of them, the spit-cobra, shoots his venom to a considerable distance; if it should strike the eye, it will produce blindness unless washed out at once. I reached the store in time for dinner, and

afterwards walked on with a man I met to Brown's Store, seven miles farther up the road. It was a moonlight night, or we should not have ventured to do it for fear of the lions. We had a number of *pagamisa*, or carrier boys with us, who kept up a monotonous chant during the whole time to frighten them away, and still more to keep off spirits, of which they have a great dread. In India the natives do exactly the same thing. I have often heard them in the Central Provinces, when walking along a solitary road at night, shouting at the top of their voices to scare away the ghosts.

When I got back to Umtali I found the Sessions had begun; Judge Vintcent being the presiding judge. He was appointed in 1894, and has done much to enforce order and respect for the law. He is always severe when oppression of the natives is proved. In Bulawayo, not long ago, he condemned a man to seven years' imprisonment for going round to the various kraals, and giving out that he was the new native commissioner, and, on the strength of it, practising various kinds of extortion. He had a case of oppression by a native policeman to try during these Umtali Sessions, and gave the man a heavy sentence; the prosecution being instituted at the instance of a prospector, who had come in, at great inconvenience and expense, to give evidence.

The days of lawlessness are happily dying out with the pioneers. In Mashonaland it is a great thing to have formed part of the original expedition that took possession of the country, and the title of pioneer is assumed by numbers of men who have no right to it, and who advance the most preposterous claims to indulgence and assistance. As a rule they drink heavily, but one learns to look leniently on drunkenness after a personal experience of the climate. It is not merely that it is trying, but there is hardly any fresh meat to be had, and tinned salmon and bully beef do not seem to nourish in the same way that fresh food does. One gets tired of the perpetual tea and condensed milk, and a craving is set up for some kind of stimulant. There is no doubt, too, that a little alcohol is a safeguard against fever; the difficulty is not to take too much.

But though there is a good deal of drunkenness, the use of the revolver, as in America, is unknown. In Chicago and the mining cities of the West, for a man to be shot in a brawl is an everyday occurrence. I saw two men kill each other, in the middle of the day, in a crowded street in Chicago, and it hardly excited attention. I don't think there has been a single instance of the kind in Rhodesia. Moreover the law prohibiting the sale of liquor to the natives is very strictly enforced, and natives are rarely seen the worse for drink, as is so frequently the case in Cape Colony and in the Transvaal. Their liquor legislation is much to the Chartered Company's credit.

A Mr. Fischer, who has a farm with his brother on the high veldt between Le Sapi and the Inyanga, asked me if I would walk out there with him, and Mr. Creech

kindly lent me two of his boys to enable me to do so.
Before I started I met Mr. Rainey, one of my missionary
friends, who had not been able to get away from Umtali.
He told me they had had the same difficulty as myself
in getting boys, and that eventually Mr. Kidd and Mr.
Coupland had gone on without them. Mr. Coupland's
tragic death I have already mentioned. Mr. Kidd subsequently made his way back to Massi-Kessi by a direct
path over the hills instead of returning by Umtali.
He nearly died there of fever, and was still weak and
ill when I saw him in Johannesburg three months afterwards. Mr. Rainey has remained at Melsetter.

The first night we stayed at Old Umtali, Mr. Caul-
field, the English Church clergyman, kindly putting me
up in the church-house, as there was no room in the
hotel. The next day we were delayed in starting until
four o'clock, so the heat was over before we began our
walk. We followed the Inyanga road until six o'clock,
when we reached the Odzana River, a lovely clear
stream that comes down from the Inyanga and flows
into the Odzi. Here we halted, and had supper, and as
before long the moon would be up, Mr. Fischer suggested
that we should go on to the Odzi, ten miles farther.
We left the Inyanga road on our right, and crossing the
Odzana, followed a Kaffir path to Echainia, a lofty cone-
shaped peak beneath which was the pass by which we
were to cross the range that divides the two rivers.

Kaffirs always walk in single file, placing one foot
before the other, so their paths are narrow and slightly

concave. A European finds them tiring at first, as his boots do not rest flat upon the ground, and until they are hardened to it, the sides of the feet become tender. I did not like walking behind a string of boys, as they intercepted the view, so I generally walked in front, and Mr. Fischer caused much merriment by telling them that my camera contained dynamite, and that I must go first to throw it at any lion we might meet. They quite believed what he said, and when we sat down to rest kept at a respectful distance from it.

The sun had set when we reached the foot of the pass, and the moon having not yet risen, it was very dark, and every rustle in the grass made me start, though Mr. Fischer assured me that there were no lions about, as the game had all been cleared off by the rinderpest, and there was nothing to attract them ; that they kept to the main road, where they could pick up oxen and donkeys. They had become so ravenous, on account of the scarcity of game, that a day or two before one of them had actually killed a horse in the middle of the day, whilst trotting behind the cart to which it was fastened. The main road was only seven miles away, and as they had killed three donkeys and a native there that week, I did not feel very confident that we might not come across one on his way to his hunting ground.

The moon rose when we were half-way up the pass, and even in the Himalayas I have seldom seen a grander sight. Towering up above us on the left was the pointed granite peak of Echainia, on the right was a deep ravine, and below us, stretching away for miles towards Umtali, we could see the level veldt shimmering under the yellow rays of the tropical moon.

We halted at the top for half-an-hour, lit a fire, and had a smoke and a rest. We gave the boys (we had nine with us) a cigarette each, and they were quite happy, sitting chattering and laughing round the fire like children. The Odzi was four miles farther on, the road descending steeply at first, but for the last two miles going on the level through deep sand, which the boys found very trying. It was then quite a little stream, which we could wade through easily, but in the rains it overflows its banks, and becomes a deep, impassable torrent. We camped a little way from it, more from fear of lions than of malaria, made a roaring fire, and had supper before going to sleep. The boys were in great spirits. They had plenty of *oojjoo*, the name they give to the roughly ground meal they obtain from a kind of millet called *ripoko*, which is the staple food of the Mashonas. It makes a dark brown viscous porridge, which to a European palate is not appetising, but the Mashonas say it is wonderfully sustaining. I daresay it is, for it seems to contain a considerable amount of oil. We also gave them what we did not finish of our tinned provisions, the jam being especially appreciated. Mr. Fischer's boys were Mashonas from a kraal near his farm, and they held themselves entirely aloof from my two boys, who were Shangaans. I noticed that if we gave a boy anything he did not keep it to himself, but shared it with the others. Mr. Fischer told me they always do this. The boys were quite raw and untrained, and it was very amusing to watch them. I had an unused kettle with me, and one of them came in much perplexity to ask if he was really to put it on the fire; that it would take all the brightness away.

It was the hottest time of the year, but it was chilly at night, so we undid a bale of the blankets which Mr. Fischer was taking back for trading purposes, and rolled ourselves up in them with a rifle between us, in case a lion should come prowling around. At daybreak we started again through a beautiful, well-timbered valley with great stretches of open grassy sward; on our east being the magnificent serrated outline of the Inyanga mountains, and on our west the low range of granite hills that separated us from the Salisbury road, weathered into every kind of strange and fantastic shape.

CHAPTER V

The Mashonas are a very superstitious people. I noticed that they would often throw a branch as they passed by on to a bundle of branches lying by the side of the road, and was told they did it for luck. When starting on a journey, an unmarried man will put a stick in the ground by the side of a path, and pile a few stones round it. If, when he returns along that path, possibly a month or two later, he should find the stick covered with branches by passers-by, it is a sign that he will have many children. After all it is not more foolish than our counting our cherry-stones.

We walked for several hours through lovely wooded country, until we came to a kraal, belonging to a chief called Rukui. The men were all out at work, but there were three or four women in the kraal, one of whom went and called the chief, an old grey-headed and very feeble man. He came supporting himself on a stick, held up by his son ; but, old as he was, there was quite as much respect paid to him by his people as if he were young and active, for so long as a Mashona chief is alive, his authority as chief continues. When the natives spoke to him, they clapped their hands softly together as a mark of deference. He gave us some Kaffir beer in a gourd calabash, but it had only just been made, and we were unable to drink it, though our boys drank it greedily. I have tasted it several times since, and cannot say I like it. It is made from Kaffir corn, and has a sour, sickly taste, but it is said to be very wholesome, and men who live long in the country grow to like it exceedingly. We gave Rukui a cigarette, which he pulled at so vigorously that it nearly choked him, and he was glad to hand it to one of his indunas. He told us that they had killed an eland the day before, so they had plenty of meat. We had seen occasional tracks both of eland and of sable antelope all the morning, but, since the rinderpest, game has become scarce. One of our boys had eaten so much the night before that he was taken violently ill, and we had to leave him behind with his load, with another boy to look after him, but they managed to come up again with us before nightfall. About five o'clock we arrived at another kraal called Chaganguru's. We did not go up to it ourselves, as it was late, but sent one of the boys to barter salt for ooffoo, and the chief came down to have a smoke and a talk. He was a remarkably fine-looking man, with regular features, and a well-shaped head, quite unlike most of the Mashonas. I think he must have had Arab blood in him, for he had a finely shaped nose, thin lips, and smooth hair; there was hardly anything of the Kaffir type about him.

For half a bar of salt, worth threepence, we got more ooffoo than I had bought in Umtali at a store for two shillings. The storekeepers, I was told, will not sell to the natives under a certain price, so that for salt for which a white man only pays sixpence, a native has to pay a shilling. In the same way there are two prices for blankets, and for the other articles which the Kaffirs principally buy. I do not know how this can be stopped, but it is an unfair system, and naturally makes the natives feel that they are unjustly treated.

We encamped that night by the side of a rippling mountain stream, at a place called Nia Tandi, taking the precaution to build a *skerm* or barrier of thorn bushes as a protection against the lions. A few yards away there was a camp of boys returning to their kraals from Umtali, where they had been at work, and they and our boys kept on chattering and eating till the middle of the night. Kaffirs only begin to amuse themselves in the evening; in the daytime both the men and the women are out of the kraal, the women grinding corn, fetching water, and doing other domestic work, whilst the men are harvesting, hunting, or fishing. In the evening they sit round the fire and talk and sing until far on in the night.

Next morning we had a steep hill to climb, which we were anxious to get over before the sun became too powerful, so we started an hour before sunrise. It

consisted of a long stretch of at least a mile of perfectly
bare granite, inclined upwards at a steep angle. When
we reached the top, we found ourselves on a level plain,
stretching as far as we could see, which is known as the
high veldt. On our left was a deep valley, on the far
side of which we could see Makoni's demolished kraal,
and beyond it the hills that form the Devil's Pass on
the Salisbury road. We reached Mr. Fischer's farm in
time for breakfast, and had a warm welcome from his
brother, who had been laid up with a bad attack of
fever. The brothers had been obliged to abandon their
farm when the rising broke out, and to go into laager
in Umtali; but as soon as the country seemed fairly
safe, they had returned to it, though they were warned
that they did so at their own risk. They had always
been on good terms with the natives, and were confident
that they would not be molested. To be on the safe
side, they did not go back into the huts which had
previously formed their homestead, but built a fort
between two huge granite boulders, in which they felt
they could resist any attack. They inserted a layer of
clay between the thatch and the rafters, to make the
roof fire-proof, so that they could not be burned out,
and they slept in a little room they had built up with
stones on the top of one of the boulders, the only access
to it being by a ladder which they could draw up after
them. Their principal difficulty, if they should ever be
besieged, would be to obtain water, as the spring is half
a mile away. The fort itself is strong enough to enable a

couple of resolute men to resist any number of Mashonas, but it would be an easy matter to starve them out.

When they went back to their farm the natives were still in open revolt around Salisbury, and it required no little courage to isolate themselves in a place a good fifteen miles from the nearest police-camp. It is men like these who are wanted as settlers. They are Americans, who came out three years ago, and Mr. Rhodes, who does all he can to encourage agriculture, gave them this farm, rent-free I believe, and they have done very well with it. Last year they raised a quantity of oats which they sold as forage to the troops, and they have also grown mealies and tobacco. They gave me some tobacco to try, manufactured by themselves, which they always smoked, but though pleasant in flavour, I found it far too strong; probably with continued cultivation it would become milder. They told me it grows luxuriantly, and so, too, do the castor-oil plant, which is indigenous, tomatoes, and grenadillas, the latter being imported from Natal. Vegetables they found difficult to raise, chiefly on account of the insects.

Farming is attended with many difficulties, and though they had no rent to meet, they could not make it pay by itself; where they have made their profit has been in trading with the natives, in buying mealies and ootfoo to sell again in Umtali. The principal difficulties with which they had been confronted in the way of farming had been the temporary difficulties of the limited market, which will improve as the country becomes more populated, locusts, which have been very bad for the last three years, and rinderpest, as well as permanent difficulties which are more serious. To begin with, the rainy season is too short, so the ground cannot be tilled until December. This drawback could be got over by a proper system of water conservation, for which the country is admirably suited. The ground does not remain fertile unless manured, and at present manuring is not possible as there are no cattle. That is only a question of time and of re-stocking when the rinderpest has been effectually stamped out. Moreover, cattle manure is a coarse, hot manure, and the red soil, which is the general soil in Mashonaland, has a tendency to bind, and requires bone-dust to open it. Cultivation will also clear away the insects with which the farmer is at present plagued. They abound in every new country. What is wanted is energy, even more than manure.

The country is well watered, with frequent streams which give plenty of water for stock, but there is little available for irrigation, as it lies in deep hollows. This obstacle, however, could easily be got over, as it has been in other countries, by pumping it up either by windmills or by steam power and leading it over the land. In Australia, for example, the farms in many districts are dependent for water solely upon artesian wells.

Again, in some places the ground is so sandy that it is difficult to lead water through it; but in Australia a similar difficulty has been overcome by leading it through pipes, and in the early days through the hollowed-out trunks of trees. Another trouble caused by the sandy nature of the soil is that, after it has been ploughed, it is so loose that a heavy shower of rain will wash the seed away; but with proper manure to bind it together a loose soil can often be made exceedingly productive. Then there are any number of insects—locusts, grasshoppers, beetles, and underground and overground borers; these are found in every new country and will disappear with cultivation. With regard to stock, the rinderpest is only a passing visitation and may be left out of the question. The cattle, it is true, are subject to lung sickness, red-water, and other diseases peculiar to South Africa, and in places the grass is coarse and sour, but taken as a whole the country is well suited for stock. This is shown by the fact that before the rinderpest broke out there were more than five hundred thousand head of cattle in Rhodesia. Almost everywhere in Mashonaland there is a sufficiency of water for them even in the driest seasons, and there is little probability of a scarcity of grass. In case of an unusually severe drought they could easily be driven from one pasturing ground to another. It is said that sheep will not do well; that the grass is too rank for them, and that they become poor and die in numbers from no apparent disease. This remark applies to the whole of South Africa, for with the exception of the Karroo, no part of it is a sheep country. I was told, however, by a man upon whose opinion I could rely, that the Inyanga and Melsetter districts will probably suit them admirably. The grass is short and turfy, and water so plentiful that there would be no risk of the droughts which are so great a danger to the Australian sheep-farmer.

Pigs, it is generally acknowledged, do well; they can be turned loose to feed on roots, and rapidly grow fat. A long-legged greyhound breed is indigenous to the country, but English pigs have been tried, and have been found to thrive capitally. Curiously enough the Mashonas will not eat them, though they will eat almost any other kind of flesh. It is probably because, like vultures, they are natural scavengers.

The country is not at present a white man's country, for when new soil is turned over fever is nearly sure to result. That, however, has been the case all over South Africa. It was very bad in Kimberley when the mines were first started, and is not uncommon in Pretoria even now. Men complain, too, that they soon lose their energy, and cannot do hard manual work. That is due, I think, more to bad food than to the climate, and to the presence of the natives, for a supply of black labour always spoils white labour; white people will not exert themselves when it is possible to make black people work for them. The worst of it is that the Mashonas are unwilling to work, and the general rate of wages is so high, owing to the excessive wages paid to boys for carrying loads, that it is impossible for farmers to pay the wages demanded and yet work their farms at a profit.

All these are very serious obstacles to any one intending to settle in Rhodesia at the present time, but they are all obstacles that can be overcome. The country so far has not had a fair chance. The incidental difficulties of the rebellion, the rinderpest, and the locusts, have been perfectly heart-breaking, and, in addition to all that, the majority of the so-called farmers have not been farmers at all. They are simply men who have taken to farming, and expect with little or no knowledge to make sufficiently large profits within a few years to enable them to come back to England. If they do not get these profits they say the country is not a farming country. Another temporary hindrance is, that the cattle being dead, there is at present no means to till the ground. Salted oxen are expensive, and horses even more so; and the latter will not live through the rainy season—very few survive it. They die both of horse sickness, and of lung sickness, and the same diseases attack mules. Donkeys are not affected, but they cost too much, and are too slow, and the expense of getting up steam-ploughs is prohibitive. The truth of the matter is that farming in Rhodesia requires capital. For a poor man, or a man with even moderate means, to emigrate there under present conditions, is simply folly. He will only lose his money, and probably also his health. He will certainly have a time of terrible struggle and hardship.

Mr. Wallace Broad, in the evidence he lately gave before the Bulawayo Chamber of Mines, summed up the question very fairly. He is a geologist and mineral surveyor, and a Dufferin gold medallist of the University of New Brunswick, and as he has been in Rhodesia some time, he is well qualified to judge. "The chances of making a fortune are greater here," he stated. "You cannot get very rich in Canada in farming, but are always sure of a competence. If a man comes here with capital and intelligence, he should do much better than in Canada. A man with £20,000 here cuts a small figure; in Canada, in one of the smaller sized towns, he would be considered a nabob. From what I have seen of the country I have great faith in it as a mineral region, and I think it will be heard of one of these days as a great gold-producer. It is difficult to make a comparison with Canada; we have an abundance of water there, and irrigation is seldom necessary. Generally speaking, the conditions are quite different; for instance, here it is possible with irrigation to have two crops in one year; there you can only have one; here you have native labour, there you have none; here you have locusts and drought to contend with, there early frosts, and often bad harvest weather. Each country has its advantages and disadvantages. On the whole Rhodesia offers as many inducements to the agriculturist as Canada, but here he requires by far the larger capital."

And he might have added that for some years to come the market for produce in Rhodesia must be infinitely more limited than it is in Canada.

CHAPTER VI

Mr. Fischer's farm is on a well-watered plain, over 5000 feet in height, but the hard granitic soil is not particularly well suited for agriculture; possibly it might do better for stock. The Inyanga plateau is only twenty-five miles distant, and I was assured by people who had been there, that it is admirably adapted for both; but like most things in Rhodesia, the Inyanga is still a region of possibilities; its capabilities have not yet been actually proved. Mr. Rhodes had recently bought several farms from a Mr. Fotheringham, an Australian, the only person who had really tried to farm there. I met him at Umtali on his way back to Australia; a lucky man, as he had been paid a good price for his land. He spoke well of the country, but nevertheless seemed glad to be leaving it; and the conditions of life in Rhodesia are so hard that I think most men would be glad to get away if they could. I met very few who wished to settle there permanently; almost every one was anxious to make a little money and clear out.

I was sorry that want of boys prevented my visiting the Inyanga, as the scenery is said to be more beautiful than in any other part of Rhodesia, the plateau itself being over 6000 feet in height, and the peaks attaining to as much as 8500 feet. It is said that traces have been found of such extensive irrigation that it must at one time have been thickly populated, but that must have been long ago, for it is now almost uninhabited.

Behind the hut in which the Fischers originally lived, is a kopje in which are the ruins of a remarkable fortified kraal. The Mashonas say it was not built by them, but by the Balosi, a people who lived in Mashonaland before they came into it. It has four separate circles of defence, composed of sconces formed by massive granite boulders connected together by strongly built walls, the masonry of which is peculiar, the stones fitting closely into each other without mortar. On the top of the rock which crowns the kopje was the chief's hut; it could only be reached by a ladder, as the rock has precipitous sides. At the foot of the kopje, a few yards outside the kraal, is a spring of excellent water, reached by a couple of strongly fortified underground passages, so that a rush could be made for it at night with comparatively little risk. The fortifications altogether betoken a high order of intelligence.

A mile or two away, on the road to the Inyanga, is a kraal belonging to a famous witch-doctor called Chirimba. We went over to see him but found the kraal empty, with no one in it except an old and

CHIRIMBA, MASHONA WITCH-DOCTOR, IN THE MIDDLE, WITH MASHONAS STANDING

marvellously wrinkled woman. I was sorry to have missed Chirimba, and was glad when he came the next morning to pay me a visit. He said he had heard there was a white man in the country with no hair on his face (to be clean-shaven is unusual in Rhodesia), so he presumed I was a white witch-doctor. I photographed him, and he went away, quite convinced, I believe, of my supernatural powers. I also took this photograph of the messenger of one of the native commissioners who passed by the farm, attended by a piccanin to carry his things, on his way to convey a message to a neighbouring kraal. He was fully armed, and besides his rifle carried another emblem of authority in the shape of a *sjambok* or hippopotamus-hide whip. In Matabililand these men are no longer permitted to go about with arms, but as Mashonaland was only just emerging from rebellion, it was not thought safe to send them to distant kraals unarmed. That may be so, but they certainly ought not to be allowed to go alone; they should always be accompanied by the native commissioner to whom they may be attached. As it is they are the scourge of the country, and like the zaptiehs in Turkey, do more than any one else to make the lives of the people wretched, and to foment rebellion. They were especially bad before the recent rising, when no trouble was taken to keep any check on them, and they are not much more trustworthy now. I was told of one who had gone into a kraal, and assaulted a Mashona woman.

The husband came running back to the kraal to protect her, and the police boy seized his rifle and shot him dead. Since I have been in England there has been a telegram in the papers saying that a chief in the Marandella district had killed another police boy for the same offence.

A great deal has been written about the ill-usage of the native women both in Mashonaland and in Matabililand, not only by these police boys but by the white men. I think, so far as white men are concerned, it has been grossly exaggerated. Of course there have been isolated cases, and there are also a certain number of white men who live with native women; that is not peculiar to Rhodesia, it occurs in every country where a white and black race mix. It was far more common in India, and in the other parts of South Africa, in their earlier days, than it is in Rhodesia. In Mashonaland, especially, it is rare, and morality altogether is, on the whole, higher than in most parts of England, certainly than in London. The women as a rule are well treated, and are very seldom Mashona women, who, though they are exceedingly immoral, are prevented from living with the white men by a prediction of Nyanda, the witch-doctress, that if they do they will beget snakes. In Salisbury and Umtali it is scarcely known for a man to have a black mistress, it is chiefly men who are living by themselves in the outlying districts. They generally get a woman from Zumbo in Portuguese territory, paying about £5 for her, and she almost

always has a happier lot with her white owner than she would have in her own kraal. The settlers have felt most deeply the charge of wholesale immorality that has been levelled against them. As a matter of fact they are less to blame in this respect than any people I have ever come across.

In Matabililand the social conditions are altogether different from those prevailing in Mashonaland. There the Maholi women have always been lax in their conduct, but the Matabili women have not, because unchastity was punished with death as amongst the Zulus and the Swazis. Now that the death penalty can no longer be inflicted, there is an almost universal demoralisation, the women offering themselves voluntarily to the white men. In most cases they are better treated than before, and no sympathy need be wasted upon them; but the fathers and husbands have a very just grievance, which no doubt was one of the chief causes of the rebellion. The fathers lose the *ukulobola*, the cattle which have to be paid for a wife, and the husbands lose their wives, for they naturally turn them away. In Natal exactly the same demoralisation is taking place. The Zulu women are not by nature moral, but, until Zululand came under our rule, they were enforcedly chaste, for the penalty was death to both parties for the seduction of any woman, whether married or single. Now the whole country is becoming corrupt, not, as so many people assert, because of the evil effect of Christianity upon the native character, but because the tribal authority, and with it the death penalty, have been done away with, and the women are no longer afraid to give free play to their passions. To check the rapidly spreading immorality a penal clause was inserted in the Natal Native Code, making the seduction of any woman, married or single, punishable with six months' hard labour; and some such law ought to be enacted for Rhodesia. How necessary it is to prevent a widespread degradation may be judged by what Mr. Cross, the magistrate of the Alfred Division of Natal, says in his yearly report, dated January 9, 1897: " I regret to say that the morals of the natives in this division are not improving (except with those coming under the influence of the missionaries), and they are bound to get worse now that the police have received orders not to prosecute men for contravening the provisions of section 277 of the Code, unless complaints are made to them by the parents of the girls who are seduced, or the husbands of the women who have committed adultery; this laxity to enforce the provisions of their own long-established law to the native mind means that they can do as they like. If the morals of the natives are to be improved the law of seduction and adultery should be enforced, especially as fear of punishment is the only means of impressing a thing on a native mind. This fact should not be lost sight of, viz., that the natives have to be treated like children in many ways, and if they are to be raised in the scale of morality under our government, then the law must be enforced, and not be a dead letter as it is at present."

Mr. Blake's description of the outraged modesty of the Matabili women is absurd: the difficulty is to keep them away from Bulawayo. So too is his assertion that cruelty and outrage are universal in Rhodesia. Some perfectly damnable things have been done, by men in high places, and the doers of them have not been punished—that is what has been so bad: it has established a sort of precedent of immunity; but these deeds have been the exception and not the rule, and they have not been worse, or more frequent, than similar deeds that have been committed during the reduction to submission of every savage nation.

Still the Matabili men have a very poignant grievance, for which a remedy ought to be provided by law. The curious thing is that it should never have been thought of, for the whole question was carefully gone into in 1881 by the Commission appointed by the Cape Government to inquire into native laws and customs. The neglect of the High Commissioner, and of the Chartered Company, to enact a law similar to that which exists in the Colony or Natal, is but another instance of the necessity of having a separate official appointed by the British Government, whose especial function it shall be to look after native interests. The evidence given by Pombani before the Commission, on behalf of the Fingoes, is both instructive and interesting. It explains the whole matter in the clearest possible way from a native point of view: " In giving our daughters in marriage we do not look alone to the cattle but to the character and standing of the man to whom we give her. We don't allow a girl to choose a husband for herself, we choose for her. Now the girls are giving us trouble in this respect, and this trouble arises through a thing called love. We parents do not comprehend this at all. In regard to the treatment of the women much depends on the character of the man. Even when ukulobola is not paid the treatment may be good, though it is sometimes not so. Ukulobola may be paid, and the treatment may be unkind, but it is worse where ukulobola has not been paid. A man can turn round on his wife and say, ' You are only a cat, I did not pay for you.' A cat is the only living animal which we natives never buy, and cats are passed among ourselves as presents. In former days we used to compel our daughters to marry the men we selected for them. Now we have learned this is not right, and the girls' wishes are consulted ; of course I cannot answer for every one, because it might create anger. But one evil which we see resulting from leaving the choice of a husband to the girl is that they are very often seduced, and that after seduction it may appear that the man is not a fit man to marry the girl, and so we have to keep the girl at our kraals. If we complain we are told what colonial law is; that it was by mutual consent, and the girls say it was by love. No fine is imposed on the man. According to our laws, when a man has seduced

a girl, she is depreciated in value and becomes an
idikazi.[1] It is not right in our opinion that this should
be so, and the man who seduces a girl should be fined,
because a father cannot get cattle for her, and he would
have done so had she not been seduced."

In consequence of this, and the other evidence that
was given, both seduction and adultery were made the
ground for a civil suit by the father or husband, the
measure of the damages being the custom amongst the
natives in the Transkei to punish seduction by a fine
of from three to five head of cattle, or more if the girl
be the daughter of a chief. If the Natal law of imprisonment be considered too stringent, there could
surely be no objection to making seduction a ground
for damages, as in the Transkei. A law of the kind is
absolutely necessary. In India, to prevent the natives
taking punishment into their own hands, adultery has
been made a criminal offence, punishable with five
years' penal servitude. In connection with this subject,
I must add that the Dutch, as a race, are singularly free
from reproach; partly from the contempt for the natives
derived from the unforgotten traditions of slavery,
partly also from the austere character of their religion.
There are, of course, a certain number of Dutch half-
castes, but the majority of the Dutch, especially of the
upper classes, are of unmixed blood. Around French
Hoek, and in the Ceres district, where the Huguenots
originally settled, it is curious to note how the purity of

---

[1] *Idikazi*—*i.e.* dowerless.

the race has been maintained through all these generations. Not only have most of the people French
names, but I noticed in many of them the dark eyes
and hair, the small well-shaped ears, and the delicately
chiselled features which they brought with them from
their native Languedoc.

Another urgent question is that of corporal punishment. I asked Mr. Taberer, the chief native commissioner for Mashonaland, under what authority the
native commissioners are empowered to flog. He replied that they are strictly prohibited from doing so,
that it is illegal, and that they can be punished for it.
I said that I had heard from prospectors and transport
riders all the way up the road that they do flog, however illegal it may be. I was told that if a boy will
not work, or tries to run away, the usual thing is to
take him to the native commissioner, and have him
given twenty-five, and I found that the word "twenty-
five" said in English to any of the boys was sufficient
to make them grin in a sickly way—they quite understood what it meant. I asked a man who was ex-
patiating one day on the excellence of the system for
what offence it was inflicted, and he replied, for breaking a contract. He put it in this way: " A boy engages
to serve me for a certain time, and I give him food,
and so if he bolts before his time is up, naturally
I can have him flogged." " But," I suggested, " if you
have given him food for so many days, he has also
given you labour, so if he goes off without his pay

you are about quits." "Well, I can't argue about it," he replied; "all I know is, that is what is done." After a flogging, he said, a boy would do his work all right and give no further trouble, and he assured me it is the only way to treat natives.

Most men I met told me the same thing, but Sir Theophilus Shepstone, whose knowledge of the native character was unrivalled, gave the following evidence before the Commission to which I have already referred. He was asked by Sir J. D. Barry, "What would you consider to be the best penalty for disobedience on the part of a servant to a master? Would you fine and imprison him, or would you enforce corporal punishment?" He answered, "*Fine or imprisonment would be the most suitable punishment for such an offence.*" "Would you give the magistrate the right to flog?" "I think that in many cases of theft the magistrate should have that power." "Do the natives attach any disgrace to it?" "Yes."

There is a criminal breach of contract act both in the Colony and in Natal, but there must be a regular trial before a magistrate, and formal evidence must be given in proof of the contract; moreover, flogging cannot be inflicted, only imprisonment, whilst in India a breach of contract is not a criminal offence at all. It is not right that half-educated men of no social position, many of them mere boys, whose only qualification for the work is that they know the native languages, should be entrusted with such arbitrary powers, or rather that the illegal exercise of these powers should be winked at by the authorities, for it is idle to suppose that they are not aware of what is going on. Is it a matter for wonder that labour is so difficult to obtain for the mines, or for any other purpose? Mr. Rhodes told some interviewers lately that the original supply of labour had been stopped owing to Sir Richard Martin's report and to the efforts of Exeter Hall faddists. That is certainly not a true statement of the case. It was stopped by the rebellion long before Sir Richard Martin's report appeared, and the rebellion was directly caused by the oppressive treatment of the natives. I will go more into detail later on, when I come to sum up the general results of the Company's rule. Mr. Rhodes also stated that when the railway is extended to the coal-fields of the Zambesi, there will be no difficulty in obtaining boys from there. When that occurs, it is to be hoped that the High Commissioner will take measures to insure that the same treatment is not meted out to them as has been meted out to the unhappy Matabili and Mashonas. It is not pleasant to notice the way in which the latter avoid coming into contact with the settlers, and to recollect that when we first went up to Mashonaland they welcomed us gladly. Colonel Wood, who travelled there in 1887, says: "We were pleased to notice that the Mashonas seemed an honest people, as articles I lost from the waggon were found and restored by them. Their conduct was in contrast with that of the Matabili"; and again, "This part of the country (near the Umfuli River) is peopled by industrious, happy people who reap good harvests. There is no missionary of any sort," he continues, "among these poor people, and they are so fond of the white men that one would exercise a good influence."

When one looks back over the history of South Africa, it is sickening to observe how the same farce has been re-enacted time after time. First the missionary goes up, and if he is a good man, his influence becomes so great with the tribe that he seems to it almost like a god. An entrance having been thus obtained into the country, and white men received with cordiality and friendship, the chief is wheedled into giving a concession, by which, before long, the ruin of the tribe is effected; it may not be deliberately intended, but it is nevertheless effected. The missionaries have, as a rule, acted in accordance with their tenets, and so long as they have not been followed up by other white men, their influence has been almost always for good. Look at the result of their labours in Khama's country. But they open the door to other white men, and the net result in most cases has been subjugation and drink and national degradation: and in some instances rebellion and partial extermination. Of a truth the African missionary may say, "I come not to bring peace but a sword."

However much one may admire the character of the individual missionary—and I for one do admire it in all sincerity—it is hard to see in what way civilisation as yet has been of benefit to the Kaffirs. A man who knew them intimately said to me in Cape Town, "Why should we intrude our religion upon a people like the Zulus, who until we unsettled them in their religious beliefs were really a very virtuous people." It is a knotty question—that of the heavenward way—but in South Africa we generally succeed in keeping the feet of the natives off it, and not upon it.

The Zulus are an essentially logical people. "You say it is a wicked thing to drink and lead immoral lives," a Zulu said to one of my friends, "and that if we do we shall go to hell. Well, hell can't be a very bad place, for you white people don't seem to be afraid of going there. We see that you do all these things."

We argue about the natives, and lay down rules for their improvement, but we seldom try to see through their eyes, or to understand how *they* feel about all that is being done for, and to them. Yet it is interesting sometimes to glance into a native's mind, as the following little essay enables us to do. It was written by a Zulu school-girl: "We often wonder if the English and the Dutch did right to take the country away from us. I don't know whether they did right to come here or not. It was right to help us to be better, and it was not right to take our land from us, and give us nothing but English government and taxes. I think they did right a little, but much more wrong. They have also brought many things that trouble us. They make us pay taxes for our own houses. They do not make our houses for us either; they give us a little piece of land and we stay on it, and never go on to what they call theirs, and yet they make us pay taxes. Before the English came, the natives' wants were few and easily supplied, and they were not troubled about what they should do with their money, for they had none. Their children would play in the sunshine and dirt until they were satisfied, with no one to tell them not to soil their clothes, or to trouble them by calling them into school. In this way the Abantu lived."

The question of locations to which this little Kaffir girl called attention, has been the cause of most of the rebellions that have taken place. A tribe when conquered is placed on a location, often of poor ground and insufficient for its needs. This has been the case in Matabililand, where the Chartered Company were compelled by the Matabililand Order in Council of 1894 to set aside land for this purpose. That order did not, however, apply to Mashonaland, and I believe that there an apportionment of locations has not yet been made, but that the whole of the land has been pegged out for farms, the Mashonas being allowed to remain in their kraals upon them at the sufferance only of the new owners, one of whom told me that he had endeavoured to obtain labour from a certain Mashona chief by representing to him that as he and his tribe were living upon his farm, he ought to supply him with boys. I was told, too, that Makoni, the greatest of the Mashona chiefs, whose capture and execution I will shortly describe, felt it as one of the greatest of his grievances that his land should have been given away to strangers up to his very kraal.

It must be remembered that the natives are not systematic cultivators; that they have neither the knowledge nor the means for bringing poor land under cultivation. They only sow in patches where the conditions are favourable, and they require large tracts for their cattle to wander over. To restrict them unnecessarily in their migrations is the most serious injury that can be inflicted upon them. If there is to be permanent peace in Mashonaland, an amount of land sufficient for their needs must be set aside for them without delay.

Sir Andreas Stockenstrom, Lieutenant-Governor of the Eastern Province, in the evidence he gave in 1852 to the Committee of the House of Commons appointed to report on Kaffir affairs, laid great stress on the neglect of this elementary act of justice as having conduced to the recent Kaffir revolt. "You must leave them the land; no tribe can do without land: barbarians less than civilised nations. The Kaffirs are not manufacturers nor sailors; if they have no corn and pasture-land they must rob or starve."

In any arrangement, moreover, that is made to set aside land in Rhodesia for the natives, watch will have to be kept by the High Commissioner, to prevent it being taken from them again upon some frivolous pretext. That has been the cause of almost all the native troubles in South Africa.

The *Financial Record* at the end of the Matabili war foreshadowed clearly what has since happened. On the 7th April 1894 it remarked: "Reuter reported from London on Thursday that Sir Henry Loch has arranged with Lord Ripon a settlement of the Matabili question that will be conducive to the prosperity of the natives, and that the text of the settlement has been wired to the administrator of the Cape. South Africa generally will read this with much interest, and will be curious to see in what respect the settlement will benefit the natives. If this means that the Matabili are to be deprived or filched of their farms, that is of all those that are worth anything, and driven into locations within the boundaries of which they will find it difficult to subsist, we may take it for granted that the native trouble in the Northern Transvaal will have its replica in Matabililand." It is exactly what was done, and the predicted result has followed. Mr. Carnegie lays especial stress upon this matter. "Two districts," he says, "were also reserved for native locations, but these being on the whole unhealthy, have up to the present not been occupied by the natives, who dread the fever from past experience." Whether other locations have yet been assigned to them I was not able to ascertain. It is not a question that can safely be left in abeyance.

CHAPTER VII

The labour difficulty had followed me even to this remote farm, and Mr. Fischer was unable either to procure me boys, or to get them for himself for a trading trip he was anxious to make to the M'toko country. I had therefore to leave my luggage behind, and to walk down to the Le Sapi store, twelve miles away, to see if I could obtain boys there. The storekeeper kindly lent me one of his own, and told me to call at the farm of Frank Xigubu, the Zulu mission boy who was brought up to Mashonaland by Bishop Knight Bruce, and ask him if he could help me. I did so, and got a boy from him also. I found him reading to a mixed class of Mashona men and women, who seemed to be listening with an absorbed interest. I noticed many little things whilst I was in Mashonaland which showed that the natives would eagerly grasp at any means of improvement if it were presented to them.

For instance, two men in Salisbury told me they had overheard their boys teaching themselves the English alphabet. Every one spoke of Frank as an honest reliable man who is doing his best, but the means at his disposal are small. He is, I believe, no longer in the service of the mission, but is farming on his own account. From there I walked on towards Makoni's kraal, accompanied part of the time by a man I had chanced to meet. On our way we met a native carrying a rifle, and asked him how he came to have it when it is strictly forbidden. He explained that he had been given permission by the native commissioner, because one of Makoni's sons was reported to be in the neighbourhood, and anxious to avenge his father's death, and it was not deemed safe for friendly natives, who had sided with us, to go about unarmed. This explanation seemed sufficient, so we let him go, but several men to whom I related the incident said that it was lucky it was not they who had met him, as they would certainly have shot him on sight; and one man, who, although a mere boy, had been an assistant native commissioner, assured me that it was an unwritten but perfectly understood law that any one coming across an armed native was justified in shooting him. When I reached Bulawayo I asked Captain Lawley, the deputy-administrator, if this was really the case, and he gave me a copy of the Arms Act of 1897, by which it is provided that a native or Asiatic found with arms or ammunition shall be liable to a fine not exceeding £50, or be imprisoned, with or without hard labour, for a a period not exceeding two years. This is not nearly so severe as the Arms Act in force on the Indian frontier. The Act, moreover, lays down that not every one, only a justice of the peace, field-cornet, or member of a duly constituted police or defensive force, may apprehend any one found in possession of such arms or ammunition, and convey him before the nearest magistrate.

When I left my companion it was still early in the afternoon, and, as I had the two boys with me, I felt sure I could not miss my way. But the view from the kraal was a glorious one, and I remained looking at it so long that it was dark hours before we reached the Fischers' farm. The boys had not been there before, and only vaguely knew its whereabouts. They lost their way completely, and we wandered on and on in the darkness until I began to think we should have to camp out—not a particularly cheerful prospect with lions about. About nine o'clock we came to a kraal high up on the side of a hill; the dogs barked and the women shrieked, and we could see torches being carried hither and thither. The rebellion had only just been put down, and I was afraid to go up and ask the way, so I motioned to the boys to keep straight on. Luckily the kraal had put them right in their bearings, and they knew from it where they were, and in another half-hour piloted me safe through to my destination.

It was not a pleasant walk, for I had no firearms of any kind with me, not even a revolver—only my camera

CAPE CART AT THE DEVIL'S PASS IN MANICALAND.

—and I felt nervous about snakes, and still more about lions; but when it was over I felt glad to have gone through it, and to have experienced the intense, silent loneliness of the open veldt. The natives were burning the long grass before the rains, and the hurrying, crackling columns of flame, leaping along the mountain side in the moonless night, had a sublimity that I shall never forget.

On the following day I bade good-bye to my kind friends, the Fischers, and started with my boys for Le Sapi. There I took advantage of a Cape cart, on its way down to Umtali, to return to the Devil's Pass, which I was anxious not to miss. On the way we passed by Mount Zonga, an odd sugar-loaf hill, which the Mashonas assert was transported bodily from Gazaland, and deposited where it now stands. The Devil's Pass I thought disappointing, and the view from it not nearly so grand as that from the Christmas Pass, but it has as bad a reputation for lions as that pass had in the pioneer days of Umtali. The night before my arrival they had killed a mule thirty yards behind the store. The mules for the coach are kept at the top of the pass, and the storekeeper, hearing a great noise in the stables, got up to see what it was, and was standing at the door of his tent when they broke loose, and stampeded wildly past. The lions must have been amongst them at the time, for on the following morning he found the spoor of two, and the remains of a mule they had killed and eaten immediately behind the hut. In addition to the store there is a police camp on the pass, in which the men were discontented and wretched, badly housed and utterly uncared for. The same state of things existed in the police-camp at Old Umtali, where things might surely be better managed. The food served out was insufficient, and there were no arrangements for having it properly cooked; and the men had no proper kit. They were sleeping on the ground instead of on stretchers, which might easily be made at a very small cost; or the men might be employed to make rough stretchers for themselves; they would be a great preventive of fever. In Umtali they have the advantage of a doctor and a hospital, but in the isolated police-camps there is neither, and I heard many sad stories of untended illness and death. What is particularly hard is that recruits from England have to undergo a medical examination at Salisbury before they are finally taken into the force, and if they fall sick on the way up from Beira, before they reach Salisbury, they have to pay for their medical and hospital expenses out of their own pockets, and if they are finally rejected, they have to find their way back without pay through a country in which travelling is phenomenally expensive.

The hardships experienced in the pioneer days were intelligible; there were no means of communication; but the men understood before they enlisted that they would have to rough it, and bore their privations cheerfully. Now they are led to believe that they are going out to a settled country, with a proper administration; and if a little trouble were taken, there would really be no necessity for the way in which they are treated. Other people in Mashonaland do not have to suffer as the police are made to suffer. It is entirely a matter of faulty administration, for in Matabililand the police are in a very different state. The result of their treatment in Mashonaland is that almost the whole of the force is in a state of dangerous discontent, and I think if men in England knew the kind of life they would have to lead that very few would enlist.

The principal defect of early Rhodesian administration was want of system, but now, in the reaction from the original rough and ready methods, there is a great deal of useless red tape in all the departments of the Civil Service; it needs thorough overhauling from beginning to end.

From the Devil's Pass I returned to Le Sapi, and from there walked on to Headlands, with a couple of boys kindly obtained for me by Mr. Ross, the native commissioner. I sent them on by the main road and walked myself across the veldt with a Mashona guide, through the exquisite mountain scenery of which Professor Bryce has given so vivid a description. At Headlands, which is 5200 feet in height, I found a Mr. Pretorius and his brother combining farming and store-keeping. They have built for themselves one of the few brick houses between Umtali and Salisbury, and have a comfortable homestead with a fair amount of stock, upon which they have chiefly relied for a livelihood. They have not done much in the way of cultivation, but the soil around them is rich, and they mean to make a beginning this year. Their farm is situated in an extensive valley, the greater part of which is composed of rich black loam which they say is exceedingly fertile. They have already made a little garden to which they have led water from a distance of over half a mile, and have grown with success peaches and apricots and most kind of vegetables.

There used to be a kraal on the hill at the back of the store, but the natives attacked the store during the rising, and the kraal was demolished by the volunteers. The Mashonas in consequence have moved farther away, making labour difficult to procure. Mr. Pretorius was not able to get me boys, but I managed to arrange with a transport driver to take my luggage up on one of his waggons. Owing, however, to a misunderstanding with the boys who had come with me from Le Sapi I was obliged first to return there. I had reached Headlands late in the evening, and they did not turn up till the following morning, having stayed at a kraal on the way for the night, for Kaffirs will never walk at night if they can possibly help it, for fear of the wild beasts. They arrived just as I was going to breakfast, and patted their stomachs in token that they wanted food.

Mr. Pretorius gave them some ooffoo and told them to go to the boys' quarters to cook it. He also told them that I should probably require them to go on to Macheki, another twelve miles. He said they did not seem very willing, but thought we might be able to induce them to go after they had had their food. When I came to an arrangement with the transport rider, I sent for them to give them their pay, but found that after eating their breakfast they had gone off without saying a word to any one. They were to have been paid two shillings each, a very fair wage for a day's work; it was the price I had been told to pay by Mr. Ross, and is the ordinary rate of wage in that part of Mashonaland. The natives certainly have no ground of complaint with regard to the prices paid them for their work. They are much better paid than labourers in England. The difficulty is that they have no desire to work for any wage, however great, and have practically to be forced into doing it. I was a good deal vexed when I found they had gone, for they were Mr. Ross's own boys, and I did not like him to think I had swindled them out of their pay; I was curious, too, to discover the reason which had prompted them to go away unpaid after a hard day's work, and I knew I could catch up the waggon in a day or two, if I went back first to Le Sapi to see him, and explain the matter.

Mr. Pretorius was going part of the way to get a plough and some other things from a farm belonging to a Mr. Williams, which lies a little off the main road, and I was glad to accompany him. I think I have never seen a more beautiful stretch of country, and in places it seemed very fertile. It was here that the first settlement of Dutchmen and Afrikanders was made in 1891. Fate has been adverse and there are none of them left: they have all died or gone elsewhere. Before the rising Mr. Williams' farm was the model farm of Mashonaland. He had a considerable area under cultivation, and was really doing well; but during the rebellion everything went to rack and ruin. The house, a well-built brick house, was still standing, though with broken windows and smashed-in doors, and with weeds choking up the little garden. It was a sad picture of the harm wrought to the country by the rising. We saw a few buck on the way, and found afterwards that we had just missed a herd of sable antelope, two of the men from the police-camp getting several of them. On the way Mr. Pretorius showed me a Mashona game-trap, a deep pit, filled at the bottom with sharp-pointed stakes on which the animal is impaled, and covered over by a deceptive network of earth and boughs.

I reached Le Sapi at midday, to find that Mr. Ross had shifted his quarters to the police-camp six miles away, on the new road along which the railway is to come, and when the heat of the day was over I set off by the Kaffir footpath, which I was told would lead me to it. I found it difficult not to lose my way, for in places there was a regular network of intersecting paths, but I knew the direction and the telegraph poles helped to keep me right. I mention each day's wanderings because I was told in Beira, and even in Umtali, that it would not be safe to go off the high-road, and that between Headlands and Salisbury even the high-road was insecure. Certainly, so far as Headlands, the people seemed perfectly submissive: for, a stranger to the country as I was, and absolutely ignorant of the language, I never met with the least unpleasantness. And there are really very few natives. One may travel for miles without meeting one.

Mr. Ross was surprised to see me, as his boys had not said a word about not having been paid. They had told him I wanted to take them on to Macheki, but that as that would bring them into the territory of another chief, they had declined to go. They never like going out of their own district, Mr. Ross said, and that was in itself a sufficient reason for them to forego their pay. I found afterwards there was probably one which was even more powerful. In not a few instances men have taken boys on and on beyond the place to which they originally agreed to carry, and have then not paid them, and these boys not unnaturally said to themselves, "When this man gets to Macheki, he will probably want us to go on to Marandellas, and perhaps even to Salisbury, and he may not pay us at the end of it. We have worked a day without pay, but it's better to work a day for nothing than to work a week." They had gone back to their kraal, so all I could do was to give Mr. Ross the money, and he kindly arranged to send it out to them.

The weather was lovely, not too hot, for there had been an occasional thunderstorm, and the forest was so beautiful that I would gladly have wandered about in it for several days longer: but it was uncomfortable being separated from my things, so I went straight back to Headlands: this time by the new road. It was the Mashona spring, and the trees were in full foliage. I noticed one covered all over with a delicious-scented mauve flower, but no one was able to tell me its name, or if it has any use. Many of the trees in Mashonaland seem to be unknown both in the Transvaal and in the Colony. Fig-trees were numerous, the figs growing oddly enough not on the branches, but clustered thickly upon the roots and trunk. Kaffir oranges, too, were very common. They are a species of strychnine with a vivid green fruit, about the size of an orange, which turns when ripe into a brilliant yellow. The pulp is refreshingly acid, but it is not safe for a European to eat many of them. They do not seem to hurt the Kaffirs, for their hard shells may be seen lying about wherever the natives have been camping: I often used the broken pieces as a drinking-cup. I did not see many flowers, though I was told that the veldt would be covered with them as soon as the rains had fairly set in: but I came across a good deal of the pretty but dangerous little blue tulip, which works such devastation among the cattle and sheep. The Dutch call it "snakehead," from the resemblance of the flower to the erected head of a snake. Almost all the waggons in the road had been delayed by it, and some had lost a number of their oxen. It seems to contain an irritant poison, which makes the animal swell up, and causes great pain. Sheep are affected as well as cattle, and care must be taken to keep them from grazing on land where it is likely to be found.

Sunflowers grow to a great size, and when people begin to turn their attention to something else than gold, they might be cultivated profitably for the sake of their oil, as they are in Russia and Sclavonia.

The country was looking its worst, although it was spring, for the locusts had destroyed every green thing. There are several kinds, but all equally destructive. They seemed to me a little smaller than the Indian variety. The agricultural department in Salisbury have tried to destroy them with a fungus, with which a few are inoculated and turned loose amongst the others, but I believe without much success. At night they settle on the trees, and become torpid with the cold, and in the early morning, before the sun has awakened them, they rest on the branches with folded wings, turning the whole forest into a rich brown, like the russet tints of autumn. The natives eat them greedily, and so do most animals; pigs, dogs, and fowls especially, are all ravenously fond of them. After all they are only essence of vegetables, but white people have an aversion to them, much like that of the Scotch to shrimps: they do not seem quite canny. The principal forest-tree is the M'sassa; the wood is good for nothing but firewood, for

it is subject to the attacks of a boring insect, which
renders it unfit for timber, but the bark is stringy
and exceedingly tenacious, and the natives make an
excellent cord from it. There is another tree called
by the natives "Gonte," from the bark of which they
also make game-nets, and neatly woven bags, so close
in texture as to be almost waterproof. Mr. Lingard, of
the agricultural department, told me that experiments
are being made to test its commercial value. There is
also a curious tree with a hard, woody pod, which bursts
with a spiral twist, and shoots out the seeds with a sharp
crack. The first time I heard them bursting I fancied
some animal near me was treading on loose branches,
the noise is so loud. There are a great number of other
trees, acacias, mimosas, and euphorbias, and a large
variety of the sugar-bush, a species of protea. The
castor-oil plant grows luxuriantly everywhere, and the
natives use the oil for smearing their bodies and hair;
it makes them smell most vilely. I bought a Mashona
pillow to which the smell of the oil still clings tenaci-
ously. It is a curiously carved piece of wood, about nine
inches in height, with a slightly hollowed out cavity for
the neck to rest upon. Mr. Pretorius also gave me a
Mashona battle-axe and a beautifully carved tinder-
box, made out of the end of a pumpkin, and filled with
an inflammable pith. This is held in one hand with a
piece of flint, which is struck sharply with the other
with a circular bit of iron. They carry it, as they do
their snuff-boxes, in a hole pierced in the lobe of the

ear. I succeeded in getting a pretty little snuff-box made of horn, but the Mashonas have now taken to making them of empty cartridge cases, and snuff-boxes of their own make are becoming uncommon.

Wild cotton is abundant, and is of good quality. Mr. Lingard showed me some in Salisbury that had fairly good staple. In Cape Colony oaks are an important industry, and there is no reason why they should not do well in Mashonaland. In Ceres the forty-year-old oaks are magnificent, and the oak avenues in Stellenbosch are known all over Africa. The Dutch plant them in the Ceres district, for the sake of the acorns, upon which they feed the pigs. They will only grow trees which yield a crop. What timber they require they obtain as a rule from the poplar, and firewood chiefly from a species of protea; but they only use fires for cooking, and not to sit by as we do. When it is cold they go to bed with their clothes on, and cover themselves over with skins and blankets. They say it is not healthy to sit by a fire in a room, and as they hermetically seal their rooms, which have no chimney, I daresay it is not. When a fire is made in a room, it is made on the hearth, and the smoke finds its way through the rafters. They cook in an annexe on an open hearth. I am now talking of course of the Boer farmers, who live in out-of-the-way districts, and come little into contact with civilisation.

The great drawback to South Africa is the backwardness of the Dutch, and the restless, floating character of

the English.   The only remedy is the gradual education
of the former, which will result, and is every day resulting, from the opening up of the country by railways, and
by the consequent increased intercourse of the rural
population with that of the towns.[1]

---

[1] It may be asked what proof there is, beyond floating gossip, that
even in the early days the Mashonas were treated harshly or with
injustice.   In a letter dated 26th April 1892, addressed by the High
Commissioner, Sir Henry Loch, to the Secretary of the British South
Africa Company, with regard to the shooting of N'Gomo, Sir Graham
Bower used the following words : "I am to add also that the punishment inflicted in this case, involving the loss of some twenty-three
lives, appears utterly disproportionate to the original offence, which
was the theft of some goods from a Mr. Bennett ;" and Mr. Fairfield
on 31st May 1892, wrote on behalf of Lord Knutsford, "The full report
would, in Lord Knutsford's opinion, have justified much stronger terms
of remonstrance than were used by the High Commissioner."

CHAPTER VIII

I HAVE mentioned that I spent some time at Makoni's
kraal. He was the principal chief in the district that
lies between Manicaland and Mashonaland, between
which the Odzi River forms the border. Originally
M'tasa claimed to be his overlord, but Makoni for a
long time past had succeeded in making himself independent. Neither he nor M'tasa had ever paid
tribute either to Lobengula or to Gungunhana. These
powerful monarchs had attacked both of them many
times, but had always been obliged to retire discomfited.
When Mashonaland was taken possession of in 1890,
M'tasa coquetted for a while with the Portuguese,
with a syndicate of Natal merchants, and with the
Chartered Company. Ultimately he accepted a payment of £100 a year from the Chartered Company,
and placed himself under its protection. This the
Chartered Company construed to give them authority
over Makoni also. Makoni always chafed under the
seizure of his country, and in 1894 he killed a native
policeman who had been misconducting himself, and in
various other ways showed a restive spirit. He seems
throughout to have been on bad terms with the autho-

rities, but to have uniformly treated individual settlers with kindness and consideration. What annoyed him most was the pegging-out of the whole of his territory for farms or gold claims. This made him justly indignant.

Such was the position of affairs in June 1896, when the Mashonas around Salisbury broke into revolt, and murdered Mr. and Mrs. Norton and their child, the governess, and an American who was staying with them. Mr. Norton had gone to a neighbouring kraal, and was shot on his way back by order of the witch-doctor. At the same time another party of natives attacked the house and killed all the inmates by volleys from the outside. It is believed that they defended themselves heroically to the last, and killed a great number of their assailants, Mrs. Norton shooting several with her revolver. The bodies were not touched, and were buried by a patrol sent out hastily from Salisbury. Mr. Norton's body was only found in November, when Major Harding rode out and buried it by the side of his wife. These murders were the first intimation the people in Mashonaland had of the serious character of the revolt. Other murders followed in rapid succession, and all around and to the north and east of Salisbury there was a general feeling of alarm, which gradually spread into Manicaland. But even before that there had been symptoms of disaffection, and on the 3rd April the settlers had been ordered to come into Umtali, because fires had been seen at night near M'tasa's kraal. It was generally believed that he was going to rise, but one of the settlers with great gallantry rode out alone and had a conference with him, and was assured that the fires were only bush-fires. His coolness probably saved M'tasa from meeting the same fate that befell Makoni. The people went back to their farms and mining camps until they were electrified with the news of the murder of the Nortons at the end of June. On the 25th of that month they were all warned to come into laager again, but those who were nearer Headlands than Umtali were directed to form a laager there.

Next day all the people in the laager moved down to Umtali without being attacked on the way, though there were many positions on the road which they would have found it difficult to get through had they been defended. For a whole month the district was deserted, and the abandoned stores and farm-houses were naturally looted by the Mashonas, but they were not destroyed; three traders, however, Metcalfe, Richards, and Hitchman, were murdered at a kraal not far from Headlands, by one of Makoni's sons, and by the son of another chief called Tandi. But Makoni's son had been on bad terms with his father for some time past, and there was no evidence to connect Makoni with the murders; indeed, there was no time for him to have given any orders in connection with them, for the men had gone unexpectedly to the kraals to get food, and their murder was sudden and unpremeditated. Up to the moment, too, of his death, Makoni disclaimed all responsibility for them; and as a rule when a native is face to face with death, if he has done the thing of which he is accused, he will confess to it.

On July 28th, Colonel Alderson, who had arrived from England with imperial troops, attacked his kraal with 350 men. Major Haynes of the Royal Engineers and two men were killed, and, as Makoni had retreated into the caves below the kraal, and could not be got at, the troops retired after burning the kraal and driving away the cattle. Makoni's loss is said to have been heavy. Colonel Alderson then marched up the Salisbury road, leaving fifty men of the West Riding regiment and some volunteers at Le Sapi, about eight miles from Makoni's. This garrison remained there inactive for nearly a month, and not only did Makoni take no hostile action, but on the 13th of August he sent in two of his indunas with an offer of surrender if his life were spared, but the High Commissioner wired that he would be tried, and would have to show that he had no complicity in any of the murders.

On the 20th of August Major Watts arrived from Matabililand with sixty volunteers and fifteen waggons. It is said that on the 26th Makoni again sent his head induna to sue for peace, and that shortly before the second attack he made a last despairing effort to save himself by sending in yet another induna with half-a-crown, as a token that he was ready to pay his hut tax. The money was refused, and again no attempt was made by those in authority to confer with him in person. On the 30th, Major Watts made a night march, and attacked his kraal at daybreak with one seven-pounder, 130 of the Umtali volunteers, and fifty men of the West Riding regiment. Makoni retired at once into his caves without firing a shot, nor did he attempt to make any resistance until the caves were assaulted. For four days they were surrounded, and every effort was made with dynamite to force him to surrender, and he was told repeatedly through Tom the Cape boy, who acted as interpreter, that if he came out his life would be spared.

On the 3rd September Tom again urged him to give himself up, and he decided to do so; but as he was coming out of the cave, one of the volunteer officers caught hold of him by the arm, and dragged him out, asserting that he had taken him prisoner. His people then gave in, and came straggling out of the caves. The effect produced by the dynamite had been terrible, and the stench from the dead bodies was overpowering. Makoni was put in a hut by himself, and the indunas had a separate guard placed over them, the remainder of the natives being surrounded by a ring of sentries. During the night several of the indunas succeeded in effecting their escape, and it was feared that if Makoni should escape also, the whole district would be in a blaze, and that the safety of Umtali itself might be endangered. A court-martial was therefore convened to try him, one of the native commissioners being appointed to act as interpreter, and as his defender. In spite of his assertion that he was innocent, he was found guilty of being a rebel, and of having caused the murder of the three traders: he was therefore sentenced to be shot, and the sentence was carried out at once. He was placed with his back to a corn-bin, on the edge of the precipice on which his kraal stood, and died with a courage and dignity that extorted an unwilling admiration from all who were present. One of the best known men in Salisbury, when talking to me about it, said, "I know of nothing grander than Makoni's death, than the quiet way in which he spoke to his people, and told them to abstain from further resistance; for himself he only begged that he might be buried decently. 'And now,' he said, 'you shall see how a Makoni can die.'"

He fell dead at once, and was buried under a tobacco-tree close by where he was shot.

He complained bitterly at his trial that he had not been given a fair chance; that no one had ever attempted to confer with him, or to accept his overtures for peace.

I believe he does not lie where he was buried, for I was told by a man who knows the tribe well, that his body has been removed secretly, and lies with his fathers in the place where the Makonis have been buried for generations.

Major Watts, without doubt, acted honestly for what he deemed the best to insure the safety of a number of helpless people. What he did was much like the shooting of the princes at Delhi, an act concerning which the judgment of India is still divided. He was put under arrest by order of the High Commissioner, was tried by court-martial and was acquitted, but was not finally released until the High Commissioner had gone through the papers, and had satisfied himself that his acquittal was justifiable. The evidence brought before the court which tried him has not been published, but presumably it shows that he acted in good faith, and that he and the officers who constituted the court believed that Makoni did not give himself up to the Cape boy, Tom, but that he was taken prisoner by the officer who brought him out.

It is true that Makoni was a rebel, but the High Commissioner's proclamation, dated 13th October 1896, declaring *that from that time* continuing in armed resistance would be punishable with death, had not been issued, and apparently the only law in force was the Matabililand Order in Council, dated 10th September 1894, clause 25 of which enacts that " In case of a revolt against the Company or other misconduct committed by a native chief or tribe, the Administrator and Council may impose a reasonable fine upon the offender. The Administrator shall forthwith report every such case to the High Commissioner, who may remit the fine in whole or part; the Administrator shall give effect to any such remission."

The punishment seems curiously inadequate, but it was evidently anticipated, when this Order in Council was framed, that the natives might possibly not always submit quietly to the foreign yoke which had been imposed upon them, though not that they would rise to the extent they did; and it was apparently intended that, after they had been reduced to subjection, they should be treated with leniency and consideration.

The words are explicit, "in case of a revolt against the Company, or other misconduct, committed by a native chief or tribe." When Makoni had been taken prisoner, the only penalty, therefore, to which he would seem to have been legally liable, was that imposed by this clause; and it must be remembered that before the attack he offered to surrender if his life were spared.

Subsequently a proclamation was issued by the High Commissioner, dated 22d October 1896, by which any officer or any other person who had committed any act during the rising, which might have been illegal, is exonerated and protected from any consequences to which he might have made himself liable by such act, provided that it was done *bonâ fide.* This was only right and fair, for at that time the attitude of the imperial authorities towards the natives was one of extreme severity, and officers cannot well be blamed for having acted harshly. The proclamation does not, however, make the treatment of Makoni any the more legal, if it were not so originally, or lessen the harshness of his execution. It only shifts the onus of it directly upon the High Commissioner and the British Government.

Mr. Rhodes has been ruthless in his dealings with the various native chiefs—I mean in the way in which he obtained his concessions, and then broke down their power—but during the rebellion he has always pleaded earnestly for clemency. I have been assured by those in a position to know that the severity that has attended its suppression is directly referable to the punitive measures adopted by the imperial authorities in opposition to his advice; that from the first he has urged the expediency as well as the justice of mercy— that bygones should be bygones, and that a general amnesty should be granted. His advice has not been followed, and the consequences have been disastrous, as I will show when I come to deal with the treatment of those accused of murder during the rebellion.

However one may try to palliate what was done to Makoni, it is impossible to blind oneself to its injustice, or to the effect likely to be produced upon the other chiefs. Naturally they were afraid to give up their arms, or to surrender when attacked; they preferred to take the chance of escape, or to be dynamited in their caves. They have lost all faith that we will keep our plighted word, for, in common with many of the white people, they believe Makoni was coming out under the impression that he had been promised his life, and it will be a difficult matter to regain their confidence.

Sir George Cathcart laid down in 1852 the only true method of dealing with natives. " It is evident," he wrote, "the main secret of governing these native tribes is inviolable good faith, an innate sense of justice and truth being perhaps the only virtue they can appreciate, and for which they have among themselves, as well as in their intercourse with others, a natural respect. This opinion is perhaps contrary to colonial prejudices. It is nevertheless true, and should be respected, not only on motives of justice, but of policy."

Of course equally harsh things were done in the Indian mutiny; and had it not been for Lord Canning's vigorous action in putting a stop to them—Clemency Canning, as he was called in India—they would have gone on being done for some time after the mutiny had been quelled. I was always being told this in Rhodesia, but I do not think one wrong excuses another. The revenge we took in India was terrible. It always is when there is a conflict between races of different colours. It is the outcome of the amazed anger of the dominant race, that the subject race should dare to oppose them. But in India there was far more excuse for this anger than there has been in Rhodesia. There the rebels were soldiers who had sworn allegiance to us, had eaten our salt, and had been in our pay for years. In Rhodesia they were a people struggling bravely to regain possession of a land of which they had been forcibly dispossessed, and who had many grievous wrongs to avenge. I can quite understand that the settlers in Rhodesia, when they heard of the murder of white women, and came upon their mutilated bodies, should have seen red, as the phrase goes, but it

is only fair to the natives to remember that they also
had been seeing red for some years past, and that they
naturally avenged themselves when their turn came.
It is a vicious circle, that will go on until the country
is placed under a firm and responsible government. A
man said to me once, a man, moreover, holding a good
position: "I look upon the natives as merely superior
baboons, and the sooner they are exterminated the
better. If you had seen the bodies of murdered white
women—women whom you had known—you would
feel just the same." I have not the least doubt that I
should, but when one judges the matter dispassionately,
one cannot but perceive that the murder of these poor
white women lies not at the door of these ignorant
savages, but at the door of those who believe that the
natives are merely superior baboons, and who, unhappily,
have too often treated them in accordance with that
belief.

When I think of Makoni's dynamited kraal, of all
the tragic horror of his death, of the silent valley once
the habitation of an inoffensive and happy people, where
now not a sign of any human habitation is to be seen,
Pringle's indignant words, written more than sixty years
ago, but as true, alas, as they were then, come into my
mind :—

> "From Keisi's mead, from Chumi's hoary woods,
>   Bleak Tarka's dens, and Stormberg's rugged fells,
>   To where Gareep pours down his sounding floods,
>   Through regions where the hunted bushman dwells,
>   That bitter cry wide o'er the desert swells,

> And, like a spirit's voice, demands the song
> That of these savage haunts the story tells,
> A tale of foul oppression, fraud and wrong,
> By Afric's sons endured from Christian Europe long."

Time after time, after each successive Kaffir war, whether waged by imperial troops or by the colonists themselves, similar deeds have been pointed out, but again and again they are repeated, until one despairs that a stop will ever be put to them.

What strikes most any one used to Indian methods of dealing with natives, is the lack in South Africa of any effort by Government to insure for them impartial justice. The colonists look mainly to their own interests, and the natives have no one to represent them, or to fight their battle. Men like Mr. Rose-Innes, Mr. Solomon, Mr. Merriman, Mr. Sauer, Mr. Beard, Major Tamplin, and Mr. Hay in Cape Town, and Mr. Escombe and a host of others in Natal, as individuals, do all they can to stem the tide of injustice, but there is no recognised official to represent them, standing altogether aside from party politics and the promptings of self-interest; and until the office of High Commissioner is separated from that of the Governor of Cape Colony, and the interests of the natives are placed under his especial control, so long will rebellions and native wars continue. In India the civilians have a tradition jealously handed down by each successive generation, that the welfare of the natives has been committed to them as a trust, and they scan in the keenest possible way any proposals that may prove prejudicial to them. In Africa no such tradition exists; on the contrary, the tradition is not of protection but of spoliation, and disgraceful episodes, like Langabilele's and Galishwe's rebellions, are the result.

The natives of South Africa vastly outnumber the white people; they are as much the Queen's subjects as the natives of India, and deserving of the same just and equitable treatment. They have never received it, but it is not yet too late to give it to them. "Under the rule of the colonists," says Mr. Froude, "the natives would be doomed to inevitable degradation. Under such a rule as that which we maintain in India, they will have a chance of rising if it be in them to rise."

Ask the natives themselves, and they will tell you that they always prefer to be under imperial control. Look at the supreme effort made by Khama, when he visited England, to prevent his being placed in subjection to the Chartered Company. Look at the fate that has befallen the Bechuanas directly they were handed over to the Cape. Look at the Basuto war, and at the prosperity that has prevailed in Basutoland since it was again placed under the imperial authorities.

Tengu Jabavu, the Kaffir editor of the *Imvo*, a newspaper printed in the Kaffir language in King Williamstown, said to me, "Pray God that Basutoland never passes from out of the hand of the Queen." It is the prayer of every native who has studied the treatment of his race during the last fifty years. It was Lobengula's desire to deal directly with the Queen, and to place himself under *her* protection. It was Gungunhana's desire also. Had their wish been complied with they would not have met the fate they did. In 1889 the former sent two of his indunas to England under the charge of Mr. Maund, and he sent with them this letter: "Lobengula desires to know that there is a Queen. Some of the people who come into this land tell him there is a Queen, some of them tell him there is not. Lobengula can only find out the truth by sending eyes to find out whether there is a Queen. The indunas are his eyes. Lobengula desires, if there is a Queen, to ask her to advise and help him, as he is much troubled by white men who come into his country, and ask to dig for gold. There is no one with him upon whom he can trust, and he asks that the Queen will send some one from herself." The Queen sent a gracious reply, but the Chartered Company, before four years were over, had forced him into war, and obtained possession of his land. Lobengula was brutally cruel both to his own people and to the Mashonas, but nothing can justify the way in which he was treated by the Company. If any one doubts this, let him read the blue-books, and read also what has been said about it by Mr. Mackenzie, who, more than any one else, was in a position to know the truth.

Is it to be wondered at that the natives all over Africa are beginning to lose the faith they once had in

English honour, and in English fair-dealing, and to believe that their interests count for nothing in the commercial scale? It is not a question of little Englandism; every one who has studied the matter is agreed that in the interests of the natives themselves Africa must be opened up, and that we are the people best qualified to do it. We have permitted some dreadful things to be done, but nevertheless we have never treated the natives with anything like the cruelty or the injustice with which they have been treated in those parts of Africa which have come under the control of the other European nations. There is no reason why we should shrink from the work before us; we have put our hands to the plough, and we must keep them there until we plough a straight furrow: it is a great and a noble work—only let us do it in a cleanly way. We are perpetually being told that we shall produce a dangerous irritation amongst the colonists if we interfere with or criticise their native policy, but in these new territories that we have taken over it is we, and not they, who have made ourselves directly responsible. "We should maintain firmly and resolutely," said Mr. Chamberlain, "our hold over the territories that we have already acquired, and we should offer freely our protectorate to those friendly chiefs and people who are stretching out their hands towards us and seeking our protection and our interference."

By all means let us extend our empire, but let us insist that the people whom we incorporate shall be treated justly, and that their condition shall on the whole be bettered. It is a bastard imperialism that thinks of the interests of the few rather than of the interests of the many: it is a truer, broader feeling which embraces our black fellow-subjects as well as our white. Unfortunately in the absence of any special person to watch over their interests, and to represent their case in England (for the High Commissioner as Governor of the Cape Colony insensibly becomes identified with the Cape colonists, and adopts their views), the natives can seldom obtain the fair hearing to which they are entitled. For that reason it is desirable that the two offices should be separated, and without delay. The proposal was, I believe, seriously considered some years ago, but was negatived on the ground of the expense to the English ratepayer. If we look upon our imperial obligations in so mercantile a way, we ought to be more chary about the acquisition of fresh territories, for if we permit them to be acquired we clearly become responsible for the welfare of the people whom we find in occupation.

The native question, and not the antagonism of English and Dutch, will before long become the most vital of South African questions. Upon the way in which both the colonists and ourselves deal with it depends the country's happiness and progress. The colonists must answer for the treatment of the natives in those territories over which we have given them control, but it lies upon us to see that in those that are

still subject to us our rule is upright and just; that, to
use Sir Walter Hely-Hutchinson's words at Bulawayo,
their administration is entrusted to "men trained in
and imbued with the great traditions of British liberty;
men who will be just and straightforward in all their
dealings; men who will not be turned from the right
path by sudden and temporary gusts of popular passion;
men who will not be afraid, in spite of adverse criticism,
to condemn that which they know to be wrong, and to
cleave to that which is right." But to bring this about
we must not content ourselves with barren criticism.
We must give our criticism practical effect. Rhodesia
is passing through a terrible financial crisis. There is
very little money in the country, and it seems likely
that for some years to come very little money will be
got out of it. If we are sincere in our Imperialism we
must take over the administration, and we must pay
for it. To govern a country well there must be a high
class of officials, and to obtain a high class of officials
there must be good status and high pay. That is what
India taught us long ago.[1]

[1] Sir Charles Warren wrote in 1884 with regard to the taking over
of Bechuanaland: "(a) It can be done in a manner actually beneficial
to the native; (b) It can be done by violence and by the destruction
of the native races. The carrying out, however, of such a policy as
that under (a) is a matter of the very greatest delicacy. It can only
be carried out by Imperial officers, who must have no stake whatever
in the commercial interests and speculations of the country."

CHAPTER IX

UNEASINESS OF THE SETTLERS, BUT POSSIBILITY OF ANOTHER
RISING VERY REMOTE—SALISBURY DISTINCTIVELY AN ADMINI-
STRATIVE TOWN—COLONISATION SCHEMES OF THE SCOTTISH
AFRICA, LIMITED, AND UNITED RHODESIA—SIR GEORGE
CATHCART'S PROPOSAL IN 1852 FOR A MILITARY COLONY IN
KAFFRARIA—SIMILARITY OF THE AMATOLAS AND THE INYANGA.

FROM Headlands to the Macheki River is a stretch of
twelve miles of flat, marshy country, which looks as
though it might prove very fertile under cultivation.
I had joined a prospector who was bicycling up to
Salisbury, and as we started late, it was night before
we reached the store. Here and there the roads are
too sandy to cycle over, but as a rule they are not
at all bad. Bicycles, however, are not common; they
cost so much. I met a man who told me he had
exchanged his for two cows, which, at that time, were
worth £35 each. Now that the railway has reached
Buluwayo they will become cheaper, and on account
of the scarcity of horses will be a veritable godsend.

My companion was evidently nervous, for he declared
that a bush-fire we saw in the distance was in reality
a beacon-fire, like those which were lighted at the
beginning of the rising. He told me he had been out
prospecting a fortnight before on the Odzi River, and

had come back because of the threatening attitude of the natives : that a number of them armed with assegais had collected round him as he was sitting down to smoke, and had told him, in a very insolent manner, that several of the chiefs had not yet been knocked out. All the way up the road I found the same uneasiness prevailing. At Marandellas a man told me he had been fired at from a kopje only the morning before, and he strongly advised me not to walk on alone to Graham and White's, the next store, twenty miles away, as I should not reach it before dark, but to stay the night with the waggons on which my baggage was. I knew they were about half-way between the stores, and, on consideration, I thought it safer to do so. The transport riders had heard the same reports, and sat up half the night with their rifles, to be ready in case the natives should attempt to steal the cattle. When I reached Salisbury the police officers all laughed at these fears. They said they were utterly groundless, as the natives had quite given in, but I found that the prospectors did not feel at all confident that they had. I met two who had just returned from the Mazoe district who said that the natives there were most hostile in their demeanour, asserting quite openly that they would not pay hut-tax. There was a good deal of feeling among the prospectors that the country should have been reported to be safe when it was really not so at all. Many men had been thereby induced to come out from England, thinking they could get to work, whereas they had been obliged to stay for months in Salisbury, where everything is exceedingly costly, doing nothing, and using up what small capital they had. They said that Mr. Rhodes ought never to have announced, as he did, that the rebellion was over when Colonel Alderson left the country in December, eight months before: that, in fact, the Mashonas at that time had not been subdued at all.

Not far from Marandellas is the kraal of a chief called Chewara, where Lieutenant Morris, of the Umtali volunteers, was killed whilst gallantly rescuing Lieutenant Leigh Lye, who had been shot in the leg just in front of a cave. Morris and Lieutenant Hampton jumped down to pick him up, and managed to get him away in safety, but in doing so Morris was killed. His brother is a native commissioner in the Marandellas district, and is liked and respected both by the English and by the Mashonas.

In spite of his brother's death he seems to have acted throughout with the most admirable humanity and self-restraint. The majority of the native commissioners have not been fitted for their work; but some, like Mr. Morris, have, as Lord Grey says, done their duty under circumstances of great difficulty.

In the little graveyard near the store is the grave of Major Evans, of the Sherwood Foresters, who was killed during the attack on Gadzi's kraal.

Marandellas lies very high, considerably over 5000 feet, and is the highest point between Umtali and Salisbury. Beyond it the scenery alters in character, losing

the variety and beauty of Manicaland, and becoming flat
and monotonous. Marandellás is, in fact, the extreme
end of the vast plain that stretches from Buluwayo to
Salisbury. How little this plain varies in height may
be judged by a comparison of the heights of the principal places—Bulawayo, 4900 feet, Charter, 4750, Salisbury, 4960, Graham and White's, 5130, and Marandellás,
5600. The rise from Umtali, which is only 3705 feet
in height, is very gradual, and the railway will have
an easy gradient. It should be an easy line to construct,
for the country offers few natural difficulties. There is
plenty of water, and no necessity for tunnelling.

I found it slow work staying with the waggon, so I
walked on ahead, carrying the few things I required
with me. As far as Marandellás there was plenty of
water along the road, but from Marandellás to Salisbury
scarcely any. It was a year of exceptional drought, I
believe, for even the Makabusi was stagnant, and in
places quite dry—a very rare occurrence. All the way
the road was strewn with skeletons of dead mules and
oxen, and the streams were full of the whitened bones
of the animals that had just had strength enough to
crawl into them to die. At first I felt some repugnance
to drinking out of these streams, but I soon got over
any squeamishness of that kind. Still, the less one
drinks of the water in Mashonaland the better, however thirsty one may be: it is sure in time to produce
fever, and for the same reason also it is dangerous to
bathe in the rivers, especially in the daytime when the

sun is on the water. It almost invariably brings on an attack.

Salisbury is a pleasant little town, very different in tone from the restless youthfulness of Umtali; it has all the sedateness of a seat of government. There is a charming, though rather a limited society, and a good deal of social intermingling. I stayed there nearly a month, and enjoyed my visit immensely. I can quite understand the strong feeling of attachment to the place which all Salisburians have. The climate was delightful, for the rains were just beginning. An occasional thunderstorm kept down the heat, and there was generally a strong breeze, which, with the clear atmosphere and bright sunshine, made life a pleasure, and not a burden, as it is in so many tropical countries.

Towards the end of my stay Sir Alfred Milner passed through on his way to Beira, and was entertained at a luncheon in the town-hall. It was an interesting function, more so in many ways than the railway festivities at Buluwayo. There the people were in all the elation of a long-hoped-for boom, whereas in Salisbury they saw no chance of relief coming to them for many months. But there was a resolute hopefulness in the speeches, that made one feel what grit there is in the country, and brought with it a conviction that in spite of all its difficulties it will go ahead and prosper whether gold is found in it or not.

Exclusive of the police, Salisbury has a population

of not more than seven hundred people, but it is not in the least like a pioneer town. There is very little drinking, except occasionally when a prospector comes in for a fling. It has quite a character of its own, being neither commercial nor provincial, but purely official. As soon as the railway reaches it, and the cost of living is lessened, it ought to become a charming little place.

Mr. Milton was acting as deputy-administrator. He has had a long experience of South Africa, and in his capacity of Permanent Secretary in the Prime Minister's department in the Cape he drafted the Glen-Grey Act (the measure on which Mr. Rhodes' reputation as a legislator chiefly rests), for the enforcement of compulsory native labour. The Chartered Company are to be congratulated on having induced him to transfer his services to themselves—though what is their gain is the Cape's loss—for no man is more likely to deal fairly with the black population as well as with the white. He has a herculean task before him, but the general feeling was that he would prove equal to it. I was glad also to meet Mr. Orpen, the surveyor-general, who all through his life has been an indefatigable worker in the cause of the natives. I found him an ardent imperialist, holding that England, although she has made many mistakes, has used her influence in the main for the true interests of South Africa, and more particularly of the natives. His son, who had just come up from Melsetter, where he has a farm, spoke in the most hopeful way of the future of that district – an opinion,

I may add, endorsed by various transport riders whom I had met along the road. They all agreed that in time Mashonaland would be a fine agricultural country. Half the people who decry it are wastrels who would do no good anywhere. I am indebted, too, for much information to Mr. Fairbridge, the editor of the *Rhodesia Herald*, and the first mayor of Salisbury. In spite of all that has occurred, he has a buoyant and contagious belief in the ultimate prosperity of Mashonaland.

Whilst I was in Salisbury I went out to the Jesuit mission station at Chisha-washa, about twelve miles away. It is a charming little place, and the fathers have endeared themselves to every one by their kindness and hospitality. They are doing wonderfully good work too; the same kind of industrial work that the Trappists are doing in Natal. The general system of Jesuit teaching is by having day-schools if possible, so that the home influence may be maintained; but in Rhodesia, where the kraals are at great distances from the mission stations, and are comparatively small, it is necessary to take the children in as boarders, which is the Trappist system. This will be gradually changed into a day-school system as soon as the home influences are improved by means of the converted children, who will gradually marry, and introduce a better condition of things into their kraals. The married converts are the basis of every Jesuit mission, and as yet there has been no time for them in Mashonaland. At present they trust chiefly in incessant work. They say if the children are not at work they are in mischief, so they are taught to read, to sing, to carpenter, and to garden. In spite of all the drawbacks of insects, and a hitherto unbroken soil, they have done great things in the way of cultivation, and are full of hope of the agricultural future of Mashonaland.

Before I left for Bulawayo I had also several long talks with Mr. Duncan, the late Surveyor-General, who is now managing the affairs of the Scottish Africa, Limited, and with Colonel Raleigh Grey, who had just arrived from England to look after the interests of the United Rhodesia Company. These companies are determined to devote their energies to agriculture as well as to mining, and both Mr. Duncan and Colonel Grey were deliberating about advising the adoption of some scheme of colonisation by which a desirable class of settlers could be attracted into the country. Some such scheme was contemplated as that which is frequently adopted in America; by giving alternate blocks to settlers on condition that they will bring them under cultivation in a certain stated time. The terms offered will have to be very liberal, for life in Mashonaland is too uncomfortable for any Englishman to care to settle there, unless he sees a chance of making a competence within a reasonable time, which will enable him to return to England.

In America the way railways have often been made is by promoters selecting a tract of country which, in their opinion, will yield a handsome return under cultiva-

I

tion.   A grant is then obtained from the Government of alternate sections of land, on condition that the railway shall be constructed within a certain time.   A portion of the company's capital is thereupon set aside for the purpose of assisting desirable emigrants, and a plough, cows, seeds, and such-like things are advanced to them upon credit, together with a small plot of land, which becomes absolutely their own after a certain number of years of occupation; the money expended for these .purposes being recovered by the company by graduated payments.   The ground is allotted in alternate plots, one on each side of the line.   The railway is thus begun, and by the time it is completed there is a demand for carriage of the grain already grown by the settlers, which at once brings in an income; and the settlers having proved the capabilities of the land, the intermediate plots can be sold for an enhanced value.   In this way whole districts are populated with great rapidity.   A somewhat similar method will have to be adopted by the Rhodesian land companies, if they wish Rhodesia to become rapidly developed.

Here, however, they would be met with the determined opposition of the Chartered Company, which, for some reason, will not permit any one to build railways except itself.   But it has given away the land wholesale, so that there is none available for any wholesome scheme of government immigration, and colonisation can consequently only be worked through the agency of the various companies to whom the land has been alienated. One of the worst features in the development of a new country by a chartered company is the concentration of interests in the hands of a few powerful companies or persons. It mortgages its capabilities from the outset, and disheartens and cripples healthy individual effort. This is particularly noticeable in Rhodesia.

The Austrians had much the same problem before them in Bosnia when they occupied it in 1878. The land there in olden times was renowned for its fertility, but the Turks had allowed it to go out of cultivation, and it had become swampy and malarious, and the market, as in Mashonaland, was extremely limited. It did not seem an encouraging field for emigration, but Austria established thrifty colonies of Poles, Bohemians, and Germans, giving them the land on easy terms, and liberal assistance for the first three or four years. Now they are doing well, and the whole country has increased in value, their example giving a wholesome stimulus to the original inhabitants. Settlements of the same nature, and of the same kind of people, might possibly succeed in Rhodesia.

Sir George Cathcart pondered over a similar difficulty after the Kaffir war of 1852, and the conclusion he came to is in many ways applicable to Rhodesia generally, and especially to the Inyanga and Melsetter districts: " Outside of this hilly region, and to the eastward, but bounded on the north side by a ridge of hills, a spur from the Amatolas called the Kabousie Range, there is an extent of some fifteen miles by ten of pasture-land, where the river Kabousie, an important tributary to the Kei, receives its sources. This is plain open grass-land, only slightly undulated, and to the south-ward some equally good pasture-land brings the verge of this territory, heretofore belonging to the tribe of Sandilli, within a few miles of this place. I am thus particular in describing the locality, as it is that in which I should propose the experiment of locating a military population of Swiss emigrants, formed in the first instance of two regiments of 700 or 800 men each, with a view to ultimate colonisation, according to the scheme which is already under your lordship's (Earl Grey) consideration, and based on a system some-what analogous to that of the enrolled pensioners in New Zealand. British military pensioners in this colony have not been found to thrive, possibly owing to their unsteadiness and want of combination, whereas a national colony of people, who proverbially cling together, and are thrifty as well as expert marksmen, and accustomed to mountain districts, when organised in villages would, I firmly believe, be able with due assistance and support at starting to keep their own afterwards and thrive. Their almost immediate contact with the place, and easy communication from thence with the port of East London, would open to them a market, and insure supplies; and such people, uncon-nected with politics and prejudices, which distract the mixed community within the colony, would, as the loyal garrison of a great central citadel, control and secure the whole of British Kaffraria, and supply the place of several regiments which must be otherwise required for its occupation." And in a despatch to Sir John Pakington he says: "British military pensioners have been tried in this country, and have proved a failure, and in two out of three villages which were established close to the border, nearly all the male inhabitants were murdered at the opening of the war. Although I am inclined to think the precaution of establishing some rallying-post in the midst of each of these villages might have effectually prevented that calamity, the intemperate and idle habits of too many of the class of British military pensioners, and a natural carelessness and contempt of danger, would render them unfit to be placed with safety in an alpine district, the nature of which renders constant vigilance peculiarly essential to security.

. . . . . .

"From what I have seen, the country is so analogous to Switzerland, and so capable of feeding sheep as well as cattle on the most luxuriant pastures, and abounding with the finest water, I am convinced that such a colony, if it could be formed, would not only flourish and maintain itself, but prove the means of rendering this territory ultimately remunerative, instead of a burden to the British nation, and serve at little expense as a secure barrier for the protection of this portion of the extensive frontier of her Majesty's South African dominions" (Correspondence of Sir George Cathcart, pp. 46 and 60).

From all I have heard of the Inyanga and Melsetter districts, Sir George Cathcart's description of this valley in the Amatolas might very well apply to them. It will be seen that his scheme is much the same as that of the armed agricultural settlements suggested by M. Hoffer to the Mozambique Company.

The Scottish Africa, Ltd., were deliberating about getting settlers up from Natal and the Colony, but I doubt if they would succeed as well as a colony of thrifty Poles, or of Bohemians or Swiss. English settlers are out of the question; they would never submit to the hard conditions of life that must prevail in Rhodesia for many years yet. They would not have the necessary patience. If Rhodesia is to be colonised, it must be either by colonials or by Boers who are willing to put up with the rough lives of pioneers. But the colonials have in great measure adopted the customs of the Dutch, who are essentially a pastoral and not an agricultural people. Like them they covet enormous tracts of land where their stock can graze unrestrained, and they will not cultivate the land acre by acre as the continental nations do. That is why the German colony near Grahamstown has been one of the few successful experiments of the kind in South Africa. The Inyanga may of course prove valuable for huge sheep-runs, worked with large capital, in which case it will remain in the hands of the companies who have monopolised it, and men with moderate capital will be unable to compete with them. But South Africa as a whole, except perhaps the Karroo, cannot be said to be a promising field for sheep, as compared with Australia, New Zealand, Uruguay, or the Falkland Islands, and it is more likely that these districts would succeed, not as sheep-farms, but as the home of a frugal agricultural population—working, not to make a fortune, but to make a living; not for a foreign market, but for the wants of their own community. It is only in that way that a really prosperous country can be built up out of Rhodesia; it is too far from the seaboard to compete with India in wheat, or with Australia, or New Zealand, or Canada, either in wheat or in stock, and its products are excluded from the Transvaal, by far the most lucrative and the most constant of the South African markets, by the prohibitive import duties.

But in spite of all these drawbacks an Afrikander population, aided by a few thrifty Germans or Poles, with no rapid ambitions to distract them, will make Rhodesia prosperous just as they have made the Free State prosperous, and their task will be one of less difficulty.

That state was abandoned by England in 1852 because it was believed that it could never be made of any value, and, yet, though it will never be a rich state like the Transvaal, it is now one of the most quietly well-to-do, contented, and well-governed of the South African States.

CHAPTER X

Composition of the Force under Sir Richard Martin and Captain De Moleyns — Attack on Seki's Kraal — The M'toko Patrol — The taking of Shaungwe — Assault on Mashanganyika's Kraal — Death of Paris.

When I left Umtali at the beginning of October the Mashona rebellion was hardly over, the last of the important chiefs only surrendering about the 15th of September. Colonel Alderson had effectually secured the safety of the towns, but though he had driven the chiefs into their fastnesses, he had not broken their spirit. His instructions had been to restore communication between the towns, and then to evacuate the country, leaving the police to deal separately with the various chiefs, kraal by kraal. It would have been too expensive for the Chartered Company to retain the troops longer than was absolutely necessary. When therefore Captain de Moleyns, of the 4th Hussars, took over charge under Sir Richard Martin, in December 1896, of all the troops and police then in Mashonaland, it was found that it was not only impossible for prospectors to go out alone to the mining districts of the Mazoe and Lomagundi, but that it was even unsafe for them to venture more than a few miles out of Salisbury itself without an armed escort. It was evident that this state of affairs could not be allowed to continue, and that, whatever the causes might be which had led to the rebellion, and whatever sympathy might logically be felt for the Mashonas, it was absolutely imperative for the future well-being of the country that they should once and for all be effectually subdued. Natives always attribute forbearance to weakness, and if Mashonaland were to be retained in white occupation—of which there could be no question—it was necessary to deal sternly with the chiefs so long as they remained in opposition, and to defer treating them with indulgence until they had been reduced to absolute submission.

Captain de Moleyns was not, I should mention, under the orders of the administrator, but of Sir Richard Martin, who had succeeded Sir Frederick Carrington as Commandant-General, and who in addition was the deputy of the High Commissioner, and the representative in Rhodesia of the British Government. After careful consideration, Sir Richard Martin came to the conclusion that, with the meagre force at his disposal, it would not be safe to take the offensive until the rainy season was over, and the men under Captain de Moleyns' command had become in some measure habituated to the climate, and to the nature of the work before them.

His whole force consisted of 200 of the British South Africa Company's police, fifty of Colonel Alderson's mounted infantry, who had elected to join the police when Colonel Alderson left the country, 400 of the Umtali volunteers, and 130 natives. The police were totally untrained, and unused to the country and its ways. They had been enlisted in England, and when Captain de Moleyns assumed command they had, as a matter of fact, not arrived, but were on their way from Beira to Salisbury. Many of them had contracted fever, and all were undrilled and unaccustomed to discipline. The natives, too, were equally undisciplined and unreliable; most of them having to be disbanded, and fresh men enrolled. The volunteers formed the garrisons of Salisbury, Umtali, and the different laagers, and were not available for service in the field.

A patrol was sent out early in December to Nyam-medha's kraal, on the Hunyani River, eight miles to the south-west of Salisbury, to ascertain the attitude of that chief. He remarked ironically that if the white men would pay *him* hut-tax, he would allow them to remain in Salisbury, and several other chiefs were equally insolent. They were not anxious, they said, to fight, but they declined positively to pay hut-tax, or to give up their guns. This being the disposition of the Mashonas, it was apparent that a serious struggle was ahead. The total force available for offensive operations amounted in all to one hundred of the police, and seventy-five of the native contingent; and, until May, they suffered so terribly from fever and dysentery that the sick-list varied from 25 per cent. to 50 per cent., and in the low-lying districts rose sometimes to as high as 75 per cent. Obviously nothing could be done until the health of the men had improved, so Sir Richard Martin wisely determined to defer continuous operations until the rains were over. The natives, however, were not allowed to regain confidence by being left altogether unmolested, various kraals in the immediate vicinity of Salisbury being attacked, and in most cases destroyed. Seki, the chief of one of these kraals, about twenty-five miles from Salisbury, promised to surrender, and to give up his guns on a certain day, and Lord Grey went out in person to receive them. But when the day came Seki made excuses, and declined to give them up, asserting that he was afraid of the other chiefs who still remained armed. Lord Grey thereupon said to him, "We shall not come to talk any more ; next time we come it will be in a different way." He then left for Salisbury with a trooper as escort, but on reaching Ballyhooly, a store about half-way, he changed his mind and returned to the police who were encamped five or six miles from Seki's. It was in the middle of the wet weather, and raining hard, and he did not get there till midnight. Nevertheless he started with the men at 2 A.M., and himself led the party that stormed and took the kraal. This may have been rash, and not quite the recognised thing for a man in Lord Grey's position to do, but it put heart into the police, who were labouring under terrible difficulties at the time, and I think there are few men who will not admire him for acting as he did.

Everywhere it was apparent that the natives were not in a submissive mood, and as the police force was manifestly inadequate to cope with them, a patrol was sent out in March to the M'toko country, which lies ninety miles to the north-east of Salisbury, to try and raise a contingent of friendly natives. The patrol was commanded by Captain Harding, who was accompanied by the Honourable H. Howard,[1] at that time acting as Lord Grey's secretary. They took with them a month's rations on pack mules, and marching rapidly, reached the M'tokos in four days. Negotiating with them proved to be ticklish work ; they naturally thought the white men must be in great straits if they were reduced to coming to them for assistance, but eventually Harding succeeded in inducing Gurupila, the chief of the tribe, to join him with five hundred of his men, armed with muskets and assegais. He started back on 13th March, and was attacked at once. Several men were wounded, with the result that three hundred of the M'tokos deserted ; Gurupila, with the other two hundred, remaining staunch. The Mashonas increased rapidly in numbers, and the position became critical, so Harding halted about fifty miles from Salisbury, and sent Howard in for reinforcements. It was an exceedingly plucky ride, for Howard had been wounded in the foot, and was so prostrated with fever that he could hardly sit on his

[1] *Times* correspondent, killed at Omdurman, 2nd September 1898.

horse. He had to make his way through hostile country, and did not reach Salisbury till late at night, but De Moleyns started in a couple of hours after his arrival with only twenty-five men. Howard was too ill to return with him, and the native guide losing the way, it was several days before Harding's camp was reached, when nearly the whole force was found to be down with fever. The Mashonas had made several attacks, and in repelling them one or two of the men had been wounded.

The camp was in the midst of what is known as the granite kopje country, and it was difficult to get at the enemy, or to dislodge them from their strongholds. The granite kopjes are massive hills, rising abruptly from the granitic plateau which composes the intermediate formation between the high and low veldts. Huge boulders are piled one on the top of the other in a weird jumble that makes them look like the strongholds of the genii. The colouring, especially at sunrise and sunset, is delicately beautiful, and I have often felt, when looking at them, as though I were in fairyland. I have had the same feeling before in mountainous countries, but never so strongly as amongst these fantastic hills; a feeling due, I fancy, to the false impression their castellated summits give of supernatural agency.

A fortnight was spent in reconnoitring, and in allowing Harding's men to regain their strength. They had been sent out without a doctor, and with no proper stock of medicines—an inexcusable omission, considering the nature of the work entrusted to them. An attack was then made on a kraal called Shaungwe, situated on the summit of a hill 850 feet in height. This kraal had been repeatedly assaulted by the Matabili, but had never been taken, and the Mashonas believed it to be impregnable. It had, however, two fatal weaknesses; there was no water, and it could only be descended by one side—the other side being precipitous—so that it was an easy matter to invest it. This was done, and a continuous fire was maintained both by night and by day. Soon after the investment Gurupila was shot through the lungs, and died in a few hours. His death was of serious consequence, for it naturally shook the constancy of his men. Moreover, he had shown such cheery coolness and pluck that his loss was a matter of regret to the whole force. His body was carried away by his people to be buried in his own country; they would not permit any one to touch it, or to go near it. Their devotion to their chief was remarkable. When he lay dying they crowded round him, and many of them spat on his wound in the hope of making it heal (the Kaffirs chew a certain herb, and spray the juice over a wounded place with their mouths); but Gurupila told them that his time was come, and that he was going to join his fathers. When he was dead, his body was swathed in matting, and borne away on his followers' shoulders.

As a rule when a man in the native contingent died, or was killed, his companions asked for the English funeral service to be read, and for a firing party—a request which was invariably acceded to, for it is only by attention to little details of this kind that the affection of native troops can be retained. This, however, was after they had been with the white men for some time; when they were quite raw they liked to take their dead away, and bury them unseen.

Before long it became clear that the Mashonas were suffering terribly from thirst. The cattle bellowed incessantly, and tried to break through the picket to get at the water at the bottom of the hill, and the men called out to the sentries, "How can you expect us to fight if you won't let us get at the water?"

After ten days they could hold out no longer, and twelve men and two hundred women surrendered, the rest of the men escaping down the precipice of the un-invested side; many of them, ninety altogether, so the prisoners said, being killed in the attempt. Maramisa, the chief, was badly wounded, but managed to get away. The self-restraint shown by the women when they were brought into the camp was extraordinary. They had been many days without water, and their thirst must have been terrible; yet they sat quietly in a circle, and when water was brought showed no unseemly eagerness to drink. There was no struggling; each woman took a sip from the calabash, and handed it on to her neighbour; their stoical composure was astonishing. As soon as the kraal was taken, Captain De Moleyns returned with the patrol to Salisbury.

On the 10th June another patrol was sent out under Major Gosling—De Moleyns being ill with fever—to attack Mashanganyika's kraal. As it was known to be strongly fortified, he took with him a hundred and fifty of the police, the native contingent, three seven-pounders, and three maxims. He succeeded in taking it with the loss of one man killed and two wounded, and then moved farther to the eastward to attack Kunzi's stronghold, which was believed to be even more formidable. This kraal is about forty miles from Salisbury, in the same broken granite country as Shaungwe. The attack was made at daybreak. During the first rush two men were killed or wounded, and there was some danger of a repulse, but Harding and Lieutenant Feltham forced their way over the stockade under a heavy fire, closely followed by twenty or thirty men. Six more men were killed or badly hurt, but a lodgment was effected within the kraal, and command obtained of the entrance to the caves. Towards the evening the Mashonas withdrew to a kopje half a mile distant, which was also stormed and taken, the natives retiring into the hilly country. still farther to the eastward.

During the attack on this kraal, one of Makoni's sons was badly wounded. After their father was executed, two of his sons, about eleven and twelve years old, took service with Harding, who at that time was acting as galloper to Major Watts. He took a fancy to the boys, and asked their mother if he might have them, and she consented willingly, merely stipulating that they should be allowed to come back to see her once a year. One of the redeeming features in the Mashona character is their genuine affection for their children, and the respect the children pay to their parents, and to old people. The boys became greatly attached to Harding, and he to them. They accompanied him on all his patrols, and became the privileged pets of the camp. I don't know what their real names were, but they were always known as Archer and Paris. They were both of them nice boys, and the younger one, Paris, had an impulsively affectionate nature. Harding told me a story about him which is worth recording, now that the poor lad is dead. They were out on a patrol in bitterly cold weather, and one morning when Paris brought him his coffee, Harding said, " How cold it is, Paris." That evening when he went to bed, he felt he had more clothing on than usual, and on counting his blankets found that Paris, without saying anything, had quietly put his own blanket on the bed when making it up. He was killed whilst bringing Harding some food from the camp. His brother was with him, and as they reached the fighting line, a bullet whizzed close by them, and Archer said, " Let us go back." " I can't," answered Paris, " I have the chief's food, I must go on," and he went on, and had his thigh shattered directly afterwards by a bullet. He was carefully nursed, and in a couple of months had all but recovered, when inflammation suddenly supervened, and he died.   His brother felt his loss deeply, for the two boys had been inseparable. He is still with Major Harding, and bids fair to turn out a smart, dependable boy.   He is now the bugler in the Black Watch, as the native contingent is generally called in Mashonaland.

Still it must not be supposed that many of the Mashonas are capable of the feeling shown by poor little Paris.   As a rule they are singularly unresponsive to kind treatment, but I was told, by those who have lived amongst them, that the women are more easily influenced by sentiment than the men.

CHAPTER XI

ATTACK UPON CHESUMBA'S—CHARACTER OF THE MASHONA CAVES
—KARUBI, THE WITCH-DOCTOR, AND NYANDA, THE WITCH-
DOCTRESS—TERMINATION OF THE REBELLION—IS THE USE OF
DYNAMITE LEGITIMATE?

ABOUT the middle of July Captain de Moleyns decided
to attack the kraal of a chief called Chesumba, twelve
miles from Salisbury, where some fifteen hundred
natives were known to be congregated. It was built
upon the banks of the Rewa, a little stream flowing
into the Hunyani a few miles below Chesumba's.
Another kraal of almost equal extent was situated at
the junction of the two streams, and it was thought
unwise to permit this large body of natives, whose
attitude moreover was most hostile, to remain un-
subdued at so short a distance from the town.

I will relate what took place with some detail, as I
went out from Salisbury, and made a careful examination of the caves ; my reason being that when I came
up to Mashonaland I had a strong impression of the
unnecessary cruelty involved in the use of dynamite
against these poor creatures, who, after all, were only
making a last gallant stand for the possession of their
country. I will try to describe the kraal, but my

description can convey only a vague impression of its
appearance, utterly unlike as it is to anything I have
ever seen in any part of the world. The country for
the first ten miles from Salisbury is flat and scantily
wooded, but about two miles from Chesumba's it
changes altogether in character. Groups of enormous
boulders are strewn about in a confused tangle; the
ground between them being heavily timbered.

De Moleyns took with him 100 of the police, the
native contingent, two seven-pounders, and two maxims.
From the information he had received of the strength
of the kraal, he felt that his only chance of success,
except with great loss of life, was by making a surprise
attack immediately before dawn. He moved out of
Salisbury therefore at 2 A.M. and marched steadily until
four o'clock, when his guides told him the kraal was
within a quarter of a mile. On reconnoitring he found
this to be the case, and as the day was beginning to
break ordered an immediate assault. The Mashonas
were taken by surprise, but had he delayed half-an-hour
longer they would have been on the alert, and the loss
must have been considerable; and in Mashonaland at
that time, the life of every armed man was of consequence.

The kraal was situated to the east of the Rewa, the
banks of which are composed of huge masses of granite,
piled one on the top of the other to a height of several
hundred feet, forming a series of natural cavities, the
mouths facing towards the stream, and the hillside at

the back forming the terminus of the caves. The kraal from the side of the stream was practically impregnable, but from the other side, where the troops were halted, it was more accessible, and the artificial fortifications were therefore stronger and more extensive. The ground all the way from Salisbury is, as I have mentioned, quite flat until it breaks precipitously away into the bed of the stream. The huts were clustered together at the extreme edge of the plain, with a little ground in front of them, which had been cleared for cultivating mealies and tomatoes. Around the huts was a palisade fifteen feet in height, formed of the trunks of trees driven into the ground, and held firmly together with creepers and thorn bushes; an aperture being left in the middle of sufficient size to allow one person at a time to pass in or out. This aperture was closed when not in use, not by transverse bars, but by movable tree-trunks, having exactly the same appearance as the others, so that it was impossible for an attacking party to discover in what part of the palisade the entrance was. When the troops delivered the assault, the Mashonas, who were awakened from their sleep, bolted hurriedly down the side of the cliff, and disappeared in the crevices of the rocks, from which they kept up a constant but ineffectual fire, two of the police being killed and one wounded. The storming party cleft their way through the palisade, and rushed past the huts to find themselves confronted by a second and still stronger line of defence, consisting of natural sconces formed by the granite boulders; the intervening spaces being filled up with a stockade several feet in thickness. This line of defence was right on the edge of the precipice, in an angle of the rocks, and was commanded by the mouths of the caves, so that when the men reached the other side, they came under a raking fire from an unseen enemy—always a trying thing for troops.

The natural defences were so strong that the inner stockade could easily have been held by a dozen resolute men against any number of assailants, but the Mashonas are not a courageous people; they can endure heroically, but can neither defend nor attack. They have always been hunted down by the Matabili, and other tribes, and their refuge has been in flight, and in the difficulty of getting at them in their interminable burrows. Like the conies they are a feeble folk, and dwell in the rocks, and into them they retire when danger threatens, emerging again when it has passed. They reminded me of the little red Himalayan marmots, which sit by the side of their holes, keeping up a shrill, incessant "dring," but directly they are approached dive out of sight, and even when wounded tumble into their holes to die.

The predecessors of the Matabili ground down the Mashonas terribly, far worse than the Matabili, under whom they increased both in numbers and in cattle, always a sure sign of the prosperity of a Kaffir tribe. They say themselves that they preferred the Matabili rule to ours, because under them they were troubled but once a year, whereas now their troubles come with each day's rising sun. It is the regularity of toil, and the constant intermeddling in their lives, that they find so irksome. They would rather endure the risk of sudden onslaughts and death than the constant supervision and interference of the white man's rule.

In ordinary speech the word "cave" denotes simply an underground cavity of greater or less extent, but these Mashona caves far more nearly resemble burrows. They are merely the crevices underneath the granite boulders where they do not rest flush with the ground, and are often only just large enough for a man to lie under, flat upon his stomach, like a lizard; though here and there there are bigger spaces formed by the leaning together of two boulders, which resemble true caves. These crevices connect naturally, and are easily got into, and as easily got out of: the collection of boulders forming, in fact, an underground fortress of enormous extent. This of Chesumba's was about a mile in length by half a mile in width, and many, Kunzi's for instance, are even larger. They are nearly always situated by the side of a stream (there is a theory that the boulders have been hurled together by a strong current), so there is never any lack of water, the stream generally flowing underground through the caves; and the Mashonas have always been in the habit of storing their grain in them, so that in case of an attack, they can hold out for an indefinite time. The Matabili indeed gave up trying to take them: "What is the use," they said, " of fighting against people whom you cannot see, and who shoot you out of a hole in the ground, so that the bullet travels up your body and comes out at your head?" (At the attack on Thabas Imamba, a trooper stooped to pick up a bit of a Kaffir pot to see what it was. It covered a hole communicating with a crevice, and a man lying inside it shot him through the shoulder.) They depended for their loot in women and cattle and grain upon the result of the first attack, before the Mashonas had had time to take refuge in their caves: after that they could inflict but little damage, but passed on their way like the dust-storms that spring up suddenly all over Mashonaland, and die as suddenly away. The Matabili raided this part of the country systematically, but they never succeeded in making the people slaves as is commonly supposed. Most of the Mashona chiefs purchased a precarious immunity from attack by the payment of a tribute, but one or two of them, like Makoni and·M'tasa, did not even do that.

To go back, however, to the attack on Chesumba's. When the inner stockade had been taken, De Moleyns made his interpreter call out to the Mashonas to surrender—that they would not be hurt, but that if they did not come out he would dynamite them until they did. Their only answer was a shower of bullets. It was not that they did not understand what dynamite is: they understood thoroughly, so much so that Kunzi is said to have actually used it himself to enlarge some of his caves. De Moleyns then told them they should have two hours in which to send out their women and children, and as none were sent out, he was reluctantly obliged to blow up the nearest of the caves, and a number of women and children then crawled out, and were sent to the camp to be looked after. This went on for four days, cave after cave being blown up, whilst repeated requests were made to the people to surrender. At last they did so, and the caves were destroyed as far as possible. One hundred and eleven men gave themselves up, and five hundred women and children; the rest managed to get away. It is believed that comparatively few were killed. The dynamite, though terrible enough, has not the invariably awful effect that it might be expected to have, because the twists and turns of the caves break the force of the explosion.

The prisoners were located on a piece of ground five miles from Salisbury, with the exception of eight men who were put on their trial for murder. Among the prisoners was the chief Maramombo, whose arm was badly injured. He refused to allow it to be amputated, saying he would rather die than live without it, but he ultimately made one of those marvellous recoveries noticeable amongst savages all over the world.

Whilst Captain de Moleyns was occupied with this kraal, Major Ridley with a squadron of the 7th Hussars attacked and took Umzwitze's kraal, sixteen miles from Charter, three of the Hussars being killed, and Major Ridley himself wounded. In August many other fortified kraals were taken and destroyed, but the only

serious resistance that was made was at Mashayan-
gombi's, where Sir Richard Martin himself took command. It was taken with a loss on our side of four
men killed and six wounded. Three hundred and
twenty women gave themselves up, and were sent to
the location with the others.

By the end of September the whole of the chiefs
had submitted, the only persons of consequence still
remaining at large being the witch-doctor Kakubi, and
the witch-doctress Nyanda. I was in Salisbury when
Kakubi was captured, and brought in to stand his trial
for murder. He was a half-starved, miserable-looking
wretch, but he, and still more Nyanda, had exercised
immense power, and they, and a witch-doctor who had
come up from Matabililand, seem to have really been
the main instigators of the Mashona rising.

Late in September Harding was sent to patrol the
M'Toko country, and went right through it to the
Inyanga mountains near Umtali. He reported that
everything was quiet, so prospectors and farmers began
once more to venture out, though with an excusable
hesitation.

How greatly the war has retarded the development
of the country may be judged from the fact that all
through the summer absolutely nothing was done, the
settlers remaining in enforced idleness in the towns, and
at the stores along the main road.

I may say frankly that my preconceived opinion was
entirely changed by what I saw at Chesumba's, and that

I satisfied myself, though I confess with considerable hesitation—its effects are so fearful—that the use of dynamite under proper supervision is legitimate, and, on the whole, perhaps more humane than the alternative process of investing the caves, and starving the natives out. The question is of importance, because protests have on various occasions been made with regard to its use in South African warfare. Those who have studied the history of the subject will remember Bishop Colenso's indignant and eloquent protest against its employment in Langalibale's revolt in 1873, and in 1882 such powerful representations were made regarding its adoption by the Boers that the British Government instructed Mr. Hudson, the British Resident at Pretoria, to report to them upon the matter. The conclusion he came to was that what was done was done with the greatest possible humanity, every inducement being used to persuade the natives to come out of the caves before they were blown up, and the British Government therefore declined to interfere further.

Still it is evident that with dynamite in the hands of a harsh or indiscreet man, unless the strictest supervision is exercised, regrettable excesses will occur. That, on the whole, it has been used humanely during the Mashona rising is proved by the fact that most, though not all, of the missionaries approved of its use. The fact, too, that it was employed by Sir Richard Martin and Captain de Moleyns, who are known for their punctilious regard for humanity, is a sufficient guarantee that it was made use of when they were present in a proper way, but, if rumour is to be believed, it was not always employed with an equal sense of responsibility.

The Mashona caves, as I have explained, are really vast underground fortresses with interminable ramifications, and it is argued that to use dynamite to blow them up is as legitimate as to blow up the gate, or to blow in the wall of a town, preparatory to an assault, or to blow up a man-of-war with a torpedo. There is, however, this difference, that in civilised warfare the opposing forces are both furnished with the same weapons, whereas in savage wars only the civilised force is provided with these powerful engines of destruction. The distinction is surely material, and it ought only to be used with the greatest reluctance, and as a last resort, and ample time ought to be given to the women and children to come out. Otherwise we shall deserve the censure deservedly bestowed upon St. Arnaud by Mr. Kinglake. "St. Arnaud had warmly approved the destruction of life which had been effected in 1844 by filling with smoke the crowded caves of the Dahra: but he had sagaciously observed that the popularity of the measure in Europe was not coextensive with the approbation which seems to have been bestowed upon its author by the military authorities. These counter-views guided M. St. Arnaud. . . . 'Then,' he writes to his brother, 'I had all the apertures hermetically stopped up. I made one vast sepulchre. No one went into the caverns. No one but myself knew that under there there are five hundred brigands who will never again slaughter Frenchmen." There has been nothing of this kind in Mashonaland. Whether the use of dynamite is legitimate, in cases where women and children are assembled, is a point about which there will always be a difference of opinion; but supposing it to be so, it seems to have been used, on the whole, with due precautions and in a proper way.

The point, however, that I am anxious to emphasise, is that the word "caves" is misleading. It conveys the idea that the people collect together in extensive underground chambers, which are blown to pieces with them in it. This was what I thought myself, before I had seen Chesumba's, and as I fancy many other people have the same idea, I have taken more pains than I should otherwise have done to explain how essentially erroneous it is.

CHAPTER XII

Splendid Work done by the Police in Mashonaland, and by the Native Contingent under Major Harding—Bravery of the Mashonas—They are Treacherous, but not Incapable of Gratitude—The only way to Govern them is by Justice, not through Fear.

THE work done last year by the police and hussars in Mashonaland has really been very fine. The former were a mere handful of men, who had to operate under the most trying circumstances over an enormous extent of country of an exceptionally difficult character; one so bare of supplies, that everything had to be sent up from the base. There were not many casualties at each particular attack, but the constant fighting from January to September, and still more the incessant exposure to sudden and violent alternations of rain and heat, which, with the bad and insufficient food, brought on fever and dysentery, tried the men severely. The majority were gently born, and unused to hardship and exposure; many were scarcely more than boys, and all were unacclimatised, so disease played havoc with them from the first. In spite of it the pluck they showed was splendid; the more so that the operations being of a guerilla nature, they had little to encourage them in the way of recognition, either in England or in South Africa.

Only those who have been in Mashonaland can rightly appreciate what they have done; but the total amount of the casualties will convey some slight idea of the arduous nature of their work. Out of a force of 250 police, and 120 of the native contingent, 26 men were killed, and 35 wounded; 21 died from illness, and 20 more were sent out of the country incapacitated and utterly broken down. Including illness, therefore, the total loss amounted to rather over one-fourth of the men engaged—an extraordinarily high percentage. This does not include the loss of the hussars either by sickness or in action, but only those incurred by the police.

It was the long days of camping in the wet, when many of them were prostrate with fever, but unable to be put on the sick-list until the fighting of the moment was over, that tried the men's fortitude the most. Continual attacks of fever shake a man to bits, and break down his nerve as nothing else will, and I could quite understand Captain de Moleyns' feeling of compunction when he looked back upon it all. " I am really sorry," he said to me, " for the awful time the men have had. It couldn't be helped—the work had to be done —but I have felt for them all the same, and I confess I am proud of the way in which these mere lads responded to every call we made upon them." I think Captain de Moleyns' personal influence had a good deal to do with it; the men followed because he led them himself.

But splendidly as the English police behaved, they could never have effected what they did had they not been loyally backed up by the native police (organised during the rebellion), whose services have been simply invaluable. It is composed chiefly of Zulus, with a sprinkling of men from Chinde and Zumbo. When Sir Richard Martin took over charge, he found the existing native police in a state of utter disorganisation, so he disbanded most of them, and raised what was practically a new corps, and placed it under the command of Major Harding of the B.S.A. Company's police, who has succeeded in making them a thoroughly reliable, efficient, and well-disciplined force. He obtained a remarkable influence over the men, and was able not only to make them follow him to a difficult assault, but to retain control of them afterwards—a much more difficult matter. He has shown what grand fighting material lies ready to our hand if entrusted to men who are in sympathy with the native character. They require a man who can be stern as well as just, but who understands them sufficiently not to wound their feelings in matters of native custom and etiquette. They are only grown-up children, and must be humoured without being spoilt. With proper leading there is no reason why they should not prove as good soldiers as the Sikhs. We conquered India, not with white troops, but with native regiments led by English officers, and if we chose we might conquer Africa in the same way, to the exceeding benefit both of the natives and of our-

selves; but to evoke the necessary feeling of devotion
we must be inflexibly just. That is what gave Gordon
his marvellous power.

Harding deserves all the more credit because he
had to work his men into shape, not in time of peace,
but in the midst of a most arduous and trying campaign. He has been ably assisted by his sergeant,
a mounted infantry man, who lives in the camp with
the men, and has them always under his eye.

The police say that so far from the Mashonas being
cowards, they fought in their own peculiar fashion with
magnificent courage. During several of the attacks,
when the dynamite was thrown into the caves, they
rushed forward and snatched away the fuse, although
they knew too well from what they had seen what the
awful effect of the explosion would be. They were naked
savages, fighting with the most primitive weapons, and
they naturally took refuge in their caves, but that does
not mean that they were cowards. Even the few guns
they had were charged with self-made powder of an
inferior character. A ludicrous exemplification of this
occurred during the M'toko patrol. Gurupila's men had
been supplied with English powder, and used the
same charge as they were accustomed to use of their
own powder. The consequence was that the guns
kicked tremendously, and several of the men had their
faces damaged, whereupon they laid the guns down on
the ground and let them off with their toes.

After the inhuman talk about the natives to which

I had to listen during my walk up from Umtali, it was a pleasant relief to meet once more with that feeling of respect for a brave enemy which does so much to lessen the unavoidable brutalities of warfare.

A little incident that took place during an attack on one of the kraals is worth recording. A cave was about to be blown up, when one of the native contingent heard a child crying just inside it. He called out to the officers who were bringing up the dynamite to stop, jumped into the cave at imminent risk of being shot, and brought the child out. Colonel Alderson relates how Major Harding did exactly the same thing. It shows the force of example: no troops are more influenced by it, for good or for evil, than native troops.

In fighting against savages treachery must always be expected, and it requires considerable self-restraint not to resort to similar methods. Indeed, all over South Africa I was assured, and not only by the irresponsible critic at the wayside canteen, but by men of position and influence, that when dealing with savages the only possible way to succeed is to behave as they do: that they do not understand anything else, and sometimes the temptation to yield to this kind of reasoning must be overpowering. At one of the kraals, for instance, two of the police officers were asked by a Mashona to come up to the rock under which he was lying to have a conference. They came within hearing distance, but he called out, "Come nearer, I can't hear;" and when they did so, he fired at them from a few feet off, luckily hitting neither. It did not make them feel very amiably disposed towards him. Poor young Coryndon, a brave lad of nineteen, who had hurried out to Mashonaland when the rebellion began, was killed when going unwarily to capture a goat tied up on the veldt as a decoy, being shot by a Mashona who was lying in ambush near by.

The Zulus and the Matabili, who are an off-shoot of the Zulu race, may generally be depended upon to keep their word, but the Mashonas have all the evil characteristics of a down-trodden people, treachery amongst them. The frequent conferences, or " indabas," as they are called, held by Lord Grey with the different Mashona chiefs, were attended, therefore, with a very real risk of assassination. And Lord Grey shirked neither fatigue nor danger when he thought his presence on a patrol might be of service in effecting a peaceful surrender. Moreover, to his infinite credit, he never allowed himself to be carried away by the wave of vindictive feeling against the natives which was passing over the country. The better tone which is everywhere noticeable in Mashonaland is largely due to the restraining influence exerted by him, by Sir Richard Martin—of whom I never heard any one speak except with respect—by Judge Vintcent and Mr. Duncan, and by Captain de Moleyns : they have been resolute without being harsh, and England has every reason to be grateful to them.

But though the Mashonas are treacherous, it is absurd to assert, as men so often do, that they have no finer feelings, and no instinct of gratitude. So far as I have been able to ascertain, they are quick and intelligent, and capable of much devotion to their masters. It is all a matter of how they are treated. A prospector, with whom I was walking along the road, told me it was impossible to do anything with them, they are such ungrateful brutes. "I will give you an instance," he said: "I and another man were out prospecting. We had had a rough time and not too much food. Most of the boys behaved all right, but one chap was always grousing, saying that he could not carry so heavy a load, and that he wanted more food when there was none to give him. We had always treated our boys well, and his going on like that riled me, so one night I said, 'Come here, I'll give you some food,' and when he came, I caught hold of him and gave him a jolly good hiding. He didn't say anything, but the next morning we found he had cleared without his pay or anything. He had just gone off, leaving us there on the veldt without any one to carry his load. What are you to do with brutes like that ? If the country is to be developed we must have forced labour, by whatever name you may choose to call it ; that is what people in England can't be got to understand."

Men of this kind expect natives to stand kicking and abuse and insufficient food, and yet be grateful and attached servants. They almost always pay dearly for their conduct, for in South Africa as in India, the natives have a marvellous system of communicating

with each other, and it rapidly becomes known all over
a district who is a good man to work with, and who is
a bad one; and a man who has once established a
bad reputation will find it next to impossible to obtain
boys, so he naturally calls out for forced labour. The
natives sing a funny little song. It was made by an
Englishman, but they have quite adopted it, and, what is
more to the purpose, they act in accordance with it—

> " Ikona mali, piccaninny scoff,
>   Meningy sebenza—this nigger's off,"

which may be translated thus :—

> " No pay and little scoff,
>   Too much work—this nigger's off."

I believe, from all I have heard, that if the Mashonas
had been properly treated from the beginning there
would have been no rebellion, nor would there have
been any difficulty in procuring labour; the settlers
have in great measure brought their troubles in this
respect upon themselves. I do not mean for a moment
to make a sweeping assertion that all the settlers in
Mashonaland have treated the natives badly. Many of
them, and I sincerely believe the large majority of them,
have treated them kindly and well, and they have been
rewarded for it by the natives behaving well to them in
return; but the minority has been sufficiently large and
sufficiently brutal to involve the innocent majority in
the discredit attaching to their deeds. A native has
little to think of, or to talk about, and an act of cruelty

will make a deep and lasting impression which will obliterate the recollection of many acts of kindness, and will spread suspicion and distrust over a whole district. That is why it is so necessary to make a native understand that though he will be punished severely if he does wrong, the white man will be punished also if he behaves to him with cruelty or fraud. Absolutely impartial justice is the secret of our rule in India, and to make the natives of Rhodesia contented, to do away with the danger of rebellion, it must be enforced there also. That is now being gradually done, for Judge Vintcent is making it felt, quietly but firmly, that he is no respecter of persons, and that the law must be obeyed. In the early days, however, there seems to have been but little justice for a native.

Rhodesia is a young country, and it will not do to be hypercritical ; most of our colonies have had a similar struggle, and in nearly all of them similar things have happened. That they have not happened in India is due to the inherent difference between a colony and a dependency. In the former the main endeavour is to repress the natives, so that they may be used as a servile race ; in the latter the great object is to educate and raise them, so that the country may eventually be governed by and through them. The difference of aim must be allowed for when considering the difference of government ; so too must the difference in character of the people. Nevertheless, in endeavouring to ascertain the cause of the Mashona discontent it is impossible to ignore the injustice with which they were originally treated.

All whom I have talked to, who have taken the trouble to study the Mashonas, agree that they have in them much that is good. They are degraded in many ways, dirty, and filthily immoral, but the germ of better things is there; it is only cultivation that is needed to bring it out, and that so far it has seldom received. Father Rickartz, the superior of the Jesuit mission at Chisha-washa, told me that the induna of the neighbouring kraal came in the day before the mission was attacked to warn him of what was impending, but was unfortunately unable to speak with him alone. Nor was this the only instance I heard of, where the natives showed practical gratitude for kind treatment they had received; in many instances they remained faithful to their masters, and in some cases even met death by their side.

In Mashonaland the Wesleyan mission at Gwenda's never revolted, and the teachers were not recalled from it, though there were more than two thousand Mashonas located there. In Matabililand, too, the converts in some instances showed the greatest fidelity.

Mrs. Reed has kindly allowed me to take the following account from a letter she received at the time from her son, Mr. Cullen Reed, dated April 10, 1896: "No sooner had we got home than messengers from the Makalanga chief came bidding me fly, as he had done all he could to save me, having refused to obey the

Matabili order to have me killed; but that now a
Matabili impi from Lanabi, who had killed the Government officials of the district and the police, had come,
and I must fly. They begged me at least to go and
hide a little way off, and see if what they said was not
true. This led to another long debate in my own mind,
but I resolved that as it was the request and warning of
the people themselves, there could be no display of
want of confidence in them on my part if I fled a short
distance off for a day. Thus I went down to my cattle
kraal eight miles away, and afterwards learned that I
missed the impi by only a mile, but finding me gone,
and *no clue being given them, though my people easily
guessed where I was*, they returned to Lanabi.

"A trooper came down from Government to call me
in. He had had a really plucky ride, expecting to meet
the Matabili at every turn, and really missing Lanabi's
impi at my kraal because he had lost his way, the Hope
Fountain boy who had ridden with him not knowing
it. Both had done a really plucky thing, and it might
easily have been fatal to them."

The rebellion was full of plucky deeds of this kind:
of men going out, as Blakiston and Routledge did, to
save their comrades, with the certainty that they were
going to their death.

I suppose there was no man in South Africa who
knew the natives more intimately than the Honourable
Charles Brownlee, chief magistrate of East Griqualand and
Gaika Commissioner. This is what he says about their

gratitude: "We find that in all their wars with the Colony, women and children have been respected, and missionaries have been assisted to a place of safety, and have not been injured by those among whom they have laboured. Will the highly-civilised inhabitants of India bear comparison with this? Many cases can be adduced in which Kaffir servants gave warning to their masters of approaching danger, when they might have taken their lives and stock. There are many cases, also, in which Kaffirs who had experienced kindness from traders took them to a place of safety on the breaking out of hostilities; one case I could instance in which the trader thus rescued treated his saviour with the basest ingratitude on the return of peace."

In the recent rising in Bechuanaland, it will be remembered that when Galishwe killed the trader Blum, he sent his wife out of the country in safety. Unhappily both in Matabililand and in Mashonaland English women have been killed, and barbarously killed, but there is a passage in Mr. Rhodes' colloquy with the indunas at the famous indaba in the Matappos which throws a sinister light on the reason for this. It is given thus by Colonel Baden-Powell: "Then he (Sikombo) was asked why it was that the Matabele, in breaking out, had exceeded the usual rules of war, and had murdered women and children? And he said it was because white men had been reported to be doing the same thing." Unfortunately the retribution fell, as it so often does, upon the innocent, and not upon the guilty. The same circle of cruelty and reprisals and vengeance has gone on in South Africa, almost without interruption, from the beginning of European intrusion. What has been done cannot be retrieved, and it would be of no use to call attention to it now, were it not that Central Africa lies alluringly before us. Is it to be subjected to the same terrible ordeal, or are we going to open it out in a more Christian fashion ?

Viewed from a merely selfish standpoint, the matter is not one that we can afford to neglect. In England the *danger* of the native question is commonly overlooked, but in South Africa it is fully recognised. Speaking in the Cape House on July 1, 1896, Sir Gordon Sprigg said : " The Mashona rebellion had a material effect upon the natives of the Cape Colony. Day after day, for five months, he had received alarming telegrams from the native territories, *and he did not know how soon it would be before a great native war might break out in Cape Colony as a consequence of what was taking place in Mashonaland.* For this reason he had decided that no member of the Cape Mounted Rifles should be moved from the Transkei or Pondoland, believing that it was the presence of force on the spot which kept the natives quiet." Both Mr. Rose Innes and Mr. Schreiner warmly supported the Government's action in the matter. But if we could only bring ourselves to believe it, justice would keep the natives quiet more effectually than troops. Look how the Basutos stood by Sir George Grey during the Indian mutiny.

CHAPTER XIII

THE question which excites the keenest interest in
Salisbury, more even than the rebellion, is the Beira
railway. When the site of the town was fixed upon, on
the 12th September 1890, it was believed that it would
become the centre of one of the richest and greatest
gold-fields in South Africa. Those expectations were
doomed to disappointment, and after the Matabili war
every effort was made to divert capital from Mashonaland to Matabililand. Men who had already settled in
Mashonaland, and had obtained property there, resent
this intensely; they resent too the constant putting off
of the railroad which has been so repeatedly promised
to them; they think that it might have been in Salisbury long before the Mashona rising, had the same
energy been shown in its construction as in that of
the Bulawayo line. What with rebellion, rinderpest,
and locusts, the Salisbury people feel that their difficulties are indeed almost more than they can struggle
against, and that an undue amount of assistance has
been given to Bulawayo to the detriment of themselves.
When I was there, the price of eggs varied from 26s.
a dozen to 48s. a dozen (the price in Bulawayo being

4s. 6d.); cabbages cost 5s. each, potatoes 3s. a lb., and a bunch of four onions 3s. 6d.: Klondike prices are nothing to this. Everything was on the same scale. Nor is the reason difficult to seek. When I passed through Umtali, the freights to Massi-Kessi were £12, 15s. a ton, and from there to Salisbury, a distance of under two hundred miles, the transport rates by waggon had been as high as £11 per 100 lbs., or £220 a ton. They were falling rapidly with the introduction of cattle from Madagascar, and I was told in Beira in February that they had already gone as low as 30s. a ton, and that transport riders would still be able to make a profit if they went down even to 20s. Prices, however, had not fallen very much, owing partly to the ring of storekeepers keeping them up, and partly to the difficulty of obtaining delivery of goods by reason of the block on the Beira railway, and the excessive rates charged for freight. When I returned to the Transvaal I came across the following instructive table of comparative rates of transport, given by Mr. Hennen Jennings in his evidence before the Mines Commission at Johannesburg, on May 12, 1897, to which I have added the present rate on the Beira railway, premising that up to November of last year it was slightly lower:—

		Pence per ton per mile.	Rates.
Machinery—American		0·51	1·000
„	Cape Railways	2·34	4·565
„	O.F.S. Railway	2·31	4·565
„	Natal Railways	3·04	5·931
„	Portuguese	4·07	7·940

		Pence per ton per mile.	Rates.
Machinery—Netherlands (Cape)	. .	7·69	15·000
,, ,, (Natal)	. .	5·06	9·871
,, ,, (Delagoa)	. .	4·27	8·330
,, English Railways	. .	1·12	2·190
,, Beira Railway	. .	12·00	23·549

On the Beira line (I quote from advertised rates) the tariff is £7, 5s. per ton of 2000 lbs., or 40 or 60 cubic ft., at the railway company's option: the following goods being classified at 60 cubic ft. per ton, adding thereby enormously to the freight charged: "Timber, bedding, wire-netting, rugs, furniture, empty tanks, baths, millinery, mattresses, matting, wool," in fact, all the things most wanted in a pioneer country.

Now £7, 5s. for 153 miles is 10·14d. per mile, as against the 7·69d. charged in the Transvaal. The rate on Messrs. Pauling's construction line was even higher; for 45 miles it was £5, that is to say, 2s. 2½d. per mile. Of course there is this difference: the Transvaal line is a paying line over which there is an enormous quantity of traffic, whereas the Beira line is a new line, which has not yet overcome the initial difficulties inseparable from all new lines, so the rates must be heavy to pay the expenses; but that does not make things easier for the people in Mashonaland.

It was reported in Umtali in November that Mr. Rhodes had promised that the rate over the whole line should be reduced to 1s. a ton per mile as soon as it had reached Umtali, and I was told in Beira on my way home that this rate had actually been fixed. It is still heavy enough to crush out any attempt to get up machinery either for the mines in Manicaland, or for those in the Salisbury district. Moreover, so long as the rails are blocked by construction material, machinery and other goods will only be taken as a matter of favour at special prices, so that there is not much hope for the people of Salisbury until the railway is actually running into that town. A few storekeepers and others will make large fortunes, but the condition of the majority of the people will be but little bettered until the line is completed.

The passenger rates are not a whit less oppressive than those for freight. Through the kindness of the Cape railway authorities I have been able to prepare the following comparative table, which will show this at a glance :—

Passenger Fares for 153 miles.

(The distance from Beira to Chimoio, the terminus of the Beira Railway.)

	First Class	Second Class
On Cape and Free State lines . . .	38/3	25/6
On Netherlands S.A.R.	38/6	31/
On Beira Railway (only one class ; as a rule trucks, except by the weekly mail)	80/	

Passenger Fares for 45 miles.

(The distance from Chimoio to Massi-Kessi.)

	First Class	Second Class
On Cape and Free State lines . . .	11/3	7/6
On Netherlands S.A.R.	11/6	9/
On Beira Construction line (only one class)	40/	

Second
Class.

Rates for natives over Cape and Free State lines in batches of not less than 25, one halfpenny each per mile, that is to say for 153 miles . . . 6/5
Over the Netherlands line in groups of 20 or more . 6/6
On the Beira line 15/

I travelled up from Delagoa Bay to Beira in the same boat with Mr. Lawley, who is in charge of the line, and in discussing with him the question of English emigration to Mashonaland, I asked him how he could possibly expect families with a small capital of, say £500, to come out to Mashonaland under the present conditions—they would only manure it with their bones for the benefit of the big companies who have the land in their grip. He replied that small capitalists were the very class of people the country requires; that there have been enough and to spare of speculators in land : that it is genuine colonists who are wanted; and he felt sure that Mr. Rhodes would do all he could to assist them. But I do not see how even Mr. Rhodes is going to unravel the tangle the country has got into : there are so many vested interests to be dealt with. In time it *may* become a rich country, and it will certainly be a pleasant country to live in, but at present it would be suicidal for an Englishman with small capital to attempt to farm there.

The first thing that is needful to open it up, and to lessen the cost of living is the railway, and the Salisbury people feel very bitterly about the way in which they have been postponed to Bulawayo. The country between

Umtali and Salisbury, through which the line will have to pass, presents no such natural difficulties as the line to Bulawayo from the Cape, and they think that if faith had been kept with them the Beira line would have been in Salisbury long ago; they believe that they have been sacrificed to Mr. Rhodes' political combinations. Had Mr. Rhodes completed the line from Beira he might have found it difficult to procure the construction of that from Mafeking, but now that line is completed he will no doubt push on with the Beira line, so that he can control the rates from the Cape to Bulawayo.

I heard a member of the Cape House remark, when discussing the arrangement that had been made with the Cape Government, " We have to take it and be thankful, for Rhodes is an awkward man to deal with; if he is thwarted he is capable of shutting down the Bulawayo line, and of forcing all the Rhodesian traffic to come through Beira." On the other hand, he can now practically freeze out Beira, and as he is not at all friendly to the Portuguese, or to the Mozambique Company, he would probably not be unwilling to do so if he thought it could be done with safety. It would make him immensely popular in the Cape. The position is an excellent one for Mr. Rhodes, putting enormous power politically and financially in his hands. It remains to be seen whether he will use it for the benefit of Rhodesia, or for that of the Cape.

During his recent election campaign, he said at

Klipdam, on August 1st, that he trusted a ministry would not be returned to office hostile to the country which bore his name. If so, Rhodesia would be hostile, and would obtain an outlet through other countries.

The British South Africa Company, I should mention, have a voting majority in the Beira Railway Company, and therefore control its management.

The Anglo-Portuguese Convention, however, dated June 11, 1891, provides that "notes shall be exchanged between her Majesty's Government and the Portuguese Government with regard to the traffic rates to be charged on the railway, similar to those exchanged on the 20th August 1890."

And by Article 19 of the Mozambique Company's charter, dated February 11, 1891, that company pledges itself to construct and work during the term of the concession, without any subsidy or guarantee whatever from the State, a railway of steel rails of a minimum weight of 20 kilos per running metre, to connect the bay of Pungwe with the interior frontier of the district of Manica, passing through Massi-Kessi.

This construction must be completed within a period of four years, no extension of time being allowed, reckoned from the date when the Government ordered it to be done. The general or special kilometric rates of transport on this railway are to be equal for all, and *never, without the sanction of the Government, to be above those in force on the lines of the Cape Colony.*

I was told by one of the Portuguese officials that as soon as the railway reaches the frontier (and by this time it ought to be there), the Portuguese Government intends to insist upon the due observance of this stipulation, for the present rates are crushing out their mines quite as much as those in Mashonaland. This will mean an immediate reduction from 1s. per ton per mile to 2·34d. per ton, and presumably a corresponding reduction in the passenger rates.

Until that is effected, it cannot be said whether the Mashonaland gold-fields are payable or not: up to the present they have not had a fair chance. To get up machinery at the existing rates would be folly, and all the companies can do is to wait until transport has been cheapened.

CHAPTER XIV

FROM Salisbury I went to Gwelo by coach. It is a rising little town, the centre of what bids fair to be one of the most prosperous mining districts in Rhodesia; but the mines being twenty or thirty miles away, I was not able to visit them. The rains had just begun, and as it poured without ceasing all the way to Bulawayo, I was afraid I should not be able to go out to the Matoppos. Major Bodle, however, who is second in command of the Matabililand police, kindly sent me out in a Cape cart to Fort Usher, which is on the outskirts of the hills, about twenty miles away. It was a cool, pleasant morning, and for the first ten miles the horses trotted out briskly. Then we noticed that one of them was labouring a good deal, and that his mouth and nostrils were covered with froth, so we outspanned to let him rest. He would not eat, but staggered about in a dazed way, and finally lay down, and the Cape boy who was driving said he had horse-sickness, and that it was doubtful whether we should get him into the fort. By going slowly, and with frequent rests we managed to bring him in, and though he was still bad when I left, he seemed likely to recover: if so, he would be what is called a salted horse, worth about three times his previous value. Horse-sickness is a dreadful scourge all over South Africa, but especially bad in Rhodesia. The police have suffered terribly from it, and it has greatly augmented the difficulties of the campaign. Captain Nicholson told me that in October 1896 there were, roughly speaking, sixteen hundred horses in Matabililand, and at the end of May 1897 only one hundred and twenty. It generally comes on suddenly, as it did in this case, and ends fatally in a couple of hours, or even less. Captain Straker, who was in command at Fort Usher, told me that he was riding a favourite pony which seemed to be going all right when it suddenly flagged, and in half-an-hour was dead. There is nothing to be done for the poor beasts, no cure being known; they must simply be left to fight it out by themselves. They seem to suffer considerable pain, and to crave for human sympathy, for they will leave their companions, and come up to any human beings who may be in sight, as though craving for help, and, if grazing when attacked, they will generally approach any hut or building that may be near, and lie down against it.

In the afternoon Captain Straker kindly took me out to a valley in the Matoppos called the Cantoor, where General Carrington had a fight with the Matabili. It is several miles inside the hills, and gives a fair idea of their general character. They are a granite range, running nearly due east and west for some sixty miles, with an average width of from twenty to twenty-five miles. They are quite distinct in character from the granite kopjes in Mashonaland, which are isolated mountains of granite, dotted about on a granitic plateau. These hills consist of an immense collection of boulders similar to those at Chesumba's, but instead of being in a break of the plain, where a stream has cleft out for itself a precipitous channel, they rise up from it to nearly a thousand feet in height in a series of contorted ridges, intersecting each other at every variety of angle. These ridges are sometimes bare, but are generally covered with a scanty bush, the intervening valleys being thickly wooded, except where the natives have cleared patches for cultivation. It is a terribly difficult country for troops to operate in, the valleys being so narrow that they come under a raking fire from all sides, and it is impossible either by artillery or by rifle fire to silence opponents who can disperse themselves in an impenetrable wilderness of rocks with perfect safety, and can aim, crouching behind them like baboons, without exposing themselves in the least. Fortunately the Matabili are not skilled in hill fighting. They have always fought on open ground, in the half - moon formation invented by Chaka, and perfected by Moselikatze, and they did not seem to appreciate their strength, or to work in conjunction when not massed together, but scattered about in groups of twos and threes amongst these boulders. Moreover, they suffered from the fatal weakness of having no definite leader, each induna having independent command of his own men.

The morning after I arrived, M'twani, the most prominent of these indunas, happened to come into the fort, and in the afternoon I rode out to his kraal with Mr. Moody, the native commissioner, and Lieutenant Macgeean. We came up with M'twani and one of his men, on their way home, just where the track became too broken for us to ride any longer, so we gave our horses to his man to hold, and went on with M'twani himself as our guide: he carrying Mr. Moody's rifle, the only weapon we had with us, and a couple of knob-kerries. He is a tall, good-looking man, with the quiet, stately, unmoved manner of a Matabili induna. Before our time he was a man of consequence, his sister Loski being Lobengula's head queen. His kraal is about six miles farther into the hills than the Cantoor, the valley where General Carrington's action took place, on which occasion he was in command. His brother was killed, and he himself was shot through the leg by a Lee-Metford bullet. He showed us the scar left by the wound, and remarked that he was not badly hurt, as the bullet missed the bone. His kraal is in the middle of an almost inaccessible valley, where the Tuli River is joined by the Nyokani—(the little snake)—a lovely brook we had been following for several miles. It was here that the Matabili women and children were gathered together during the rising, the only entrances to it being by two steep and exceedingly difficult paths, along which the cattle have to be driven one by one. As it contains an abundance both of water and of arable land, it is nearly perfect as a place of refuge. General Carrington intended to attack it, but fortunately changed his mind. He could hardly have failed to meet with disaster and heavy loss.

The only effectual way to subdue the Matabili after they have taken to the Matoppos is to surround them by a chain of forts, and starve them out, for, though they are of great extent, there are comparatively few places where the ground is sufficiently open for culti-vation, or where there is pasturage for cattle, and these few places are so feverish that even the natives fear to live in them. M'twani told us that he had been suffering badly with fever himself, and that nearly the whole of his people were down with it. The Matabili themselves did not live in the Matoppos, but had their kraals on the open ground around Bulawayo; it was their slaves, the Makalakas, who lived in them under the supervision of Matabili indunas. The Matabili, it must be borne in mind, are not the original inhabitants of the country. They are the descendants of a body of Zulus, who left Zululand under Moselikatze, one of Chaka's generals, between the years 1836 and 1838, and carved out a dominion for themselves in the country that lies between the Zambesi and the Limpopo. This country must always be sparsely populated, and many districts where the forest is thick are absolutely un-inhabited.   Last year, the census showed that the entire population of Matabililand amounted only to 118,000, of whom 12,000 were pure Matabili of the original Zulu stock, the remainder being Makalakas, Makalangas, and Mashonas, who are all known by the general name of Maholis, or slaves.   The bulk of the original inhabitants were Makalangas, who are found scattered all over the country.   The south-eastern portion between the Ma-toppos and the Transvaal and Portuguese borders, is chiefly inhabited by a tribe of Mahatees, an overflow from the tribe of that name settled in the Transvaal, where they have suffered much ill-treatment at the hands of the Boers.   Not long ago their chief sent to the authorities in Bulawayo to ask if he might trek with his people into Rhodesia.   Since then he has died, but his son 'Mpefu has refused to pay his hut-tax to the Transvaal Government, and there will probably have to be an expedition to compel him to do so. These are some of the people whose rights we bound ourselves to protect under the Transvaal Convention, but about whom we have never troubled ourselves in the least.   Until Rhodesia came under English rule, they were between two fires, the Dutch and the Matabili, of whom the latter raided them so con-tinually that hardly any women or children were found in their kraals when we took over the country; they had all been killed or carried away.   I was told they are willing enough to work in the mines, or to do any other kind of labour, but unfortunately there are not a great number of them.

When Matabililand was denuded of troops for the Jameson raid, one of the indunas, a son of the famous witch-doctor Maginyamachi, perceived that if the Matabili hoped ever to regain their independence, they could not have a more favourable opportunity for rising. The Majakas, the young Matabili warriors, had long been fretting under the indignity of the forced labour exacted from them, and the Maholis were in a state of equal irritation on account of the compulsory slaughter of their cattle, in accordance with the rinderpest regulations, which, as in Galishwe's country, seem to have been carried out with a needless disregard for native susceptibilities.

Lord Grey has denied absolutely that there was forced labour in Rhodesia, and the British South Africa Company wrote to the Colonial Office that "the suggestion made by Sir Richard Martin's report that a system of compulsory labour has existed in any part of Rhodesia has astounded the directors. They cannot credit the statements made. Certainly no authority whatever, direct or indirect, has been given by the Company for such a practice, and if it has prevailed it has been wholly without the consent or knowledge of the board."

That there was forced labour, however, and of the most galling kind, is conclusively proved by the statement of Mr. H. J. Taylor, the chief native commissioner of Matabililand.

" The higher class natives—the ' Abezansi '—had a great antipathy to labour, which they considered to be derogatory to their dignity. The hard-earned wage of the ' Hole ' was often taken by his former owner in the Abezansi section. Much discontent was thus caused, and as the demand for labour in the mining districts increased, it was deemed advisable to call upon the Abezansi to contribute their share to the labour. In many instances they refused to do so, arguing that their slaves should earn money for them. This condition of semi-slavery could not be tolerated by a civilised government, and in order to deal equally with all classes, the young men of the Abezansi were called upon to work for two months in the year. This they refused to do upon the grounds of their former argument. In some cases the native police had to call out some of the young men to work. They were brought before the native commissioner, and handed over to a master to whom they were registered for a specified term and wage."

Now what is this but forced labour ? It is practically admitted to be so in Matabililand, for the Chamber of Mines are continually urging its re-imposition, and Mr. Rhodes has stated that the difficulty in the development of the mines is due to the scarcity of labour, caused by the stoppage of the original supply, owing to Sir Richard Martin's report. But if the original supply were voluntary and not enforced, it would still be available. No one who has been in the country, and has taken the trouble to look dispassionately into the matter, can have any doubt that Sir Richard Martin was fully justified in all he said, and that he might well have written far more strongly.

In view of Mr. Rhodes' avowed intention to draw a labour supply from the untapped regions of the Zambesi, a careful perusal should be made of the evidence (given by Sir R. Martin) of Mr. Carnegie, the missionary, and care should be taken that proper guarantees should be given that these Zambesi natives shall not be similarly ill-treated.

"Next comes the native labour question," Mr. Carnegie wrote, "which certainly had something to do with the rebellion. A proud, hitherto unconquered, Matabili cannot be turned in a month, or a year, into a useful servant by kicks, sjamboks, or blows. You cannot civilise him by quarrelling with him a few days before his pay is due, by stoning, or unjustly beating him, by cursing him for not understanding an order given in English, by being too kind to him. Let it be abundantly understood that none of these charges can be brought against many employers, but there were those guilty of such acts, and under the system of Government labour supply the natives were unable to choose their employers. There are many details connected with the treatment of natives, personally known to myself, which prove conclusively that the wrong men were often chosen for handling such raw material, both in the mines, on the farms, and in the Government service. Speaking then from their point of view, the natives practically said :

' Our country is gone, our cattle have gone, our people are scattered, we have nothing to live for, our women are deserting us, the white man does as he likes with them ; we are the slaves of the white man, we are nobody, and have no rights or laws of any kind.' Many reasoned thus among themselves, rightly or wrongly."

Could there be a sadder commentary upon the result of our occupation of Matabililand ?

It has been said that the missionaries have remained silent about these things, but, as a matter of fact. the majority have spoken out unflinchingly, like Mr. Carnegie and Mr. Reed.   Later on I will give an indignant letter, written by Mr. J. White to the *Methodist Times* in 1896, explaining the causes that had led to the Mashona rebellion.   Written at the time it was, by a man who had to make his life in the country, and to endure the brunt of the obloquy which it could not fail to bring upon him, it was, like Mr. Carnegie's and Mr. Reed's, an exceedingly courageous protest.

Mr. Reed says about labour : " I would respectfully suggest that whatever settlement may be made in future concerning the natives they be left free to choose what period of the year they can best be spared at home, and for whom they will work, *i.e.* to suit themselves as far as they can to the nature of their employment, wages, treatment, &c.   Any other arrangement seems to me to partake of the nature of slavery, which is surely repugnant to every English instinct."

These statements should be read in connection with

Clause 2 of the British South Africa Company's Charter: "The Company shall to the best of its ability discourage, and, so far as may be practicable, abolish by degrees any system of slave-trade or *domestic servitude* in the territories aforesaid."

On the other hand, the Rev. J. Shimmin, the superintendent of the Wesleyan mission in Matabililand, in his observations on the present state of native affairs in that country published in the B.S.A. Company's Report, which has just been issued, says: "As a Christian minister I should strongly deprecate the slightest infringement of the liberties of any subject, but to affirm that a veiled form of slavery is condoned by the officials of the Chartered Company, is a travesty of terms unworthy of reasonable men." It depends what idea one has of slavery, or rather of *domestic servitude*. The indenturing of the Bechuana rebels in the Cape Colony is looked upon by many as a veiled form of slavery; by others it is not; just as in Rhodesia some people agree with Mr. Carnegie, but others—and I fancy the majority —with Mr. Shimmin. In any case it is not desirable to approach to it so nearly that there should be any dispute about the matter, for it is, as Mr. Reed says, repugnant to every British instinct.

Lord Grey dismisses the subject in an altogether inadequate way. The hardships inflicted on the natives are too well substantiated to be dealt with so cavalierly. "Although treated with great consideration by the Government; although no taxes were levied; and although every precaution was taken to prevent harassing and unnecessary interference by the white settlers, the fact remained that a warlike and hitherto unconquered people were daily reminded that they, the former lords of the earth, were now expected to wear the livery of inferiority, and to *perform industrial duties* which formerly they had exacted from their slaves."

That they were compelled to perform these industrial duties was in direct breach of the charter, whereas any one reading Lord Grey's Report would imagine that the compulsion to labour was perfectly legitimate, and the discontent of the Matabili a consequence that could not be avoided.

How different a view was held by the late Earl Grey. "Throughout this part of the British dominions," he wrote in 1880, "the coloured people are generally looked upon by the whites as an inferior race, whose interests ought to be systematically disregarded when they come into competition with their own, and who ought to be governed mainly with a view to the advantage of the superior race. And for this advantage two things are considered to be especially necessary : first, that facilities should be afforded to the white colonists for obtaining possession of land heretofore occupied by the native tribes ; and secondly, that the Kaffir population should be made to furnish as large and as cheap a supply of labour as possible. . . . This desire for cheap labour, and what has been well called 'the hunger for land,' has led settlers of European descent to deal harshly

and unjustly with uncivilised tribes, not only in Africa,
but elsewhere. This fact must be borne in mind in
considering how the British dominions in South Africa
ought in future to be governed." (*Nineteenth Century*.)

But quite as strong an opinion against it is entertained by many people even in South Africa. The
Diamond Fields Advertiser, in a leading article upon
the Rev. John Mackenzie's criticism of the Chartered
Company in the *Contemporary Review*, speaks out
very plainly: " Mr. Mackenzie's observations regarding
forced labour in Rhodesia demand the most serious
consideration of both the home and the colonial public.
Most Rhodesian settlers who discuss the cause of the
recent rebellion—and who, for obvious and sufficient
reasons, are shy of divulging their names to the public—
say far stronger things concerning the labour system in
the new territory than ever Mr. Mackenzie has said. If
it be true that chiefs were fined, and even lashed, for failing to produce such and such a number of ' boys ' in so
many hours, it is imperative that the British Government—and still more, the British public—should know it.
Mr. Mackenzie says that this system of forced labour is
' opposed to the deepest purpose and the dearest wishes
of the British people.' Unhappily, experience both in
Africa and in Australia does not bear out this view. To
be candid with one another, do not most of us who have
come to the colonies from the mother-land undergo a
weakening of moral fibre as regards the treatment of
natives, as the influence of English ideas wanes ? If we

do, it is not surprising. The settler, aware of the vast potentialities of the land with which he has cast in his lot, his mind harassed, his energies confined owing to the scarcity of labour, naturally looks with an eye of longing upon the vast labour supplies which the native tribes represent. Only the other day, Mr. George Albu, speaking before the Mines Commission at the Rand, hinted, not obliquely, at forced labour as a possible expedient in the Transvaal. If once forced labour—another name for slavery—be allowed in any province of Africa under British over-lordship, depend upon it the poison will work its way through all the States. That it is a poison we strenuously insist; dividends are admirable things in their way, and dividends let us have, if we can possibly get them by fair means, but to get dividends out of Africa at the expense of the great moral idea which must be behind all our development will be to take a most serious step towards our failure and decadence."

The article urges that Mr. Mackenzie had formulated a case which the Parliamentary Committee could not dismiss without searching investigation, and that representative indunas from Rhodesia ought to be summoned before it. No such investigation was made, and when I was in Rhodesia both the people and the press were clamouring for the recognised imposition of some form of forced labour.

CHAPTER XV

THE rising was to have begun all over Matabililand on Saturday the 27th March, but it broke out prematurely on the 23rd, the preceding Tuesday. The white men in the Filibusi district were massacred, and the Matabili closed in around Bulawayo. From that time, until the 25th April, there were continual fights in the immediate neighbourhood of the town, and had the natives possessed any leader of ordinary military ability, they should have had no difficulty in wiping out the whole of the white population of Rhodesia. They had but to close the Tuli road to the south—an easy matter—and the Bulawayo people, having only a fortnight's provisions, and a very limited supply of ammunition, would have had no choice but to cut their way out—a desperate task in the face of an overpowering enemy, and by a road winding through continuous defiles. But instead of seizing the road, they left it open, and only invested the town on the other three sides, so that Colonel Plumer was able

N

to enter it without difficulty with the hurriedly raised Matabili Relief force. The Matabili are said to have done this deliberately, in the hope that the white men would clear out, and let them have the country once more to themselves; but it is also asserted, and with more probability, that they intended to attack the white people during their retreat through the Mangwe Pass, when they would have had a fair chance of destroying them at one blow. Whatever the motive may have been, it proved to be a fatal error in tactics. They could easily have shut off all access to the town, for it is calculated that during the last days of the fighting in its vicinity they could not have had less than twenty-five thousand men in the field. Their disorganisation was mainly due to a lucky chance. Gambo, the head induna of the western district, one of their most important men and a warrior of repute, would naturally have been in command, having led an impi during the first Matabili war, but he happened to be in Bulawayo at the time of the premature outbreak in the Filibusi district. He had been sent for to have the rinderpest regulations explained to him, and when the news of the murders arrived, Mr. Duncan, who was acting as administrator, ordered him to be arrested, and retained him in custody during the whole of the rising, his people in consequence remaining steady all through it.

There is an interesting account in the first issue of the *Matabili Times*, published on the 13th April 1894,

written with the cyclostyle, which was kindly given
to me by Mr Löwinger, the editor, which shows the
great authority held by Gambo in the country, and
how important a bearing his detention had upon the
issue of the rebellion : " Gambo, son-in-law of the
late king, Lo Bengula, and one of the last important
chiefs to surrender, came into camp on the 29th
March, attended by his indunas and followers. On
the following morning the administrator, Dr. Jameson,
received Gambo at an indaba, when Umlugulu, the
great dance-doctor Secombi, and other chiefs were
present. In reply to a question from Gambo, the
administrator said he would be looked after by the
Company till such time as the land that he formerly
lived upon was cultivated and yielded crops. He was
allowed to take up his own land again, seeing there
were no old workings there, and that it would be futile
to prospect for gold. For the present they would all
be disarmed, but later on Gambo and his indunas
would be allowed arms for personal protection and
trading purposes. They would be afforded police protection, and would have the same consideration shown
them as the white people had, and any complaint made
to the police would receive proper attention. Their
women would also be protected. Regarding the
' Amaholis,' which tribe were the slaves of the Matabili, and since the outbreak, as Gambo asserted, were
becoming insubordinate, the administrator said that the
' Amaholis ' would still have to serve them as before,

but that if they refused there was to be no fighting, but the grievances would have to be brought to the notice of the police for redress."

Does not this show how natural it was for the Abezansi—the young bloods of the Matabili—to become angry and sullen when they were called upon in the way that Mr. Taylor has described, to work for two months in the year, side by side with the Amaholis, their former slaves?   "Brought by the native police," to use Mr. Taylor's own words, "before the native commissioner, and handed over to a master to whom they were registered for a specified term and wage."   Naturally they felt that this was not in accordance with Dr. Jameson's declaration to Gambo, and that faith had not been kept with them.   That in itself is enough to induce any native tribe to rise; "two words" is what they are never able to understand; they believe in their rulers laying down a law, and adhering to it rigidly.

That the labour grievance was not an occasional grievance, but one extending to a large number of people is proved by a statement by Mr Taylor in the Chartered Company's Report for the year 1894-1895, that the total number of natives employed by Europeans was over ten thousand.   What made the matter worse was that not only were the Matabili deprived of the services of the Amaholi—that, in spite of Dr. Jameson's undertaking to the contrary, was unavoidable—but they were themselves compelled to labour side by side with them.

At the Bulawayo festivities, Captain Lawley made an important statement. "I think," he said, "that I am betraying no State secrets when I tell you that a code of laws, which has received the sanction of the High Commissioner, is now in the hands of the Colonial Secretary, which will, I hope, enable us to carry these views into practical effect. It is a simple code, but it will enable us, I hope, to wean the natives from a life of indolence, disturbed occasionally by exhilarating outbursts of war and plunder, to a life of regular habits, and regular industry."

The provisions of this new code should be carefully scanned to see whether any of its clauses can possibly be twisted into sanctioning the imposition of what, under another name, will be but a form of compulsory labour.

In all probability the provisions of Natal Act 19 of 1891 will be adopted in the Rhodesian Code. Sir R. Martin referred to them incidentally in his report, but drew a marked distinction between such powers when given to an old colony and to a new one, and I may add the distinction is even greater when they are given to a company, whose primary object is the declaration of a dividend.

One of the officials of the Mozambique Company in Beira told me that company was unable to develop the country properly because the officials were perpetually being hampered by the foolish humanitarian party in Lisbon. There, too, the inevitable conflict is going on between the governing class, who look to the interests of the whole community, and the commercial class, who think mainly of their own.   The same conflict occurs in India in the indigo and tea districts between the Indian civil servants and the planters.

Clause 36 of the Natal Act is to the following effect : " The supreme chief has power to call upon all natives to supply labour for public works, and for the general needs of the Colony.   This call or command may be transmitted by any person authorised to do so, and each native so called upon is bound to obey such call, and render such service in person unless legally released from such duty."

And Clause 39 declares that " the supreme chief, in the exercise of the political powers which attach to his office, has authority to punish by fine and imprisonment, or by both, for disobedience to his orders or disregard of his authority."

Although there may be no objection to the temporary imposition of compulsory labour for the needs of a colony in time of famine or drought, it is a very different matter if it is to be enforced regularly, and if the men are to be employed, not by the State, but to be handed over to the various companies for the development of their mines and other properties.   It is difficult to understand on what grounds compulsory labour of that kind could be defended.

Mr. Whitaker, whose father was for fifty years, on and off, Premier and Attorney-General of New Zealand, referred thus to the New Zealand system in the evidence he gave before the Bulawayo Chamber of Mines: "They (in New Zealand) adopted a system which I am very much in favour of, and that was, that when they conquered any portion of country, they gave the natives back a certain amount of land, and never asked them to work, but allowed them to live by themselves. Isolation," he said, "has been to their advantage, and that of the white man too, in that it has opened avocations for a white population to settle in the country. In New Zealand we have very few social evils, and have no rows with the natives, and don't look upon them as a factor in the community."

It is quite true that the Amaholis (not the Matabili) were accustomed to work compulsorily for Lobengula, but it is a very different thing having to turn out now and again for some special purpose to being obliged to work for fixed periods. It is the regularity of the work that natives cannot stand. In Chitral exactly the same difficulty was encountered. There the people had always been accustomed to "begar" or forced labour, but they objected strongly to being constrained to go to and fro, day after day, from village to village. "Are we to be made carriers of loads for all our lives?" they said; "it were better to fight, and be killed at once." The natives in Rhodesia have exactly the same feeling. In time they will learn the value of money, just as the Chitralis are learning it, but an enforced servitude is not the right way to teach it to them : it will only delay the educating process which is so much desired.   And with regard to the Matabili, it must be remembered that labour of any kind is entirely opposed to their habits; that it will take years before they can become resigned to it.

"Like all other branches of the Zulu race," says Sir Richard Martin, " the men were averse to labour, which they considered altogether derogatory.   It was for them to hunt and fight : the tilling of gardens and such menial work fell to the lot of the women.   Thus it may be said that, previous to the arrival of the white man in their country, the idea of work was altogether foreign to them."

How strong an objection they feel to it may be judged from the following telegram from Sir F. Carrington on 19th September 1896 : " Inderna's people are reported by officer commanding to be unwilling to surrender at Gwelo, saying they have plenty of corn, *and will not work in the mines.*"

I make no apology for dwelling at considerable length upon this subject, for its importance cannot be over-estimated; the more so, that the Colonial Office seems disposed to accede to the Chartered Company's proposals.

Speaking in the House of Commons on May 7, 1898, Mr Chamberlain said, " The corvée existing in Matabili-land was of this nature—that the natives against their will were practically compelled to give a certain time of the year to ordinary industrial labour.   It was not the whole of their time, but I think it was for three months in the year that the native chiefs had to furnish a certain proportion of labour for the mines. . . . When you say to a savage people, who have hitherto found their chief employment, occupation, and profit in war, 'You shall no longer go to war; tribal war is forbidden,' you have to bring about some means by which they may earn their living in place of it, and you have to induce them, sooner or later, to adopt the ordinary methods of earning a livelihood by the sweat of their brow. But with a race of this kind, I doubt very much if you can do it merely by preaching. I think that something in the nature of inducement, stimulus, or pressure is absolutely necessary if you are to secure a result which is desirable in the interests of humanity and civilisation." After that pronouncement of opinion, it is to be hoped that the forthcoming native code will be submitted to the keenest scrutiny before it is definitely promulgated.[1]

[1] Mr. Chamberlain will hardly venture to sanction the corvée if he has reason to believe it is against the wish of the majority of the people of Great Britain, and that it is so may be inferred from the opinion of the *Times* upon forced labour, which may be taken as representing the considered view of the nation. On September 13th, 1898, the *Times* said in a leading article : "But as a matter of practice, what colonists can be trusted to work a system of ' forced labour' among native races ? It is a mere euphemism for slavery. And if there is one principle more than another which has lain at the root of British Imperialism it is the doctrine that wherever the British flag flies the slave is free." For most people that will sum up the whole question.

CHAPTER XVI

The people in Rhodesia were living in perfect ignorance that any rebellion was impending. There was no armed force in the country, for Dr. Jameson had taken all the white police with him except five, and Mr. Duncan, who was acting as administrator, was obliged to disband the native police at once, as they were manifestly in sympathy with the rebels. The outbreak came like a thunderclap. On Monday the 23rd March 1896, Tom Maddox, a prospector, was killed in the Filibusi district. He was very popular with the natives, and had always treated them well, and that in spite of it he should have been murdered was a sign that the rising was going to be serious. All the settlers in the Filibusi district collected together, and orders were sent to them from Bulawayo to come in there at once, while the Rhodesia Horse was promptly called out.

At that time the only Imperial officer in Bulawayo

was Captain Nicholson of the 7th Hussars. After the
Jameson raid he had been sent up by the Imperial
Government to take over charge of the arms and
ammunition.

Fugitives began to pour into the town from all
directions, and the women and children were placed in
the club for safety. If the Matabili had attacked the
town at once they could easily have taken it, for
there were only about four hundred rifles in the whole
place. Fortunately there was no lack of ammunition.

The story of its defence is familiar to every one.
The difficulties the administration had to contend
with were very great. They had only these four
hundred rifles, and were afraid to render the town
defenceless with so large a force of natives in the
near neighbourhood. Yet they were obliged to send
out simultaneously a number of small relieving forces
to bring in the people from the outlying districts, and
they were also obliged to establish forts on the Tuli
road, for on the keeping of that open lay their whole
chance of relief. By the first of April the Matabili
had invested the other three sides of the town, and
constant engagements took place; the last fight in its
immediate vicinity being on the 25th April, when
Captain Macfarlane, formerly of the 9th Lancers, who
seems to have been the backbone of the defence, effectually crushed them at the Umguzi River. He had
only four men killed and five wounded, but he inflicted
terrible loss on the enemy, who twice charged right up

to the guns in the old heroic Matabili-Zulu style. After the fight they melted away, and never held together again. Numbers fled towards the Zambesi, where they suffered terribly from fever and famine, as well as from wild animals.

It is said that eighteen of them were killed by lions in one night alone in the dense forest that lies some fifty miles to the north of Gwelo.

The most probable explanation of the premature outbreak of the rebellion is the uncontrollable irritation produced by the shooting of the cattle. Whatever the cause may have been, the Matabili did not become properly organised for several weeks after it began. Their original idea was to attack Bulawayo early in the morning, and then to sweep the country, killing off the settlers one by one. Had they adhered to this plan not a soul would have been left alive. As it was, the settlers were able to get into laager not only in Bulawayo, but in Gwelo, Mangwe, Tuli, and Belingwe. The difficulties of the defence must not be estimated from the actual fighting, or from the number of men killed. The horses died wholesale from horse-sickness and want of forage. There was great scarcity of water, wells having to be sunk to procure it, and very little food. At one time there were only eight bags of meal left in the Government store, and a little bully beef. There was considerable danger of famine — all the food having to be brought up by the coach, which might have been stopped at any time. The cattle captured on the patrols were driven into the town, and died there of rinderpest, and the stench was fearful. Yet there was but little typhoid or other serious illness, showing how exceedingly healthy Bulawayo is. The chief trouble was from veldt sores, a kind of scurvy brought on by the want of fresh meat and vegetables the supply of which was altogether stopped.

The safety of Bulawayo being thus assured by the efforts of the people themselves before help could be sent to them, they began at once to take measures to bring the country again into subjection. On May 11th, Colonel Napier was sent up the Salisbury road to meet Mr. Rhodes, who was coming down with Colonel Beal and the Salisbury relief column. Colonel Plumer arrived in Bulawayo on the 15th with the Matabili Relief force, and a day or two later Sir Richard Martin, who had been sent out from England as Deputy of the High Commissioner, and Commandant of the police. Ten days afterwards, General Sir Frederick Carrington arrived also, to assume general command of the operations, bringing with him Colonel Baden-Powell as chief of his staff. Earl Grey, the newly-appointed administrator, had come into the town before that, on the 28th April, and had relieved Mr. Duncan of his duties as acting administrator. He had a narrow escape, for a Matabili impi under the induna Babyan crossed the road just before the coach in which he was came up, and crossed it again at the same place immediately after it had passed.

Colonel Plumer was instructed to move along the Guai River to attack the Matabili, who were said to be collected there in force. At the same time, Colonel Paget, who was advancing up the Tuli road with the 7th Hussars, instead of going on straight to Bulawayo, was sent with two squadrons through the thickly populated Belingwe district to Victoria, and thence to circle round through Gwelo; Major Ridley with another squadron coming straight on to Bulawayo through Maklutsi and the Mangwe Pass.

Towards the end of the rising there was a severe fight at Thabas Imamba, about seventy miles to the north of Bulawayo, at which Mr. Rhodes was present, and after that the only part of Matabililand where the natives were able to hold their own was in the Matoppo hills, into which they had retreated. They were attacked there simultaneously by General Carrington at the Cantoor, and by Major Laing, of the Belingwe field force, at the Nungweni Pass, ten miles farther to the west. It was intended that the two forces should join inside the hills, but neither was able to force its way through, and both had to retire with considerable loss. On a subsequent occasion, at the Nungweni Pass, when Captain Nicholson was in command, if it had not been for the coolness with which Captain Hoel Llewellyn worked the Maxim during a Matabili onrush, the loss must again have been considerable. A day or two later the Matabili were attacked at Umlugulu, where there proved to be some awkward caves. Major Kershaw was killed, and several of the men, and once more the Matabili remained masters of the situation.

The whole of the country to the southward and eastward had, however, been brought under control, the natives retreating either into the Matoppos, or right away to the Zambesi. The only chiefs who attempted any resistance were Wedza, whose kraal is near Belingwe, and Uwini, whose kraal is about twenty miles from Gwelo. Wedza capitulated, and is still living at his kraal, but Uwini was taken prisoner, and, though badly wounded, was tried summarily by court-martial and shot as a rebel. By order of the High Commissioner, Colonel Baden-Powell, who confirmed the death sentence, was himself tried by court-martial and was acquitted.

Lord Grey in his report makes the following reference to the capture of these kraals: "They" (the Hussars) "did valuable service in blowing up the strongholds of Monogola and of Wedza, a notoriously bad character; and they demonstrated the power of the Queen in a way that admitted of no doubt, to a large and important district, by the capture and execution of Uwini, whose death has had a most salutary influence in the pacification of the country. The fact that Uwini and Wedza had successfully withstood the raids of Lobengula, had caused the Matabili on this occasion to take refuge in their fastnesses, and then consider themselves in safety."

But many people in Rhodesia think that Uwini was treated with unnecessary harshness; that he was not in any way more guilty than the other rebel chiefs who were not shot when taken prisoner, and that as a brave opponent, who had been badly wounded in a gallant attempt to resist a vastly superior force, he might well have been accorded different treatment. Lord Rosmead felt constrained by what had happened to remind all military officers in Rhodesia that martial law had not been proclaimed there, and that prisoners ought to be handed over to the civil authorities.

The reduction of the Matoppos would have been long and difficult task, and opinions are divided as to the advisability of what was done. Most of the military men seem to think that it would have been wiser to have gone on until the Matabili were brought to their knees, and sued for peace. Instead of that Mr. Rhodes, at great personal risk, held his famous meetings or indabas, and arranged terms which at the time were a financial necessity, for the Chartered Company could not have borne the expense of the war much longer; nor would it have been possible to have got up provisions, as the rains were beginning. What Mr. Rhodes did seems therefore to have been the wisest course which could have been adopted. Still, as it is, the natives think that it was not they, but we, who asked that hostilities should cease. Their pride has not been humbled, and it is by no means unlikely that some day they may again be tempted to try conclusions with us. Mr. Carnegie, in the weighty statement which Sir Richard Martin has appended to his report — a statement the whole of which should be read and re-read — makes this remark: " As to the position of the Matabili nation in the country at the present moment, let me say that under Lobengula there were two factions, one representing the old warriors, and the other the young bloods. From all I can gather to-day these two parties still exist in the land; the one in the Matoppo hills, and the other in the bushy country in the north-west. Nyamande represents the younger men of the tribe, and he, being the son of Lobengula, and one of the Insukumini, would in their estimation be most likely a fit and proper person to be made king. Usipampamu, who some months ago crossed the Zambesi, may have a few followers, though I hear the Barotze have driven him back in two battles. But the nation as such is divided into two factions —the one under Umlugulu and Ufisela, among the Matoppo hills, and the other under Umtini, Bugwele, and the others in the bushy country. The final stand will most likely be made among the Matoppo hills."

If they should rise again, it will be a much easier matter to subdue them, for a chain of forts connected by the telephone has been built outside the Matoppos, so that they can be effectually prevented from breaking out; and, what is more to the purpose, Sir Richard

Martin and Captain Nicholson have got the Matabililand Police into thoroughly good order, and have converted what was a very scratch corps indeed into a smart and well-disciplined body of men. There is no native contingent in Matabililand as in Mashonaland, but a rather larger force of white police, consisting of six hundred troopers and twenty-one officers. Two hundred are stationed in the Bulawayo depôt, and the rest in the forts, of which there are twenty-nine, scattered about all over the country. They have seventeen machine-guns, and six field-guns, so they should have no difficulty in crushing any incipient rebellion before it has had time to gather force.

The natives have been partially disarmed, and a Disarmament Act has come into force by which it has been made illegal for any of them to possess arms without leave from the administrator; and the Chartered Company are resolved to enforce this law strictly. It is a similar law, only not nearly so stringent, as the Arms Act in force on the Indian frontier, and is absolutely necessary for the safety of the country. Moreover, the settlers are now on the alert and will not be taken by surprise as they were before.

An excellent system has also been initiated by Sir Richard Martin, by which a prospector if he wants a rifle can obtain it on the recommendation of the administrator. With it he is given the name of the fort in the district to which he is attached. Each of these forts is stocked with provisions for a couple of months, as well as with spare arms and ammunition; and should any disturbance occur in the district, the prospector becomes at once a member of the garrison, and is entitled both to ammunition and to rations. Naturally, there is still a good deal of hesitation about venturing out to prospect, and wild rumours are constantly afloat, but Captain Nicholson declares that the natives are absolutely under control.   Up to the present they have abided loyally by the terms of the agreement made with them, and have not fired a shot since the day on which they agreed to give in, or to sit down, to use their own expressive phrase.

Too great a dependence must not be placed upon native declarations, but they say themselves that they understand now that they are not a match for the white men.   Mr. Rhodes asked one of their indunas if they had really thought they had any chance of succeeding.   "Yes," he said, "we felt sure we could beat you, but we know now that we could no more beat you than we can lick our elbows."   After he had gone, Mr. Rhodes and those who were with him tried to lick their elbows, but found it an impossibility.

In spite of the financial difficulties in which the rebellion involved them, the Chartered Company, when they found the natives in a starving condition, supplied them with food amounting to a weight of over five million pounds (two thousand five hundred tons), the transport cost of which from the railway base could certainly not have been less than £100 per ton.   That is to say, they have expended on their rebellious subjects, at a time of great financial difficulty, at least £250,000.   It fully justifies Father Daignault's comment, " I must add that the action of the Company in supplying the natives with seed and food, and trying to find employment for them, after they caused the Company such a loss of life, money, and property, is highly creditable, and I cannot instance a similar case of equal generosity."

This clemency has had the best possible effect; and another great factor that makes for peace is the railway.   The natives are fully aware of its importance, one of them having been heard to say, " What is the good of fighting against the white men ? the oxen are all dead from rinderpest, but they can make their waggons run without oxen."

But by far the most effectual guarantee for peace will be the firm but just rule which there is every reason to hope is being instituted.   Of Judge Vintcent and his work there is but one opinion.   Mr Milton, who rules in Salisbury, has an admirable record in South Africa; and Captain Lawley, the deputy-administrator in Matabililand, although he has won the enthusiastic confidence of the settlers, is determined that fair treatment shall also be accorded to the natives. Let us hope that the words he spoke at the Bulawayo banquet will in time come true—he may be depended upon to do his utmost to bring about their fulfilment: " It was a tide of commercial activity and commercial enterprise, but it was a tide which bore upon its bosom the healing influences of Christianity and civilisation, and would in the end do much to diminish the sum of human suffering and of human sin."

That is as it should be, but vastly different methods of evangelisation will have to be employed in the future to those which have been adopted in the past.

The Mashonaland rising began on the 18th June, when the Matabili rebellion was practically over; so both Imperial troops and volunteers were sent up from Bulawayo to assist in quelling it; Colonel Alderson, with the mounted infantry, coming out direct from England.

The rebellion was never really serious, and soon resolved itself into a gradual reduction one by one of the different chiefs, who had no cohesion, and did not co-operate in any way with each other. Like the rising in Matabililand it was full, however, of gallant incidents of individual pluck.

Most of them have already been recounted in the Chartered Company's Report, but one, not contained in it, is, I think, worth relating, as it gives a vivid idea of the horrors entailed by a native rebellion.

A Mr. Bester, a Dutchman, had a farm about twenty miles from Enkledoorn, and was living there with his wife, his children, and his aged mother. They were attacked suddenly, and Bester was shot in the shoulder. He managed to crawl into the house, where he fainted from loss of blood. A white man who was

helping him with the farm was assegaied, and killed
before he could reach shelter. The two ladies barricaded the doors and windows, and kept off the natives
with the help of Mr. Bester's three daughters, the
eldest of whom was under sixteen. Early the next
morning Mr Botha, his wife, and two daughters arrived.
His house had been attacked also, and his son killed,
and he and the rest of his family had escaped by
night, walking more than fifteen miles. Mercifully
the natives hardly ever move from their kraals at
night, so they had been able to get away unobserved.
That afternoon the attack upon the two families was
renewed, and young Mrs. Bester was killed. Mr. Botha
was sick and unable to move, and Mr. Bester was
hors de combat with his wound; so Mrs. Botha and old
Mrs. Bester had again to conduct the whole of the
defence, and of the subsequent retreat. As soon as it
grew dark, they made their way on foot to Enkledoorn,
reaching it a little before daybreak. I heard the story
from several transport riders, but they were not quite
sure of the details, for which I am indebted to Dr.
Wiener, who was in Enkledoorn at the time (it was in
June 1896). He attended Mr. Bester for the wound in
his shoulder, and succeeded in pulling him through.

The relief, too, of the Abercorn mine, by a volunteer force commanded by Mr. Duncan, was a very fine
piece of work. Captain de Moleyns told me it was
one of the finest during the whole of the Mashona
rebellion. When Lord Grey arrived in Bulawayo, Mr.

Duncan handed over charge to him, and, as soon as it was at all safe, started for Salisbury. He and his companion, a Mr. De Preez, rode in one night from Charter, a distance of sixty-four miles. They left on Thursday afternoon at five o'clock, and arrived the following morning at seven. News came on the Saturday that the Abercorn people were in danger, and Duncan hastily got sixty men together, and started off the same evening to relieve them. The Abercorn is fully seventy miles from Salisbury, and they had intermittent fighting all the way, and did not reach it till the Monday morning, when they found seven white men in the last stage of exhaustion. They had been besieged for twenty-three days by the Mashonas, who had built a circle of stone barricades around the store. One man, who had attempted to parley with them, had been killed, and three had been wounded. They had plenty of food, but were hard put to it for water, being obliged to drink gin and lime-juice. They had suffered terribly, too, from the extremes of heat and cold, one of them dying of pneumonia soon after they were relieved. They had made a laager of provision cases, and of sacks of flour piled breast-high, but unprotected at the top, and had connected it by a passage with the store, which consisted of the usual thatched wattle-and-daub hut. The patrol started with only a bully-beef tin and a few biscuits, which each man carried in his wallet; so they were glad to find plenty of food at the store. They remained there that night, and on the following morning made a détour to avoid the Mashonas, in case they should have blocked the road along which they had come. To do this, they had to cut a path for twelve miles through the bush for the ambulance waggon and the Maxim. Jack Rowland, one of the rescued men, died that night, the funeral service being read by the Jesuit missionary, Father Bichler, who had pluckily accompanied the patrol, and who, indeed, accompanied most of the important patrols all through the rising. They got back to Salisbury on Friday without any casualties; but it was fortunate they made a détour, for it was found afterwards that the direct road had been barricaded behind them immediately after they had passed. Great holes, twenty feet in length and twelve feet in width, had been dug in it, and covered with branches and earth, so that a hostile force coming along the road at night might fall into them, like elephants into Mashona game-traps. Covering barricades had also been built on the side of the hills, so that it would have been impossible for any but a very strong force to cut its way through.

The Mashonas are not as brave as the Matabili, but they have a far better idea of fortification; and the way in which their kraals are defended shows a high order of intelligence, which it is to be hoped will be turned to advantage when peace is restored.

It is the custom now to run them down, to deride them as a base and degraded race, but that was not the opinion formed by travellers who visited

MASHONA IRON-WORKERS.

Mashonaland before we took possession of it. I have already quoted what Colonel Wood thought of them, and Baines formed an equally appreciative estimate of their character. "All hunters and traders," he writes, "who have had intercourse with the Mashonas agree in describing them as a friendly, peaceable, industrious, and ingenious people. They make fine iron from magnetic iron ore, grow cotton, construct rude textile fabrics, and in many of these particulars are entirely in advance of the surrounding tribes."

What they require is a firm but just rule—to be treated as children who have to be taught, but who require encouragement as well as severity to make them learn, and, above all things, justice.

When dealing, too, with these native tribes, we must not expect rapid results. Mr. Ritter, the magistrate of the New Hanover division of Natal, in his report of 1897, brings this out very forcibly: "The progress of any race towards civilisation in one year (if there is no retrogression) must be imperceptibly small. The races now occupying Europe required about 2000 years to rise from barbarism to their present status, and even superior races did not progress steadily, but had periods of relapsing. A nation advances similarly to a man ascending to the summit of a mountain. He cannot go up in a straight line, but he occasionally has to descend into a valley and then to go up again. One thing is certain. Teaching will not convert a savage into a civilised being. We can improve a very common fruit-tree by grafting at once; but to breed race-horses from common stock requires very many generations. Every nation has to go through the bitter-sweet school of life, like the individual, but what to the latter is a year, to the former is a century. . . . Taken all in all, the natives have many sterling qualities, and the vigour of a youthful nation. They would occasionally like to peg out a witch over an ant-heap, but I am sorry to say my ancestors have burnt a witch as late as the eighteenth century." We are apt to expect too much from the natives, and, if they do not always keep up to our standard, to grow impatient and out of temper with them, which is a fatal mistake.

They require firm and indeed rather severe treatment, but treatment which they can understand. The one thing that unsettles them altogether is *vacillation*. If they have been told that a certain punishment will be inflicted it ought to be inflicted, even though to western ideas it may seem unduly harsh. They do not resent severity in the least—they respect it; but they resent injustice, and above all things they dislike suspense. Let punishment be swift and certain, and not be kept dangling over their heads indefinitely.

CHAPTER XVII

THE B.S.A. COMPANY'S POLICE: IN MASHONALAND AND IN MATA-
BILILAND — EXCELLENT SYSTEM INITIATED BY CAPTAIN
NICHOLSON.

A NUMBER of letters have recently appeared in the
papers declaring that the Chartered Company's police
are badly fed, badly clothed, badly paid, and in general
badly treated. In Mashonaland they have certainly
had a hard time, but to a great extent it was unavoidable. The rinderpest entailed great difficulties of
transport, and as the patrols were obliged to move
quickly, they could take but little with them in the
shape either of food or of clothing. They had no tents,
only a waterproof sheet, and had to camp for days
together in heavy rain. Naturally they got fever, and
many of them died, and others have been crippled
for life. Still that is incidental to the nature of their
service. When the French took Madagascar, they lost
an immense number of men through fever and disease.
In the opening up of any new tropical country there
must always be a terrible mortality from sickness.
Where the Company have been seriously to blame, is
in not sending a doctor out with each of the principal
patrols. On many of them not only was there no

doctor, but there was no medicine chest, or proper surgical instruments. I know that on one of the most important patrols all that the officer in command had with him was a small case of fever medicines, with which he did what he could. The kit was shockingly bad, and no provision was made for the men's health and comfort when they were in camp. The pay, too, for a country like Mashonaland, is exceedingly small: for troopers it is only five shillings a day, of which one shilling is deferred pay. After the first year's service they are given an extra sixpence a day, and on re-engaging after two years an extra shilling, but with the scale of prices prevailing in Mashonland an extra sixpence is worth nothing at all. Indeed, a sixpence is a comparatively rare coin, a shilling being the usual standard of value: so much so that in most of the wayside stores, if the price of anything contains a sixpence, it is almost always tossed for to make it even money. A threepenny-bit is rarer still, and pennies are unknown. I bought some stamps at the post-office in Umtali, and when the clerk gave me my change in five penny stamps I asked him to let me have two pennies and a threepenny-bit; he laughed—" We don't have pennies here," he said; " and I have hardly seen a tickie (threepenny-bit) since I have been in the country."

I fancy this scarcity of small coin is due to the difficulty the banks have of getting up bullion, but the country will always be an expensive one till a smaller standard of value is introduced.

What has especially irritated the police is, that they, being enlisted in England, and knowing nothing about the country, were only paid five shillings a day during the rising, whilst the volunteers enlisted in Rhodesia were paid ten shillings. Five shillings a day is only £7 a month, and when one considers the wages paid to men in other occupations, it is not surprising that the police are discontented, and that few of them re-enlist at the expiration of their service. There are many natives who get quite as good or even better pay, and a clerk in a store gets about four or five times as much, from £25 to £30 a month.

The men complain especially that in the letter of introduction to Sir Richard Martin given to each man when he is enlisted, there is a clause which is really a great hardship, when the unhealthy nature of the country between Beira and Umtali is considered. It runs thus : " He (Sir Richard Martin) has been informed that all recruits enrolled in England are liable to be again medically inspected on arrival at Salisbury, and that if then rejected for any cause, they may be discharged without further claim, other than the £15, that has to be handed to them on their arrival at Cape Town or Durban, as specified in the particulars." (I am told, however, that instead of being given this £15, the men's expenses are now paid for them to Salisbury or Bulawayo, as the case may be.) They complain that if taken into the hospital at Umtali on their way from Beira, before the final medical inspection at Salisbury, they are made to pay their own expenses whilst there, by virtue of this clause. Another provision which presses hardly upon them is, that if they are discharged in Salisbury or Bulawayo they are not assisted back to the place where they may have been enlisted. It is like asking a time-expired man to find his way back from India. The agreement entered into with the men is silent on this point, so legally they have no claim on the Company, but considering the splendid work they have done, and the terrible hardships they have been called upon to endure, they might surely be treated a little more liberally. They feel very bitter about it, because the whole of their deferred pay is, they say, used up in getting out of the country.

An efficient police is above all things a necessity for Rhodesia, because, until a greater sense of security prevails, the country cannot be developed, nor will capital be attracted to it. For a man with colonial experience, it is by no means a bad thing to go for a while into the police—he has an opportunity to look around him and learn the local conditions; but it is foolish for educated men to come out direct from England. They can save nothing from their pay, and if they fall ill, as they are more than likely to do, before final enlistment at Salisbury, they will be about £30 out of pocket, and with no means of getting home. Can one wonder that there are continual reports that the men are in a semi-mutinous condition?

In Matabililand the conditions are vastly better; the country is healthier, and the police have not had the same rough work as in Mashonaland. The cost of living is materially less, and a trooper can save something substantial out of his pay. The class of men is, however, changing rapidly in character; fewer gentlemen are enlisting, though I am not sure that this is to be regretted, for steady, well-educated men of the artisan class make more trustworthy police than public schoolboys and University men, who are excellent for a campaign, when employed to do purely military work, but who cannot stand the monotonous work of a civilian police force, which is what the Matabililand police is rapidly becoming.

The curse of the country is drink. The conditions of life, as well as the climate, favour it, but until it is checked the high rate of mortality (which is generally erroneously attributed to fever) will continue. Father Daignault, of the Jesuit mission, who has a wide experience, said in the evidence he gave before the Chamber of Mines, " Yes, I have known many cases of sickness and death brought on through excess in drinking. If we compare the population of Bulawayo with that of other countries in respect to intemperance, I think we are as low as we can afford to be."

If the men can keep from drink, they can in Matabililand save a fair amount, and when they obtain their discharge ought to have from £30 to £40 in hand with which to start prospecting. For a working man, or for the kind of man who becomes a policeman at home, that is a handsome sum, but it is not a sufficient inducement for the men of good family who, up to the present, have been chiefly enlisted. Many of them are failures, who have drifted out with an introduction to Mr. Rhodes as their only stand-by, and been drafted into the police as a matter of course, and it is mostly they who have done the grumbling. It is related that one of them went to Mr. Rhodes, and said he expected to be something better than a mere trooper. "What did you expect?" said Mr. Rhodes; "to be a captain or a major?" "Well, I thought I should be a major," was the reply. "Very well," said Mr. Rhodes, "I will raise a troop of majors, and make you one of them."

There have been more than enough of this kind of men in the Rhodesian police, but there have also been plenty of boys of good family, who have gone out thinking they were going to a fair opening in a new country, and were quite unsuited by the influences of their birth and education for the rough life and coarse companionship, unusually rough even for a colony, which they have been obliged to endure. Those who have survived have come splendidly out of the terrible ordeal of fighting and exposure into which they were pitchforked immediately on their arrival, but if the nature of their service were understood in England, fewer men of this stamp would enlist: the recruits would come mainly from the flotsam and jetsam of South Africa.

Matabililand, as I have said, is more advanced than Mashonaland, and the police there have more comfort and less exposure, and consequently do not feel the same amount of dissatisfaction. This is proved by the fact that out of a total of six hundred men over three hundred have re-enlisted, and that last year there were only three desertions and three courts-martial. The savings-bank has done much to diminish crime by diminishing drink. Captain Nicholson started it about a year ago, and more than three hundred of the men have already become depositors, the total amount deposited from November 1896 to October 1897 being £5305; the amount to stand to a depositor's credit being strictly limited to £100. I went over the barracks at Bulawayo, and found a good billiard-room, a library, a well-managed canteen and a store, all run by the men themselves, and various other arrangements for their comfort. There is nothing of the sort as yet in Salisbury, where the work of suppressing the rising has absorbed all the energies both of the officers and of the men.

If properly encouraged the police might become an exceedingly powerful, colonising factor. At the end of their two years' service they should have acquired some knowledge both of the natives and of the language, which, with the little money they should have saved, would enable them to go out and prospect in a way that men new to the country cannot do. More than that, if they keep their eyes open, they will be able when on their patrols to judge which places have the best prospects to offer. What Captain Nicholson is trying to do, and what he has largely succeeded in doing, is to make the force a training-school of this kind. But for this purpose a particular stamp of man is required—of rather greater intelligence than the ordinary soldier, and able to take up a responsible position, as they will constantly be stationed in outposts without an officer, or sent on a patrol with possibly only one companion. Either this class of men ought to be exclusively recruited, or the pay should be increased, and the admissions confined to a higher class of men altogether, so as to produce a crack corps like the Cape or Natal Mounted Police. (Their pay may not be higher, but the cost of living is much less.) Rhodesia is too new for that, but more stability of character in the men enlisted should be looked for: when savages have to be dealt with, that is of the utmost importance, especially where, as in Matabililand, the country is practically under police control. The Imperial authorities, I should add, are doing what they can to second Captain Nicholson's efforts to make the force a colonising factor, the Colonial Office having allotted a certain number of trooperships to the Colonial College at Hollesley Bay in Suffolk.

General Sir Arthur Cunynghame's account of the Kaffraria police in 1876 shows how difficult it is even for a long-established colony, like the Cape, to maintain police in a state of efficiency, and one should not be too critical in judging their shortcomings in Rhodesia. I have adverted to them because they have been much commented upon of late; but what was wrong is being gradually remedied in Mashonaland as well as in Matabililand. Captain Nicholson's administrative work cannot be too highly praised, the more so when the circumstances under which it has been done are borne in mind. The force was raised temporarily in July 1896, but was not definitely organised until November of that year. Fighting was still going on, and owing to the ever-present transport difficulty it was hard work to establish anything like system; but in spite of everything being against him, and of the difficulty of obtaining suitable recruits, he has succeeded in creating a smart, well-disciplined, and trustworthy force.

The men in Mashonaland have shown what mettle they are made of, and now that the rebellion there is over, it is to be hoped that they will be looked after in the same way that their fellow-troopers are in Matabililand.

What Sir Arthur Cunynghame says about the Kaffraria police is worth recalling: "The frontier armed and mounted police, as they are distinctively called, are a special body, which was originally formed by Sir George Cathcart, when Governor of the Cape, at the termination of the war in 1852. . . . As years rolled on, the Afrikander farmers' sons would no longer enter the service. Other fields of labour presented themselves of a much more lucrative character, such as diamond and gold digging and transport riding (which means accompanying waggons to distant parts of the colony with merchants' goods). It became requisite to obtain young men from England. The selection was left to the Colonial Agent, possibly a clever man for civil duties, but not at all acquainted with military ones, having no special knowledge of our profession. He appears to have represented that the lowest standard of pay in this force was from five to six shillings a day per man, so that he had no difficulty in obtaining recruits. The men, however, found on their arrival that deductions from this pay were made for the purchase of horses and accoutrements, their own keep, that of their horses, and other extraneous expenses. They came to the conclusion, therefore, that they had been deceived, and said (with truth) that they were infinitely worse off than the British soldier, for whom all these extras were provided by the Government."

I have quoted this passage to show, what I have endeavoured to show all through my account of Rhodesia, that the purely *administrative*, as distinguished from the *political* mistakes, which the Chartered Company have made, have been made before both by the Imperial and by the Colonial Governments on almost every occasion on which fresh territory has been annexed. There is no reason why they should continue to be made; but the Chartered Company cannot in fairness be blamed for failing to attain, at a time of exceptional trial and stress, to a higher standard than that of which those Governments have hitherto shown themselves capable. Moreover, the Chartered Company, and Mr. Rhodes personally, have behaved with infinitely greater liberality than the Imperial Government has been wont to do under similar circumstances. Mr. Rhodes' generosity has been very great.

CHAPTER XVIII

TREATMENT OF THE NATIVES PRIOR TO THE REBELLION—ADVISABILITY OF A GENERAL AMNESTY.

WHAT was done to the natives during and after the rebellion, when the blood of the colonists was inflamed almost to madness by the brutal murder of their comrades, is intelligible, and to a certain extent excusable, but there can be no excuse for the treatment accorded to them before it broke out. It forced the Matabili into insurrection, and converted the Mashonas from a people who welcomed us as deliverers from Matabili oppression into a people who have dared death in its most abhorrent form in the hope of shaking off our rule; it demands therefore the strictest and most impartial investigation. Only a Government inquiry, conducted with full protection to those who are willing to give evidence, can elicit the truth of the many terrible stories with which the country is reeking; of things done for which no condemnation can be too vehement.

The men to whom the guardianship of the natives was especially entrusted were the native commissioners; some have proved worthy of their trust, but many have not. They have treated the natives harshly and with gross injustice, and are mainly responsible for the rebellion and for the brutal ferocity which was one of its saddest features.

"Sir Richard Martin," says Lord Grey, "condemns the administration for not exercising more care in the selection of the native commissioners, some of whom, he states, were too young and inexperienced, and were not calculated to inspire the natives with respect. This unqualified condemnation I resent as a slur most undeservedly cast upon the officials, who, as a class, have, under difficult circumstances, done their duty to the administration."

That Lord Grey should defend his officials is only what he is bound to do as head of the Chartered Company's administration, but is the view he takes of their conduct borne out by a scrutiny of the facts?

The Rev. John White, one of the Wesleyan missionaries in Mashonaland, wrote a forcible letter which appeared in the *Methodist Times* in January 1897, which I give in full, as it does not appear in the blue-book. From beginning to end it is worthy of the most careful consideration. I regret that I was not able to meet Mr. White when I was in Rhodesia. He was away at the time in one of the mission stations, but he has since returned to England, and has kindly given me permission to insert his letter here. So far as I am able to judge, every word of it is justified.

THE CAUSE OF THE MASHONA REBELLION.

To the Editor of the " Methodist Times."

" DEAR SIR,—As most of your readers are aware, for the last three months the settlers in Northern Rhodesia have been engaged in a desperate and bloody struggle with the natives of this country. Already about two hundred lives have been lost, two-thirds of which have been cruelly murdered. Irrespective of opinions or position, we have fought together to preserve our own, and the lives of the helpless women and children in our midst.

" Now that the back of the rebellion has been broken, and the probability of settlement seems nearer, we are better able to give a dispassionate opinion of the affair. Until the present I for one have refrained from expressing myself publicly on the question. I waited to hear what would be assigned as the cause of the rebellion. What would the press of the country say ? Would the British South Africa Company see and honestly confess its mistake ? Would means be at once adopted to remedy the evil ? The local press has now spoken. It declares the natives have been treated in the past with too much clemency. The influence of the ' Exeter Hall Negrophilists ' has been most severely deprecated. An imaginary contention that cruelty to the natives by whites had anything to do with the rising has been described as a ' cruel, cowardly, and wicked lie.' Now, sir, I presume many of these papers find their way to England; that they are read by the British public, and may do something to influence opinion on this matter. Their contention challenges a counter-verdict—they compel us, even though reluctantly, to state the truth as we also believe it. Since I have lived two and a half years in this country, and am now spending the whole of my time amongst the natives, I will be exonerated from any charge of presumption when I declare I know a little about those unfortunate people and their affairs.

What Caused the Mashonas to Revolt.

"I. *The Maladministration of Native Affairs.*—In every large district a native commissioner is appointed, who acts as Government representative to the natives. His duties are to administer justice, settle disputes, collect hut-tax, and in a general way look after their affairs. These commissioners are controlled by the Chief Native Commissioner, who resides at Salisbury. Some of these men have acted fairly and justly to the Mashonas; others, again, have proved themselves utterly unworthy of their position. Their attitude towards the great social question of this country has been such as to destroy in the native's mind that respect that he should have for the new-comer. Many of them have purchased, according to native law, women whom they keep as mistresses. Provided it were contended that these women do not regard their position as an unkindly one at present, we want to know what will become of them in the future. Many of these men will only remain here for a short time, when, in all probability, they will cast these unfortunate women and their children adrift. The effects of this upon the natives have been anything but good. But worse than this, in one case at least this has been carried to a criminal extreme. Last year an instance was reported to me in which one of these officials used the influence of his position to obtain a girl for immoral purposes. By means of threats of punishment he compelled the chief to give him his own daughter. I brought the matter to the notice of the Administrator, and the accused was found guilty of the charge. He shortly after left the country; yet so trivial seemed the offence that within nine months he was back again, and held an official position in the force raised to punish the rebels.

"In the same district (Lo Magundi's) another glaring act of official injustice and cruelty was committed in 1894. A policeman named Cooper was murdered by a large chief (Mazimba Guba) who lived in the extreme north of the district. Under the Sub-Inspector of Police a force was sent out to punish the murderer or murderers. At that time Rev. G. H. Eva was in charge of the Wesleyan mission station some thirty miles south of the place. One Sunday, shortly after the murder had been committed, this force arrived at his station just as he was concluding the service. According to previous arrangement, a number of the surrounding chiefs and their people had gathered there for the day. The officer in charge ordered the chiefs to be arrested, seven in number. Without in any way fastening them, they were told that if they attempted to run away they would be shot. They then moved on. About five minutes later Mr. Eva heard a shot, and ran to see what was the matter. He found only three of the chiefs were with the force; three had been shot, and one had escaped. The officer, by way of explaining, said, 'Your indunas (chiefs) have run away. I am very sorry for what has happened.' Mr. Eva declares, 'I am prepared to swear on oath that these chiefs were absolutely innocent of the policeman's death; indeed, they were at the time totally ignorant of its occurrence, and did not know of it until I told them.' Thus, on the pretext of their attempting to run away, these three innocent chiefs lost their lives. Although this case was reported to the Government, nothing was done in the matter. Very often, too, great injustices have been done to the natives in the way the hut-tax has been collected. The sum of ten shillings per year is charged as tax for every occupied hut. This amount, especially in the more remote districts, is often paid in kind. In the collecting of this rarely any attempt is made to levy the fee equitably. The huts are numbered, the number of cattle or goats demanded and taken. It has often happened that a lazy, unscrupulous owner of huts has had his paid for by some more industrious person, who owned none, but who had the misfortune to possess a cow. This has had a tendency to make the natives discontented and the hut-tax repulsive. In many districts where previously considerable herds of cattle were to be found, now hardly one exists. I do not say the hut-tax ought to be discontinued. I do think, however, some more just and less repulsive method of collecting ought to be devised.

"The above cases are typical. Such injustices and cruelties have had a tendency to make the natives fear and hate the Government and most of its officials.

" II. *The Native Constable Nuisance.*—Some time ago the Government enlisted and trained a large number of Mashona and Matabili police. They were placed under the control of the native commissioners. These fellows, previously the most arrant cowards, once they are invested with a little authority and armed with a rifle, develop into the cruellest of tyrants. They are sent about from place to place uncontrolled to execute the orders of their master. They never scruple to use their position to get almost anything they wish. They demand and obtain from the unwilling people as much beer, meal, and meat as they may require. One night, as I was travelling north, I arrived late at a kraal, and was preparing to sleep outside, when the chief, who happened to know me, offered me a hut for myself and carriers. About midnight I was awoke by some half-dozen people—men, women, and children—rushing into my place, apparently much distressed. On inquiring the cause, they told me a native policeman, who was staying overnight at the kraal, had attempted to force his way into the hut where these women were sleeping. I have since gathered that attempted assaults on women by these scoundrels are of frequent occurrence. Such has become the reputation of these representatives of official justice that their arrival at a 'kraal' is the occasion of the worst alarms, and often leads the people to run away and hide themselves. Recently at the Matoppo hills, when the Matabili chiefs were arranging terms of surrender, they mentioned as one of the causes of the revolt the treatment they had received at the hands of certain Government officials, but especially of the native police.

"III. *Injustices of Rhodesian Settlers.* — Scattered throughout this country are a considerable number of white settlers—farmers, hunters, gold 'prospectors,' traders, and others. The conduct of many of these towards the natives has been humane and just. Others, however, have given the heathen Mashona a very poor opinion of civilised justice and propriety. Many of them have bought, according to native custom, Kaffir girls, whom they regard as their property. The girls consider themselves, to all intents and purposes, as slaves of these men. In consequence, before many years elapse, the Government will be confronted with a most serious social problem unless it puts an end to this sort of thing at once. Many of these men are utterly unscrupulous, and when away from the Governmental control take the law practically into their own hands, and do as they like with the Kaffirs. I have often heard of cases in which wages have been refused when due, and, in some instances, the claimant been flogged for insisting on payment.

"Put the foregoing facts together, and then let me ask you whether the charge of injustice by whites to natives is a 'cruel, cowardly, and wicked lie.' Any unbiassed person must admit that for the terrible step they took they had some provocation. These cruelties and injustices have been rankling in their minds for many a long day, and only needed propitious circumstances to bring them to a most disastrous issue. 'We had better be dead,' some of them said, 'than be tormented like this.'

"IV. *The Rinderpest and Locust Plague.*—For two or three seasons unusually large swarms of locusts have visited this country, destroying large quantities of the crops, and in some instances reducing many of the people to the verge of starvation. This year a terrible cattle plague swept through the land, killing thousands of animals. In their ignorant and superstitious way of reasoning, they attributed these calamities to the 'whites' being in their country. 'The locusts and cattle disease,' they said, 'came with the "Barungu"' (the white men). Again and again they have asked, 'When are the white people returning to the land from whence they came?'

" V. *The Pernicious Influence of the Witch-Doctors.*—As is their custom, these Mashonas, when they need advice, resort to these mediums of their gods. The witch-doctors then inquire from the 'Murenga'—the Great Spirit. 'If you want to get rid of your troubles,' they replied, 'kill the white men.' That the advice was atrociously cruel and fearfully indiscriminate we will all admit. But think for a moment. These people are utterly savage, and reason accordingly. They believed they had grievances; they ignorantly thought we had brought the plagues amongst them; they know nothing of venting their grievances in a constitutional manner. According to their notions, the best way to rid themselves of an evil is to destroy the cause. Hence they listened to the advice of their prophets.

" VI. *The Opportune Moment.*—These witch-doctors, through their coming much in contact with men, are naturally shrewd and cunning. They took care to give their advice when it was likely to be acted upon. Dr. Jameson had taken away a number of the mounted police for purposes with which everybody is acquainted. Now, early this year a force of armed men had gone down to assist to quell the rebellion in Matabililand. Then, when off our guard, when the country was ill prepared for it, these naturally cowardly Mashonas rose in one dark mass, carrying death and desolation into the abodes of all within their reach. Within a few days some one hundred and thirty unsuspecting, many of them perfectly innocent, people were hurried into eternity.

"We who live here regard the future with some anxiety. Will the Chartered Company see its mistake, and make an honest attempt to amend matters? If so, they will find no more loyal supporters than the missionaries. If not, and these atrocities are repeated, then in the name of justice and humanity we must make our voice heard. We do not forget the many good qualities of the Company. As a Church, they have treated us handsomely; their occupation of this territory has done much to advance civilisation in Central Africa; they have brought many necessities of life within easier reach of the natives. These things we cannot overlook. At present the land is under a dark cloud; confusion and strife reign everywhere. Let those in authority face the position with brave and honest hearts. Where corruption and injustice are found, let them be swept away, and let the foundations of this new colony be laid in righteousness and truth, then we feel sure a bright and successful future awaits us.   JOHN WHITE,

Wesleyan Minister.

"SALISBURY,
30th September 1896."

I made inquiries as to both the cases referred to by Mr. White; they were of a peculiarly atrocious character, but I do not think any good purpose will be served by giving the details of them, beyond saying that they both took place in the Lo Magundi district, and that it is not an unreasonable presumption that it was the treatment which the natives in that district had received, which led to the murders there for which a good many men have already been executed.

Taking the previous treatment of the people into consideration, is it not time that a stop was put to the further prosecutions of those accused of murder during the rebellion, and that a general amnesty should be proclaimed? When I was in Rhodesia, native commissioners and police were out in every direction hunting down these unhappy wretches. Many had already been executed both in Bulawayo and Salisbury, and the prosecutions were still going on. I think if Sir Alfred Milner were aware of the terrible provocation the Lo Magundi people had received, he would hesitate about sanctioning the execution of any more men from that district. I am told that Mr. Rhodes has always pressed for a general amnesty, and also that Judge Vintcent has expressed a strong opinion that no more prosecutions should be instituted. Both he and Judge Watermeyer have done their best to secure fair trials; but the vindictive feeling prevailing, naturally enough, all over Rhodesia has made trial by assessors a perfect farce.

Many men object strongly to the executions altogether, for they say that the accused cannot with any fairness be held to be guilty of murder, inasmuch as the country had risen in open rebellion, and they were merely carrying out the orders of their chiefs. To take evidence, and invariably tainted evidence, as to whether the particular native under trial was the actual person who delivered the fatal blow is a perfect mockery. The man is hunted down by the native commissioner with the aid of spies and informers from his own kraal, who in most cases are actuated by personal enmity; they swear that they saw the prisoner kill the murdered person, and as a rule, when asked what he has to say, the prisoner replies, " Yes, I killed him; I was told to do so by such and such an induna."

In Matabililand most of the indunas have not only been pardoned, but have been given a yearly pension to insure their fidelity—an excellent measure —but if they have been pardoned it is monstrous that the full penalty should be exacted from their tools, who merely did what they were bid. The natives feel the injustice of this most keenly. It satisfies the natural desire for vengeance, but it may do much harm. Mr. Thomas, whose opinion is of great value, mentions the administrative difficulties due to the unrest subsequent upon the rebellion, and the frequent arrests of natives accused of murder.

At present the people are living under a reign of terror, no man knowing when he may not be singled out for prosecution. Natives cannot understand punishment being held over their heads for so long. What they are used to is a severe and instant punishment, and then that the matter should be forgotten. Sir Theophilus Shepstone, in his evidence before the Commission appointed by the Cape Government in 1881 to inquire into native laws and customs, in answer to the question, " What is the chief punishment among the natives (for treason) ? " answered, " Death and confiscation of property ; but the infliction of the former depends much on the circumstances. If the criminal can avoid confronting the first impulse to administer rough and ready justice his life is usually safe. There is nothing in native administration so coldly inexorable as that which in ours requires the trial of a criminal long after the crime has been committed, and the consequences of it have lost their first soreness."

Lord Grey's indignation at what he calls "the wanton and groundless charges so freely levelled against both the administration and the settlers " is a little difficult to understand, knowing, as he must know, the grave justification there has been for many of these charges. If he and Mr. Rhodes had frankly admitted that things had been badly managed in the past, but that they would take care they should be kept straight in the future, it would have been a more wholesome sign than the denunciations of Exeter Hall and Little Englanders and the Aborigines Protection Society. Sir Richard Martin mentions that in a speech delivered by him at Bulawayo soon after he went out, Lord Grey said that he feared ill-treatment had been experienced by the natives, and that he was informed it was one of not the least potent of the causes of the rebellion. Lord Grey in his reply merely says, " When I made the speech to which Sir Richard Martin refers, I had in my mind statements which had been made to me, that among a low class of employers the practice was not unknown of ill-treating a native, and causing him to run away a few days before his month's wages became due." He does not say that he has since found that the practice did not exist, only that those guilty of it should be punished. The important point is, not whether Sir Richard Martin put a wrong construction upon Lord Grey's meaning, but whether the practice existed. It is referred to both by Mr. Carnegie and by Mr. White, and it is matter of common conversation in Rhodesia. Lord Grey himself practically admits it, and it must have helped greatly to induce the rebellion.

Sir Richard Martin is a man of wide experience of the African natives. He is not a sentimentalist— far from it; he has had too much experience of actual work for that, but he is essentially a just and truthful man. Any one who reads his report can see that he has had reluctantly to perform an uncomfortable duty, and those who know Rhodesia, know that he might have written in a far less temperate way. It would be of better promise for the country's future if, instead of trying to traverse his conclusions, the Company had frankly accepted them, and had said, which is actually the case, that many of the things complained of were unknown to them; that with the scanty means at their command it had been impossible to prevent them; but that they would take care that they did not occur again. At one of the indabas in the Matoppos, Secombi, one of the Matabili indunas, said that the whole of the Matabili council prayed for the banishment of a certain prominent Government official, and declared that neither Mr. Rhodes nor Dr. Jameson knew of the things that had been done in Matabililand. Mr. Rhodes replied that the official was no longer in the Company's service.

The failure of the Company to govern rightly has not been wilful, but has arisen from weakness of administration and extent of territory. They have acquired more land than they can govern—that is the truth of the matter; and instead of contenting themselves with what they have, and trying to administer it properly, they are now anxious to acquire yet more land beyond the Zambesi. In that lies the danger of the situation. If Central Africa is to be opened out, let it be done by the Crown direct, and let it be primarily for the introduction of better government, and not for the exploitation of gold; and by direct dealings of Imperial officials with the chiefs, and not through the medium of concessions, otherwise we shall lose altogether among the Central African tribes the reputation for English fair dealing and English humanity which Livingstone and Moffat spent their lives in building up.

CHAPTER XIX

When I left Bulawayo the railway had been opened for some time, and though there had been heavy rain for nearly a month, I reached Palachwe siding with but little delay, and with a comfort which was in grateful contrast to the miseries I had endured on the Beira line. We had saloon carriages to travel in, and notwithstanding the haste with which the line had been completed, there was little at which the most captious sybarite could cavil. Palachwe siding is a wayside station from which Zeederberg's coach runs to Palachwe, Khama's capital. In spite of the scarcity of water, a really excellent dinner was provided for us at the station restaurant. Often, when the wells are dry, there is no water at all for washing purposes; what is required for cooking being brought in the engine from one of the stations farther down the line. Palachwe itself, which is twelve miles from the siding, is one of the largest native towns in South Africa, with a population of over 28,000 people. There is no hotel, but Messrs. Loosly & Maclaren, who have the principal store, gave me a kind welcome. I called on Khama in the *Kotla* (the open enclosure where he dispenses justice), and was glad to have a talk with him, for he is by far the noblest figure amongst all the South African chiefs. A dead set has been made against him for several years past, but all the white men who live under his rule speak of him in the most enthusiastic terms, as a sincere, upright, and kindly man. They have the right to take their cases before the English magistrate, but they seldom exercise it, preferring to let Khama settle them in his own summary way.

He said he had enjoyed his visit to England exceedingly. He spoke warmly of the kind treatment he had received, and seemed gratified when I told him he had left many friends amongst us.

In Rhodesia I heard nothing but abuse of Khama; but those who wish to know what he has done for his people should read what Lord Randolph Churchill, a singularly acute and fair-minded critic, thought of him: "Khama governs justly and severely," he wrote, "but without cruelty. Human life is, I believe, never taken. His authority is purely despotic, undisputed, unrestrained, but, exercised with wisdom, has secured for him the affectionate respect of the people."

Bishop Knight Bruce writes equally strongly of the greatness of his work, and so, too, does Mr. Hepburn, the missionary who lived with him for so long. The latter says, " He has not only stopped the introduction of brandy into the country, but he has stopped his people from making their own native beer. He has not only made a law against the purchase of slaves (Masarwa or Bushmen), and declared himself the Bushman's friend, but he has abolished *bogadi*, or the purchase of wives by cattle, and introduced the law of marriage by free choice, at an age when young men and young women are capable of forming such an attachment intelligently. Out of the ruins of anarchy, lawlessness, and general disorder, he has been building up law, order, and stability."

Compare this with Mr. Rhodes' telegram: " I do object to being beaten by three canting natives, especially on score temperance, when two of them (Sebele, Bathoen), are known to be utter drunkards."

When one thinks of all that Khama has done, of the noble struggle he has waged for so many years against the evil traditions of his tribe, and against the deteriorating influences that have been brought to bear upon him by white men from outside, of the constant unrelenting endeavour to lessen his authority and to break down his power, it is difficult to use moderate language. Nothing in Mr. Rhodes' conduct to the natives of South Africa has excited keener resentment in many men's minds than his efforts to have Khama placed under the rule of the Chartered Company. What kind of treatment he would have been likely to receive is shown by the following passage, taken from an interesting series of articles published in

Onsland, and translated into English in the *Cape Argus*, by Mr. D. C. de Waal, a member of the Cape Legislative Assembly, who travelled through Rhodesia with Mr. Rhodes in 1890, and again in 1894. After describing the prosperous condition of affairs there, he goes on to say, " But there is a Mordecai at the gates in the person of the arrogant Khama, or, as he has been baptized generally, Ham. This mighty potentate will not allow a store to be opened in his country, nor may any one drink spirituous liquor. One had to journey 300 miles through his country without being able to get a bite or a sup. He has forbidden his people to sell the Europeans anything, on the plea that he requires all the food for his own people. A fortnight since he had four white citizens driven out of Palachwe, where they were building their school, because they had some whisky with them. I should like to know who could exist in the foul-smelling Kaffir stad without a little whisky. His Kaffirs are not even permitted to drink their beer. No wonder that they become scabby, for meat and bread pure and simple do not suffice for the human constitution. The sooner this tyrant recognises his duty and is relegated to his proper place the better, and the sooner the Rev. Moffat and Mr. Willoughby leave Palachwe the better for them and the country at large."

Was Khama not fully justified in the letter he wrote, not long ago, to the London Society for the Protection of Native Races from the Liquor Traffic?

" . . . And concerning liquor I am still trying, but

I do not think I can succeed. Here in our country there are Europeans who like liquor exceedingly, and they are not people who like to save a nation, but seek that a nation may be destroyed by liquor; and they are not people who like to be persuaded in the matter of liquor; but you, who are people of importance in England, I know that you like to save people so that they may live in the land. And I cause you to know that we have seen the path of the train in our land, and concerning the path of the train I rejoice exceedingly. But I say, concerning the path of the train, there is something in it which I do not like among you; it is the little houses which will be in the path to sell liquor in them. I do not like them, for my people will buy liquor in them, and I say, help me in this matter, for it is a thing which will kill the nation. And I cause you to know, because you are people who do not like nations to be destroyed in the land."

The pressure to permit the sale of spirits at Palachwe became continually greater, and I believe it has been finally arranged with Khama by Sir Alfred Milner that a licence shall be granted to the refreshment-room proprietors, for the sale of liquor over the bar only, and not to be taken away. This arrangement has been found necessary to prevent liquor being smuggled into the country in large quantities.

Just before my visit Khama had given a small piece of ground to the London Missionary Society for a church, and, for the first time I believe in South

African history, the concession had been submitted to and ratified by the High Commissioner—an excellent innovation, upon which Sir Alfred Milner is to be congratulated. So long as he is at the Cape the interests of the natives will be in safe hands, for he is keenly alive to his responsibilities on their behalf, and he seems to have inspired them with an implicit trust that he will see that they are dealt with justly.

The Duke of Fife has said, and with very good cause, that he hoped that in the future, wherever the British flag flew, some form of direct imperial control would always be established. For many reasons that is desirable, but the most cogent of all is that otherwise we shall nearly always be guilty of a breach of trust to the native chiefs who, like Khama, are only willing to place themselves under the direct protection of the Crown.

In connection with this subject I will advert briefly to the history of the concessions granted by Lobengula, to show how necessary it is that similar concessions should be strictly scrutinised in the future. Sir Henry de Villiers, in refusing to recognise the validity of the concessions granted by Sigcau, the Pondoland chief, used words that apply with equal force to those given by Lobengula: "Native customs, such as they are, do not recognise such concessions." He declined therefore to sanction, within the jurisdiction of the Cape, dealings with native chiefs which the High Commissioner had sanctioned without demur in extra-colonial territory.

The concession upon which the charter was founded was used, in fact, from the beginning merely as a pretext for the acquisition of the country. Mr. de Waal gives an account of a significant conversation of a Mr. Greeff with Mr. Rhodes in 1890 (in his book "With Rhodes in Mashonaland"), which shows that even then the Matabili war was in contemplation. "Yes, Mr. Greeff," answered Mr. Rhodes, "I shall certainly some day be pressed to do as you want me to do, but you must remember that I have only the right to dig gold in the land. So long, therefore, as the Matabili do not molest my people I cannot declare war against them and deprive them of their country; but as soon as they interfere with our rights I shall end their game. I shall then ask your aid, and be very glad to get it; *and when all is over I shall grant farms to those who assisted me.*"

A ground of quarrel was not long in being found. In 1893 it was said that the Matabili were behaving with such barbarity to the Mashonas near Victoria that in the interests of humanity they must be reduced to subjection. That the Matabili were behaving with great cruelty is true; they had always done so. But that this was only a convenient cry for the purpose of lulling the opposition of people in England, like the appeal for assistance of the endangered women and children of Johannesburg, is proved by the war having been practically decided upon some time before Umgandan and Manyou had begun to coerce their

Mashona vassals. I will take the facts in their logical sequence. Captain Donovan, who served with Major Wilson's column, states that when he and his companion arrived in Cape Town in May 1893, intending to go to Matabililand, Mr. Rhodes "strongly advised us to adopt a totally different route, 'for,' said he, 'at the present time (the month of May) we are on terms of the greatest friendship with all the chiefs around, but by the time you will be coming through Matabililand, most probably about September or October, I should not like to answer for your safe passage through that country.' Regarded in the light of late events, this advice seems prophetic." Naturally so, when the prophet took steps to bring about his prophecy.

The more closely one looks into the matter the more apparent this becomes. The war actually began early in October, and any one who will read the blue-books carefully can satisfy himself that Lobengula was forced into it, in spite of all the efforts of Sir Henry Loch to save him; that to the very last he hoped that the Imperial authorities would intervene between him and his assailants; that it was a war of aggression, and not of defence. Lobengula himself asserted this most strongly. On 27th July 1893 he wired through Mr. Colenbrander to the Administrator: "I thought you came to dig gold, but it seems that you have come not only to dig the gold, but to rob me of my people and country as well."

The English Government was goaded into sanctioning immediate action by representations of the urgent need of protecting the unhappy Mashonas, but the Victoria Agreement reveals indubitably that the real object was the partition of Matabililand ; that Lobengula was doomed from the first ; that it was never intended that he should be allowed to come to terms. The agreement specifies the advantages and conditions under which members could join the Matabili Field Force ; it recites clearly what is to be done with Matabililand when conquered ; how the land is to be disposed of ; that each member of the force is to have fifteen gold claims, and five alluvial claims, and a farm of 3000 morgen (6000 acres), unconditionally (without the beneficial occupation clause imposed on the Mashonaland farms), with liberty to select the land within four months anywhere in Matabililand, and after that time upon any ground not reserved for its own use by the B.S.A. Company. The loot was to be divided in equal shares—one half to the Company, the other half to the men and officers of the force.

This agreement is of vast importance, because it shows the fixed determination to listen to no proposals that might be made by Lobengula. It explains also Mr. Rhodes' violent opposition to Matabililand being placed under the Crown, instead of being handed over to the Chartered Company. "On the 19th December, Mr. Rhodes addressed the forces at Bulawayo prior to disbandment," says the *Financial Record* of January 6, 1894, "in such a tone as to leave the impression that

the secession from the empire of the British Colonies
in South Africa was within the range of practical
politics. When Mr. Rhodes cited the example of the
revolt of the American Colonies as a warning to the
Imperial Government that he intended to have his own
way in the settlement of Matabililand, he was guilty
of what we can only characterise as phenomenal
imbecility."

Mr. Rhodes has been held up lately as an exponent
of the most ardent Imperialism, but he was far from
that formerly. He has played off the Cape against the
Home Government, and the Home Government against
the Cape, in the most masterly fashion, whenever it
has suited his own purposes. He declared recently
that he had prevented a Power out of sympathy with
the Colony (the Transvaal) from occupying the north.
There was never a more fallacious idea. Lobengula, at the time of Sir Charles Warren's expedition,
was most anxious to place himself under British
protection, and the administration of Matabililand
might have been directed by us in the same way
as Khama's country and Basutoland. It would have
still belonged to Lobengula and his people ; the influx
of white men being carefully regulated as it is in those
countries.

This, however, would not have suited Mr. Rhodes,
who said, in 1888 : " He held to the Government of
South Africa by its people, keeping the Imperial tie for
self-defence, and was proud to feel that such a Govern-

ment was capable of ruling Matabililand as well as Mashonaland. He did not object to the Imperial Government holding temporary responsibility *pending annexation (by the Cape)*, but distinctly objected to the formation of a British colony on the Zambesi apart from *Cape* control."

Mr. Rhodes, indeed, has dealt with Rhodesia throughout as a Cape politician, acting for Cape interests. This the Rhodesian colonists are beginning to perceive, and to resent, for the one thing they dislike is the idea of incorporation with the Cape. Mr. Hovell, Secretary of the Bulawayo Chamber of Commerce, said in his evidence before the Chamber of Mines : " I think, as a community, we suffer more by being tied to Cape Colony than by having to be governed by the Chartered Company. The Cape colonial system does not show appreciation of our needs, and besides that is not a progressive colony. They are a settled land community, and we are essentially a commercial and mining community."

Only on the 10th of June of the present year, the *Bulawayo Chronicle*, in a bitter leader upon Cape sympathy, observes: " The settlers in Rhodesia have rated the Transvaal soundly in times past, but the Transvaal retorts and tells us to set our own house in order first, and certainly the Cape can take a few lessons in fair treatment from the 'ignorant Boer régime.'"

Many things show that a very angry feeling is

growing up in Rhodesia against both the Chartered
Company and the Cape. It is certain that the rule of
the Company must come to an end before long, and if
Rhodesia should not yet be deemed ripe for independence, the settlers would assuredly prefer conversion into
a Crown colony, as a preparation for self-government,
to any form of incorporation with the Cape : that they
would resist to the utmost.

But to return to the treatment of the natives.
How necessary it is that the offices of High Commissioner and Governor of Cape Colony should be
separated, and the interests of the natives confided
solely to the former, is conclusively shown by the
proceedings in the case of Sigcau, the Pondoland
chief. Lord Watson, in delivering the judgment of
the Privy Council in the appeal lodged by Mr. Rhodes
as Prime Minister of Cape Colony and Secretary for
Native Affairs, and Mr. Schreiner as Attorney-General,
against the judgment of the Supreme Court of the
Cape Colony, used words which need no emphasising.

"The proclamation in question is described in the
appellant's case as an act of State, which is beyond the
cognizance of any judicial tribunal. Whatever may
have been meant by that expression, the character of
the document is, on the face of it, abundantly clear.
It is an edict dealing with matters administrative,
judicial, legislative and executive, in terms which are
beyond the competency of any authority except an
irresponsible sovereign, or a supreme and unfettered

legislature, or some person or body to whom their functions have been lawfully delegated. If the Governor and High Commissioner of the Cape Colony could be shown to have occupied one or other of these positions, a court of law would be compelled, however unwillingly, to respect his proclamation. If he did not, then his dictatorial edict was simply an invasion of the individual rights and liberties of a British subject. It set aside the established law of Pondoland with respect to arrest, trial, conviction and punishment; and condemned the respondent, Sigcau, untried and unheard, to imprisonment, the place and duration of his captivity being left to the uncontrolled will of the framer of the edict. It was satisfactory to find that the appellants' counsel did not, in the argument before this Board, venture to trace the power of the Governor to enact such a proclamation to any authority directly derived from her Majesty; because autocratic legislation of that kind in a Colony having a settled system of criminal law and criminal tribunals, would be little calculated to enhance the repute of British justice."

That the Governor should have issued such a proclamation, and that since the adverse judgment of the Privy Council the Cape Legislature should have passed a law expressly legalising the powers upon which Lord Watson commented so severely, is sufficient evidence of the necessity of separating his functions from those of the High Commissioner.

The two positions are evidently incompatible. But if at any time they should be separated—and the matter has often been mooted—it must be made clear that it is because the union of the two offices is deemed inadvisable, and not from any pharisaical idea that people at home are more humane than the colonists, or that any drastic changes are to be made. All that is wanted is a separate native department, responsible not to the colonial governments, but to the Crown, and composed preferably of colonials, who have been in contact with the natives all their lives, and understand their language and their ways. It is the system that is at fault, not the people. Nothing has done more harm to the natives, and has excited a bitterer feeling against ourselves, than the spasms of compunction with which we have from time to time been visited. Instead of recognising that our arrangements have been faulty, we have salved our conscience by a flood of invective against the colonists and the Dutch for the barbarities of which they have been guilty. Nothing can be more contemptible than the way in which the native question has been twisted into a party weapon by a certain section of politicians. It is individuals who have been brutal, not peoples; they have been found amongst men lately out from home quite as frequently as amongst the colonists or the Dutch, and the excesses of which they have been guilty have been made possible by faulty administration.

Look how excellent the native system is in Natal,

in Kaffraria, and in Basutoland; how wretched it is in Rhodesia, and in the Cape. It is just the same amongst the Dutch. In the Orange Free State the natives are treated on a different system from that which has commended itself to us; but nevertheless kindly and well. In the Transvaal they are treated abominably. I found the Free State people very indignant because a Mr. Venter had said in his evidence before the South African Committee that the natives in Rhodesia are better treated than in the Free State. I asked Tengu Jabavu what he, as representing native opinion, thought of the matter. He said he knew nothing about Rhodesia, but that in the Free State the natives are admirably treated, better than in the Colony, because liquor is kept strictly from them. In the Transvaal, he said, the treatment is very bad. The boys are knocked about terribly in the mines, and get scant justice from the landdrosts.

My subsequent observations confirmed both these opinions. The Free State system seemed to me admirably suited to the people, but in the Transvaal the native administration is in a perfect chaos. I found that there had been 1652 floggings last year in the Johannesburg jail alone, with 20,356 prisoners, a proportion of one in thirteen—an appalling total—most of them for trivial offences. But there are signs that a better state of things is coming about. The labour supply is falling short, and to induce an influx of the needful supply the boys must take back with them a more cheerful account of their experiences than they have hitherto been able to do. In any case we cannot interfere. We have too much that is wrong to redress within our own borders. Sir Charles Warren's expedition was undertaken in order to rescue the Bechuanas from predatory onslaughts from the Transvaal. They were placed first under the protection of the Crown, and were then handed over to the Cape, and last year— within ten years from Sir Charles Warren's expedition— Galishwe had gone into revolt, and his tribe had been broken up and condemned to forced servitude, and their land taken from them for ever. "The flail that the Dutch use to us is cold," said one of the Bechuana chiefs, "but the flail of the English is fiery." Is this description unmerited? Alas, no! Read the accounts given by Phillips and George Thompson of our treatment of the natives in the early part of the century. One extract from Phillips will suffice. "Judging from the detestation in which this country had been accustomed to hold the tyranny of the Dutch towards the aborigines of its colonies; and from the style in which their cruelty to the Bushmen was described by Barrow and other travellers, it might have been expected that the transfer of the Government into British hands was an event in which humanity had to rejoice. But what is the fact? During the last twenty-two years of the Dutch Government at the Cape the Bushmen were oppressed; yet, notwithstanding their oppressions, in 1796 they were still powerful. Since the

English took possession of the colony in 1796, what was, in the time of the Dutch Government, the Bushman country, has been brought into the possession of the colonists; and the people who were so powerful in 1796 as to threaten the Colony, are now reduced to slavery, or to the condition of miserable fugitives in what was then their own country."

The worst of the matter is that the same kind of thing has been going on without ceasing ever since, and it will go on until the Home Government recognises its direct responsibility to its native subjects.

Mr. Chamberlain, speaking on May 14, 1888, said, "It will raise, no doubt, one or two questions for discussion, and prominently among them the question of the continued retention in the same hands of the two great offices of High Commissioner and of Governor of the Cape Colony. It appears to me that this is a question which depends very much upon the personal qualities and characteristics of the man who may be chosen to fill these two offices. If he is an able man and discreet, and above all a firm and resolute man, it is quite possible that he may be able to maintain an Imperial policy in South Africa in the territories under the protection of the Crown, and at the same time he may be able to impress this policy upon the Government of the Cape Colony; but if he should be weak or incompetent, it is probable that the Government of the day, the Government of the majority at the Cape Colony, would impress him, and that they would secure the adoption of their policy in the administration of these trans-colonial territories, and once more we should be called upon to pay the piper without setting the tune."

It is impossible to state the case more clearly. It is prophetic of what has since occurred in Rhodesia. Matabililand was handed over to the Chartered Company (with the acquiescence of the Cape, Mr. Rhodes being then in his dual position of Prime Minister of the Cape and Managing Director of the Chartered Company), although the Imperial Government had expended a very large sum in the conduct of the war. Are we going to run the same risk again in reference to Trans-Zambesia? and who knows, perhaps in regard to Basutoland? The native interests are surely too vast to be subjected to so great a hazard. Sir Charles Warren stated in 1886 that the greatest impediment at that time to the peace of South Africa was the dual position held by the High Commissioner and the Governor of the Cape Colony; and owing to our enormously increased native dominions the question is more urgent now than it was then. Mr. Mackenzie brought it prominently before the Colonial Office in 1888, but nothing was done owing to the unfavourable way in which the proposal to separate the two offices was received in South Africa. From what I heard when I was there I believe that now it would be gladly welcomed both in the Colony and in the Republics.

CHAPTER XX

From Palachwe I went by rail to Mafeking, and there took coach to Krugersdorp by the same road that was taken by Dr. Jameson. Through the kindness of a friend I have been enabled to make use of some private notes taken at the time of the Raid. They contain so exact an account of what occurred that I will give them just as I have taken them from his manuscript :—

"In November, Leonard and Phillips went to Cape Town to see Mr. Rhodes. Mr. Leonard in his report says, 'We read to him the draft of our declaration of rights. He was leaning against the mantelpiece smoking his cigarette, and when it came to that part of the document in which we referred to free trade in South African products, he turned round suddenly, and said : "That is what I want. That is all I ask of you. The rest will come in time. We must have a beginning, and that will be the beginning. If you people get your rights, the Customs Union, Railway Convention, and other things will all come in time." He then added that we must take our time about this movement; that he would keep Jameson on the frontier so long as it was necessary, as a moral support, and also come to our assistance should we get ourselves into a tight place. We asked him how he hoped to recoup himself for his share of the expense in keeping Jameson's force on the border, which must be borne by us jointly. He said that seeing the extent of his interests in the country, he would be amply repaid by the improvement in the conditions which it was intended to effect.' It has since been suggested that the object of the movement was to steal the country, and to annex it to Rhodesia, in order to rehabilitate the Chartered Company. The suggestion is too ludicrous for serious discussion, but notwithstanding the ludicrous nature of the charge, it is quite certain that the Boers have a deep-rooted conviction of its truth.

"About December 19th it became apparent that the flag question must be settled. It appeared that Dr. Jameson rather thought that the Johannesburg reformers were quite indifferent to the flag, or assumed that provisions for the maintenance of the Transvaal flag were merely talk, and that the Union Jack would be hoisted at once. A trusted emissary was dispatched to inquire from Mr. Rhodes the meaning of this tampering with one of the fundamental conditions of the agreement. The messenger returned on Christmas morning, and at a largely attended meeting of the ringleaders, he stated that he had seen Mr. Rhodes, and had received from him the assurance that it was all right about the flag. In returning from Cape Town however, in company with Dr. Rutherfoord Harris, he learned from that gentleman that it was by no means all right, and gathered that in other quarters (not referring to Mr. Cecil Rhodes) it was assumed that the provision about maintaining the Transvaal flag was so much talk necessary to secure the adhesion of some doubtful people. The announcement was received with the gravest dissatisfaction, and it was instantly resolved to discontinue the preparations, and to break off the connection with Dr. Jameson.

"Messrs. Leonard and Hamilton were sent to see Mr. Rhodes, and to obtain from him a definite guarantee that, in the event of their availing themselves of Dr. Jameson's help under any conditions, the latter would loyally abide by the arrangements agreed upon. The interview took place on Saturday the 28th. Mr. Rhodes gave the most explicit and satisfactory assurances, and said, 'Well, you fellows must take your own time and do it in your own way. I will keep Jameson on the frontier for a month, or two months, or two years if necessary. His presence there will be the greatest help to you in obtaining what you want by peaceful means.'

"On the 26th December Major Heany was sent by train _via_ Kimberley, and Captain Holden across country to Pitsani, to tell Jameson on no account to move. Both gentlemen delivered their messages.

"On the Thursday, Friday, and Saturday, telegrams and messages were received from Dr. Jameson, all revealing impatience, and a desire, if not an intention, to disregard the wishes of the Johannesburgers. Replies were sent to him, and to the Cape Town agents, protesting against the tone adopted, and urging him to desist from the endeavour to rush the Committee, as they were pushing matters on to the best of their ability and hoped for a successful issue without recourse to violent measures, and stating emphatically that the decision must be left entirely in the Committee's hands as agreed, otherwise there would be absolute disaster. The Committee, moreover, wired by private code, drawing the attention of all parties to the fact that Jameson and others were using the Bedford M'Niel code, copies of which are kept in nearly every telegraph office in the country, for the purpose of transmitting or repeating messages obscurely worded.

"Dr. Wolff had arrived at Pitsani on the previous Tuesday, and states that he was greeted by Dr. Jameson with the remark that he had as nearly as possible started for Pretoria the previous night. On the 28th December the President was met at Bronkhorstspruit, some twenty miles from Pretoria, by some of the burghers, and one of them, Hans Botha, said he had heard there was some talk of a rising in Johannesburg, and that though he had five bullets in him he could find room for another if it were a question of attacking the Britishers. The President said he had heard of the threatened rising, but did not believe it. He could not say what was likely to happen, but they must remember this—if they wanted to kill a tortoise they must wait till he puts his head out of his shell.   On the same day the President said to a press reporter, ' If wiser counsels unfortunately should not prevail, then let the storm arise, and the wind thereof will separate the chaff from the grain.   The Government will give every opportunity for free speech, and free ventilation of grievances, but is fully prepared to put a stop to any movement made for the upset of law and order.'   That was on Saturday.   The President also received an American deputation, and several other deputations. On Monday Abe Bailey received this wire from Godolphin (who proved to be Rutherfoord Harris): ' The veterinary surgeon says the horses are now all right ; he started with them last night ; will reach you on Wednesday ; he says he can back himself for seven hundred.'   And the same afternoon Mr. Lawley got the following telegram : ' The contractor has started on the earthworks with seven hundred boys ; hopes to reach terminus on Wednesday.'

" The Reformers realised perfectly well the full significance of Jameson's action ; they realised that even if he succeeded in reaching Johannesburg, he, by taking the initiative, seriously impaired the justice of the Johannesburgers' cause, indeed put them hopelessly in the wrong ; whilst by starting first, he knocked out the foundation of the whole fabric—he made the taking of the Pretoria Arsenal impossible.

" A few minutes later information came that the Government had known of his starting early in the morning, and that Pretoria was now full of burghers, so all hope of the arsenal being surprised was over.

"On Monday night the Reform Committee was formed. On Wednesday Lionel Phillips, Auret, Abe Bailey, and M. Langermann went to Pretoria to meet the Government Commission, and to obtain the best terms for Jameson as well as for themselves. After they had left a telegram was received from Sir Jacobus de Wet with Sir Hercules Robinson's proclamation forbidding aid to be given to Dr. Jameson, and the following telegram was sent to Phillips and his companions : ' Meeting has been held since you started to consider telegram from British agent, and it was unanimously resolved to authorise you to make following offer to Government.' Begins, ' In order to avoid bloodshed on grounds of Dr. Jameson's action, if Government will allow Dr. Jameson to come unmolested the Committee will guarantee, with their persons if necessary, that he shall leave again peacefully with as little delay as possible.'

"The Government Commission consisted of Kotze, Ameshof, and Executive Member Kock. After hearing the deputation they reported to the Executive Committee, and in the afternoon handed to the deputation this answer: ' The High Commissioner has offered his services with a view to a peaceful settlement. The Government has accepted his offer. Pending his arrival, no hostile step will be taken against Johannesburg, if Johannesburg takes no hostile step against the Government, and no breaking of the law takes place, in terms of proclamation issued by State President, and thereafter the grievances will be earnestly considered.'

"On receipt of the above resolution, the deputation inquired whether this offer of the Government was intended to include Dr. Jameson. The Chief-Justice replied that the Government declined to treat about Jameson, as he was a foreign invader, and would have to be turned out of the country. The deputation thereupon handed the telegram from the Reform Committee offering their persons as security. The Committee in reply stated that the proclamation of the High Commissioner was being forwarded to Jameson, and that he would inevitably be stopped (whether by force or by the High Commissioner's proclamation was not then made clear). The deputation returned to Johannesburg fully convinced that the grievances would be redressed, and a peaceful settlement arrived at through the mediation of the High Commissioner, and that Dr. Jameson would inevitably obey the latter's proclamation, and leave the country peacefully on ascertaining that there was no necessity for his intervention on behalf of the Uitlanders.

"A great deal has been said about the impolicy, and even the bad faith of the Johannesburg people in concluding an armistice which did not include Dr Jameson. From the above account it is clear that in the first place every effort was made to provide for Jameson's safety, and in the next place no armistice was concluded. It was merely left to the Reform Committee to accept or ignore the terms offered.

" Captain Holden, immediately after Jameson's trial, expressed his regret at the unjust censure upon the Johannesburg people, and the charges of cowardice and bad faith which had been levelled against them, and stated that he had reached Pitsani the night before Dr. Jameson started, and that he faithfully and fully delivered the messages which he was charged to deliver, and earnestly impressed upon Dr. Jameson the position in which the Johannesburg people were placed, and their desire that he should not embarrass them by any precipitate action. . . .

" Dr. Jameson had invaded the country with less than 500 men. It must be clear from this that it was not his intention to conquer the Transvaal. It must have been, and indeed was, his idea that it would be impossible for the Imperial Government to stand passively by and witness the struggle between its own subjects, preferring legitimate and moderate claims, and a corrupt and incompetent Boer Government. Intervention of one sort or another he certainly expected—either material help in the shape of British troops, or the intervention of the High Commissioner to effect a peaceful settlement. By the false step which evoked the High Commissioner's proclamation, he had forfeited all claim to the support on which he reckoned. It was reasonable to suppose, therefore, that on the receipt of the proclamation ordering him to return, and calling on all British subjects to abstain from assisting him, he would realise the consequences of his mistake. He would also learn from the Reform Committee's messengers that the Johannesburg people neither required nor wished for his intervention, and he would elect to leave the country in accordance with the High Commissioner's mandate, rather than continue a course which, with the opposition of the Boer Government, must inevitably end in disgrace and disaster. This was the conclusion arrived at in the Reform Committee-room, and it was then considered what would be the position of the Johannesburg people, who, in defiance of the High Commissioner's proclamation, and in violation of the terms offered by the Transvaal Government, should adopt aggressive and wholly futile measures in aid of Dr. Jameson, only to find that he himself had obeyed the proclamation and had turned back. . . . The public in Johannesburg by this time knew of the letter of invitation. It had been taken on the battle-field, and news of it was wired in; and, apart from this, the writers had made no secret of it. But what the public did not know was the effort made to stop Jameson, and the practical repudiation of the letter before he had started. It was sufficient for them that Jameson had come in, and that, when almost reaching the goal, he had been taken prisoner for want of assistance.

. . . .

"The undeserved taunts levelled at the Johannesburg Committee have wounded them keenly, and an extremely bitter feeling was aroused by the tacit approval given to these censures by the officers of the invading force, for their continued silence was naturally construed to be tacit approval.

" It was left to Mr. Rhodes, whose intelligence and sense of justice prompted him to take a line which no one else had the courage to take, to say that the Johannesburg people were not cowards; they were rushed."[1]

To these notes it is only necessary to add that it would have been infinitely better if, after Dr. Jameson and his officers had been sent home to be tried, the whole matter had been allowed to remain in Sir Hercules Robinson's hands. He was liked and trusted by the Dutch, and if he had been left unfettered he could have done much towards restoring cordial relations with the Transvaal. Mr. Hofmeyr, when I asked him if any sort of good had been done by the South Africa Committee, replied, " Well, it has proved that Sir Hercules Robinson was an honourable English gentleman, as we always knew he was;" and Mr. Fischer of the Free State begged that I would say something to show how deep is the affection and regard felt for him there. President Steyn, it will

---

[1] This is hardly fair to Dr. Jameson and his officers, other than Sir John Willoughby; for until the inquiry they were obliged to keep silence for fear of prejudicing Mr. Rhodes' political position, and since the inquiry they have probably thought the opportunity for speaking was past. Mr. Rhodes, too, was compelled to be silent until the inquiry, as he had more important interests to safeguard. That he kept silence unwillingly is to be presumed by his allowing his own brother to remain for a year under the galling imputations with which the Johannesburg Committee were assailed.

be remembered, when Sir Hercules Robinson was leaving for England in May 1896, said in his letter of farewell: "For we are all aware of the fact that it is mainly due to your exertions that we to-day still enjoy the blessings of peace."

On the 16th January Sir Hercules Robinson wired to Mr. Chamberlain : "If you will leave the matter in my hands I will resume advocacy of Uitlanders' claims at the first moment I think it can be done with advantage ; the present moment is most inopportune, as the strongest feeling of irritation against the Uitlanders exists both among the burghers and members of Volksraad of both Republics. Any attempt to dictate in regard to internal affairs of the South African Republic at this moment would be resisted by all parties in South Africa, and would do great harm."

In spite of this warning, Mr. Chamberlain made the fatal blunder of sending to President Kruger the draft constitution, which caused so much anger, and of publishing it in London before it had been received in Pretoria. This, the naval demonstration in Delagoa Bay, the heated discussion as to the terms of Sir John Willoughby's surrender, the tone adopted towards the Transvaal by the South Africa Committee, and the ostentatious championship of Mr. Rhodes, have converted what ought to have been a purely South African matter into a quarrel between Great Britain and the Transvaal. The Raid itself would have done comparatively little mischief, had it not been for the attitude subsequently assumed by the British Government.

How unwise this attitude was may be judged by the telegram sent on the 2nd April 1896 by Sir Walter Hely Hutchinson to Mr. Chamberlain: " Ministers have sent me the following minute: 'Ministers have private information from London that on 30th March President Kruger was warned that he must within a few days accept the invitation to visit England without conditions, or the South African Republic will revert to the position of the Convention of 1881. Their informant adds words giving to this communication the character or significance of an ultimatum. Ministers have received this information with considerable reserve as regards its accuracy; but they consider it their duty to point out that all the Governments of South Africa favour a policy of peace, knowing what the disastrous results of a race war must be, and that an outbreak of hostilities between the European races will have a disturbing effect on the natives throughout South Africa, the evil consequences of which cannot be estimated.' "

To this Mr. Chamberlain replied on the 4th April: " Referring to your telegram of 2nd inst., I have pressed President of South African Republic for reply to our invitation, but have used no threats. Strong irritation is, however, felt here at the delay. He is, I fear, prevented by influences opposed to a satisfactory settlement of matters."

That the Natal Ministry should have deemed it necessary to take the action they did shows how inadvisable the interference of the Colonial Office was. If war had actually been decided upon it would have been a different matter; but to exert pressure without obtaining the desired result is an unnecessary humiliation, and does harm in every way.   It has not bettered the position of the Uitlanders; it has only caused the Transvaal Government to waste a million and a half upon forts, an expenditure for which the Uitlanders have had to pay.   What has annoyed the Free State more almost than anything else, is that the wave of suspicion to which it gave rise led them to expend a hundred thousand pounds upon increased armaments, which could ill be spared from education and railways, and the internal development of the State.

CHAPTER XXI

Mr. Chamberlain, during the debate that took place in the House of Commons on the 26th July 1897, said: " The Government do not intend to abolish the charter, and they do not intend to do it for reasons I have already stated in the House, and for additional reasons. They think, and probably with justice, that if you have Imperial control, and Rhodesia were made a Crown colony the development of the country would be delayed because the English Treasury would never consent to the expenditure of the money necessary for its development."

It is not a very noble reason why a great nation should shirk its responsibilities; but putting the natives altogether on one side, and looking at the question merely as one of material advancement, will it be greater under the Company than it would be under the Crown ?   Let us look a little more closely into the matter.   And in dealing with Rhodesia we must bear in mind that although the Company has been sanctified with the baptism of a Royal Charter it is nevertheless the natural offspring of De Beers, and that the methods which have been employed in Kimberley are likely to be employed also in Rhodesia. Let us examine what those methods are, bearing in mind that Mr. Rhodes for all practical purposes represents and controls the De Beers Company, just in the same way that until the Raid he represented and controlled the British South Africa Company.

Onsland, the accredited organ of the Afrikander Bond, in a remarkable article published in the spring of last year, said of Mr. Rhodes: "The politics and influence of Mr. Rhodes and his worshippers is a threatening danger to the whole of South Africa. This is the conviction of all who have observed the low tone existing in some circles, as if money were not only all powerful, but also the only thing desirable. This is felt by all who believe that no policy can be of real benefit to a land or nation if it issues from treachery or violence. Not in force, but in the course of a steady, healthy, and natural development lies the welfare of South Africa. Mr. Rhodes has declared himself directly against this natural development of our affairs. His career, he stated, only began after the Jameson invasion, and he has since repeatedly declared that he will continue to follow this course. The interest which the capitalists devise to obtain in South Africa will tend to expel from us all substantiality, probity, and principle."

In order to estimate the truth of this statement, it is necessary to make a rapid review of Mr. Rhodes' history in South Africa. He came to it a poor man, but in a comparatively short time, by his masterly amalgamation of the De Beers mines, he amassed a vast fortune, and then turned his attention to politics. He was elected a member of the Cape House of Assembly, and soon after became the Prime Minister of the Colony. From that time the influence of his genius, and still more of his money, became every year more predominant, and by his alliance with the Afrikander Bond he was able to procure the passing of almost any Act he pleased. Many causes combined to procure for him the commanding position he so long held, but I will confine myself to that of money, for throughout his career it has been the weightiest weapon in his armoury. I will keep strictly to documentary evidence available to every one, and will let the admitted facts speak for themselves in proof of *Onsland's* assertions.

In the articles of association of the De Beers Company there is a singular clause, giving the managing director power to expend on secret service for the advancement and benefit of the Company such sums, not exceeding £10,000 sterling per annum, as he may think fit without submission of vouchers : a clause that is obviously dangerous to the public probity.

But this sum of £10,000, large though it is, is not the only sum at Mr. Rhodes' absolute disposal as managing director and life governor of the De Beers Company.

It was found that large quantities of diamonds were being stolen by natives employed in the mines, and in order to check these thefts, and to keep the natives away from the liquor shops, the adoption of what is known as the compound system was authorised by a special Act of the Cape legislature—that is to say, the natives are confined for the period during which they have contracted to work (generally three months) in a walled-in and strictly-guarded enclosure, where they are supplied with all they require in shape of food and raiment. The merchants in the town of Kimberley objected strongly to this as detrimental to their trade, and to meet their objection, Act 23 of 1887 was passed, which provides that " all goods, wares, and merchandise that may be sold within the compound or building as provided in the preceding section, shall without exception be purchased in the electoral division of Kimberley, and no employer shall derive any benefit directly or indirectly from any such purchase." The punishment provided for the violation of this provision is for the first offence a fine of £5, or not more than one month's imprisonment, and for each subsequent offence a fine of £10, or imprisonment with or without hard labour for not more than two months.

After this Act had been in operation for some time, the Kimberley merchants found that it was being evaded, and that their trade was practically ruined, and a great outcry was raised; and to quiet it the De Beers Company passed a resolution that they would devote any profits that might be derived from the sale of any articles within the compound to what they termed public purposes.

Mr. Rhodes' own account of the transaction is as follows. He was speaking as chairman of the De Beers meeting held on October 22, 1894. "I myself," he said, "brought in the Bill, and there was a great deal said in the House about 'tommy shops,' profits made out of the natives, and so forth. The spirit of the Bill was that we should buy whatever we desired for the compounds locally, but that no profit should be allowed. These were the two positions, and the Bill was carried with these two principles embodied in it. The result was, as I think I told you once before, we saved £300,000 a year, and we do so now—owing to diamonds recovered through the compound system, which otherwise would be stolen and scattered through the country. . . . We cannot sell things at cost because the merchants would grumble. Besides, it is unwise treatment of the native: it makes him a dissatisfied man for the rest of his life, for when he leaves the compound he finds everything much dearer. Still, the spirit of the Bill is broken by selling at a profit. The pledge I gave to the House was that we would buy locally all that is required for the compound, and that we would make no profit. This is a subject which has been more than once brought up, and I have often been asked about it. I think the right solution of the difficulty is the following: I hold very strong views on the subject, and as it was owing to my efforts that the Bill was carried, I certainly think that we should do our best to fulfil the spirit of it. As we are compelled to make a profit, it should be disposed of in a special way. I have consulted the board, and there is a little difference of opinion amongst them, so that I would rather leave the matter to the vote of the shareholders. I beg to move—' That the balance realised by sale of goods in the compounds, after allowing for the cost of same, and all reasonable charges connected with the sale of said goods, and the maintenance of the compounds, be annually determined and made over to the chairman of the Company (Mr. Rhodes himself), and shall form a fund to be by him held and invested, and from time to time drawn upon and distributed to such public purpose or purposes as he in his discretion may determine, subject to such arrangements as he may make, and such conditions as he may impose, and that the said chairman shall annually state and render to the Company an account showing the position of the said fund, his expenses in connection with administering the same, and the amounts which have been expended by him for any such purpose as aforesaid.' "

This did not, however, satisfy the Kimberley people, and on June 20, 1895, Mr. Hay brought the matter forward in the Cape House of Assembly. He said: " On October 22nd last, at the annual meeting of the De Beers Company, according to the report in the *Cape Times*, the Right Honourable Cecil John Rhodes presided, and it was then carried that the profits received from the sale of food and other commodities should be devoted to any public object he might think fit;" and Mr. Hay asked the Attorney-General "if he intended taking any action for past breaches of the law in this respect, or to prevent breaches thereof in future" (Mr. Rhodes being then Prime Minister, as well as managing director of the De Beers Company).

The following answer was given by Mr. Schreiner, who was Attorney-General in Mr. Rhodes' Ministry: "The clause put in provided that all goods that might be sold in the compound should, without exception, be purchased in the electoral division of Kimberley, and no compounding employer should profit through the sale, which meant that no such employer should have an outside firm, or be interested in any firm supplying the goods sold in the compound." This ended the matter for the time; but in the following year, on the 16th June 1896, Mr. Hay moved—"That it is desirable to amend Act 23, 1887, so that goods sold to natives may be charged at cost prices." The profits, he said, accumulated, and it was possible for any one to use them as a bribe.

The debate that ensued is instructive.

Mr. Sauer eulogised the compound system; at the same time he thought it undesirable that a company should have a large sum of money to expend without any check whatever. Public purposes was rather a vague term. It might mean anything, even election expenses, or other purposes that were not very desirable. Mr. Innes said that the Act was bad legislation altogether, and he hoped that in future legislation they would take warning by this. Section 7 of the Act provided that all goods purchased for the compound should be purchased in Kimberley, and that no *employer* should derive benefit from the transaction. But profits were made, and he did not see how these profits could be audited without authorising the breaking of the law. This section could be amended.

Nothing, however, was done.

But the important question is, What use has been made of the money? The De Beers resolution I have just quoted provided that "the said chairman shall state and render to the Company an account showing the position of the said fund, his expenses in connection with administering the same, and the amounts which have been devoted by him to any such purposes as aforesaid." Have these accounts been accurately rendered? and has any means been provided to check the amounts actually received by Mr. Rhodes and those expended by him, and for what purpose? Nothing of the kind seems to have been attempted.

Mr. Rhodes, speaking two years later at the annual meeting of De Beers on 28th December 1896, made this statement: "I may say that having gone into the various transactions, I came to the conclusion that there roughly might be claimed £10,000 a year as these profits. You must remember there are the wages of the guards, and many other expenses in connection with the compounds. I was satisfied with

£10,000 a year. Some directors said there was no profit, but we came to a compromise." And so the matter was allowed to remain.

The resources of the De Beers Company are indeed so vast that to most people in South Africa it seems a hopeless task to attempt to struggle against them. As a member of the Cape Assembly said to me, "You cannot move a yard here without butting your head up against De Beers."

The enormous sums placed absolutely at Mr. Rhodes' disposal have gone far to obtain for him the influence he undoubtedly possesses, for there are few men that he has not been able to oblige.

During the recent inquiry a parallel has frequently been drawn between Clive, Warren Hastings, and Mr. Rhodes; but Macaulay expressly refers to Warren Hastings' honourable poverty; while of Clive he says, "When he landed in Calcutta in 1765, Bengal was regarded as a place to which Englishmen were sent only to get rich, by any means, in the shortest possible time. He first made dauntless and unsparing war on that gigantic system of oppression, extortion, and corruption. In that war he manfully put to hazard his ease, his fame, and his splendid fortune."

What Mr. Rhodes has done is exactly the opposite. When he appeared upon the scene, South Africa was a frugal and comparatively poor country. His restless and indomitable energy has done much to make it externally rich and prosperous, but at the cost of a deplorable demoralisation which has sapped the independence of the people, and will in the end render them infinitely poorer.

For the devices of modern capital have shown us how wise Sir Thomas More was when he wrote these words: "When every man draws to himself all that he can compass, by one title or another, it must needs follow that how plentiful soever a nation may be, yet a few dividing the wealth of it amongst themselves, the rest must fall into indigence."

The poor white question is already one of the most difficult problems with which the South African politician has to deal.

Is the assertion justified that Mr. Rhodes is mainly responsible for the monopolist tendency, which is the great danger of South African society? Let us see what the facts are, and what people in South Africa have said about them from time to time. In the report of the Select Committee on Griqualand West held in 1891, Mr. J. Cowie, the acting mayor of Beaconsfield (a suburb of Kimberley), was being examined, and Mr. Molteno said to him, "Do you mean to say the Government of this country is also in the swim of this gigantic swindle to defraud the poor men of Kimberley out of their débris?" (worth about a million sterling). "I will not say," he replied, "that the Government is in the swindle, but I will say this, that if Mr. Rhodes had not been in the dual capacity of premier and life governor of the De Beers Consolidated Mines, there is not the least doubt in my mind that we should have got it."

Mr. Rhodes seems never to have appreciated, or if he did, he chose to disregard the exceedingly unpleasant innuendoes to which his dual position gave rise.

How undesirable that position was for the Prime Minister of a responsibly governed colony is shown by the proceedings that took place when the Wesselton Mine was acquired by the De Beers Company in 1891. It is too long a story to go into here; but those who feel curious about it will find it set out with much particularity of detail, and much vigour of language, in a little pamphlet published by the Knights of Labour, and in a petition of the people of Kimberley to the Cape House of Assembly.

The impropriety of it was thoroughly understood, for Mr. Hofmeyr said in September 1888 that "being aware of the charitable feelings of some people, and intending to oppose the proposed tax on dividends in the interests more particularly of the colonial farmer and producer, he had at the commencement of last session sold out his De Beers and Central shares for whatever he could get, so that he could do his Parliamentary work unfettered by even the trace of self-interest."

So, too, in England Mr. Mundella gave up the position of President of the Board of Trade simply because Mr. Justice Vaughan Williams remarked in the course of a judgment that he held shares in a

Company which the Official Receiver, an official serving under him, was liquidating.   " It may be, of course, that he still holds these shares because they are unsaleable. I do not know how that is; and with regard to his investments in other companies there may be special reasons for his continuing these investments, but I do not understand that he, upon taking office, gave up all these investments."   Mr. Mundella thereupon resigned in order to avoid any possible imputation of a conflict between his interest and his duty.

What, then, can be thought of Mr. Rhodes' position ? As managing director and life governor of the De Beers Company he had a direct pecuniary interest in Acts for the passing of which he, as Prime Minister, was personally responsible.   He cannot be blamed for taking the fullest advantage of his position; there never was any concealment about it : but that the Cape House of Assembly and the Cape electorate should with full knowledge have given to it their sanction, goes far to justify *Onsland's* assertion.

The whole of this Select Committee's report will repay perusal.   I shall have occasion to refer to it again when dealing with the native question, but for the present I will confine myself to those portions which bear upon the condition of the working classes. Mr. E. H. Jones said in his examination : " Kenilworth (where the De Beers employés live) will eventually become a vast compound for white men as well as natives, where these employés may reside and the

Company may have entire control over them; and if any one does not satisfy the Company's requirements entirely, they will send him away. In other words, Kenilworth in the future will be what the native compounds are to-day."

The working classes of Johannesburg are always dreading, and with reason, the establishment of a State amalgamated compound system. They know that if it is once introduced the capitalists will have them in their power, and that the same system of company serfage will be introduced which is in force in Kimberley. They do not like President Kruger, but they dislike the capitalists more. They know that their condition would be infinitely worse under them than it is under the Boers, and that however prosperous the mines might prove, whatever dividends might be paid in Europe, the prosperity and freedom of Johannesburg, as a city, would disappear, as that of Kimberley has done.

Indeed, the struggle in Johannesburg between capital and labour has already begun. A director of one of the great mining groups, speaking to me about it, said: "We have settled the question of native labour, and have reduced the wages by one-third without any difficulty. We have now the more difficult problem of white labour to deal with. I don't at all approve of suddenly reducing wages, and so producing a strike. That is in every way undesirable. What we have to do is to shut down some of our

T

poorer mines, and let the men walk about the streets for two or three months until their feet are on the pavement. They'll be glad enough then to take whatever we choose to offer them."

To understand fully the dread which the working classes have of Johannesburg being assimilated to Kimberley, and of an Illicit Gold Act being put into operation of equal stringency with the Act in force in the Cape, it is necessary to explain what that Act is, and in what way it differs from the ordinary criminal law.

By the Trade in Diamonds Consolidation Act, No. 48 of 1882, generally known as the I.D.B. (illicit diamond buying) Act, it is declared unlawful for any person to have in his possession any rough or uncut diamond unless he is able to produce his proper permit for the same, or to account satisfactorily for, or prove his right to, the possession thereof; and such diamonds are · only permitted to be bought by duly licenced dealers—the penalty for contravention being a fine not exceeding £1000, or imprisonment up to fifteen years, or both. The operation of the Act was originally confined to Griqualand West, but by Act 14 of 1885 its operation was extended to the whole of Cape Colony. It will be observed that the onus of proof is placed upon the accused; that is to say, instead of the prosecution having to prove that he is guilty, he has to prove that he is innocent—a very difficult and often an impossible thing to do. This provision, coupled with the system of trapping which is in use at Kimberley, both by male and female detectives, have made the Act a terribly effective instrument.

In 1888, an attempt which was made to procure its adoption by Natal failed, giving rise to a good deal of acrimony between the Cape and that colony. What the Natal people thought of the Act is shown by an article in the *Natal Mercury*, dated September 3, 1888, and much the same opinion prevails now in the Transvaal: "And it was a conviction that our highest interests were being jeopardised, which led to the rejection of the Diamond Bill; not material, or speculative, or commercial interests in any sense, but the interests of a community determined to hold inviolate the personal liberties of the subject, which Anglo-Saxons and South Africans hold alike so dear. The Bill, even in its curtailed form, conferred upon the police inquisitorial and offensive powers which are wholly foreign to our experience, and wholly hostile to our instincts. The powers of arrest and of search proposed to be legalised by the Bill are powers which are undoubtedly capable of abuse; they would expose the people of the colony to liabilities and penalties of the most odious and oppressive kind, and they are peculiarly repugnant to a liberty-loving race. Cape colonists put up with them — very reluctantly — because they have been found necessary to the protection of their leading and most lucrative industry, but that is no reason why Natal, whose actual interest in that industry is practically nil, should place itself under a system which is revolting to the moral sense of the community. . . . We should fasten upon ourselves dangerous and hateful liabilities without doing anything to prevent the traffic in stolen diamonds. According to the answer given by the Colonial Secretary on Monday, the Cape Government possess the power, as it is, of opening letters or packets sent to Europe by the mail from any South African territory. It must exercise that power on its own responsibility, and it is well that it should do so, but it is surely asking too much of its independent neighbours that they should take that obnoxious responsibility upon their shoulders."

Mr. Rhodes is not responsible for these Acts: they were passed before he came into power; but he has been the chief upholder of them, and his recent action in the Sigcau case shows what his views are about arbitrary powers of arrest. He is hardly, therefore, the champion of progress and of freedom that in England he is generally accredited with being.

Even in Cape Colony, where the influence of the Company is supreme, the enormous powers granted to it have aroused an ineffectual opposition. The *Cape Times* of Sept. 4, 1888, contains this passage: "The work of the session is exhibited in a list of thirty-eight Acts passed—of these some are useful, some silly, only one we believe positively mischievous. . . . The object of the Act is to crush all opposition to the Diamond Mining monopoly, which is now assuming the position of a universal trader, exploiter, and financier. The Chief-Justice, in delivering judgment yesterday upon the amalgamation question, assigned the following reasons why the De Beers Consolidated Mines was not to be deemed, for the purposes of amalgamation, a company established with purposes similar to those of the Central Diamond Mining Company. 'He had looked,' he said, 'into the trust deed of the De Beers Consolidated Mines, and was satisfied it was not a company for the same and similar purposes as the Central. It was quite true that one of the purposes for which the De Beers Company was established was diamond-mining, but that formed an insignificant portion of the powers which might be exercised by the Company. The Company could undertake financial arrangements for foreign governments, might carry on diamond-mining, gold-mining, and coal-mining in any part of the world; it could carry on banking in Africa or elsewhere, and become a water company in the Colony or elsewhere. In point of fact, it was of public note that an Act had been passed that session empowering the De Beers Company to perform the duties of a water company. The powers of the Company were as extensive as those of any company that ever existed.' The prorogation was delayed in order to complete the legislation required to give this ambitious corporation effectual crushing powers; and this was the only instance, we believe, of successfully mischievous legislation in the work of the session."

There is another question that I must touch upon briefly, and that is the treatment of the natives in the De Beers compound. Mr. Rhodes, at the Chartered Company's meeting, appealed to what he had done for the natives in the colony to show that the interests of the natives in Rhodesia might safely be confided to him. But in the report of the Select Committee from which I have already quoted, there are various passages which hardly seem to bear out his contention. Mr. Holt in his evidence said: "What I complain of is, that they call the Kaffir a thief, and they are doing all they can to get a premium on his theft, and induce him to become a blackguard." And again: "I thought, although the Company appeared anxious to make the natives sober, there did not seem to be the same anxiety to prevent their becoming thieves. For instance, the compound manager has got an under-manager, and this under-manager is supposed to be a man who buys diamonds unknown to his superior. He has got so many runners, and the stones are bought under the pretence that the Company really knows nothing about it, although the money is paid really on behalf of the Company. The natives believe they are selling to an individual who is carrying the diamonds out of the compound, and the man leads them to think he is buying stolen diamonds unknown to the Company." And Mr. Thomas W. Goodwin, who was mayor of Kimberley in 1890, said: "There is another thing that I complain of, and that is the Company buying stolen diamonds from the natives in the compounds. It simply manufactures thieves. The sub-manager is supplied with funds to buy stolen diamonds from the natives, which they have managed to secrete."

Mr. Barnato—"Is not the money given in the shape of a present?"

" No."

" Has not this system been carried out in every compound in existence, and not alone by De Beers Consolidated Mines?"

" I believe so."

" And was it not found to be the only system of preventing the stealing of diamonds?"

" Yes, but it shows what extreme action has to be taken by the Company in order to secure their property. It cannot be defended from a moral point of view."

I inquired when I was in Kimberley whether this system was still pursued, and was told it was.

Syndicates and amalgamations and companies are the worst feature of South African life; go where you will, no matter where, you will find a fertile crop of them. They destroy individual effort, and tend to crush out the small traders, who are the real backbone of a nation. I was told a story, which, though an amusing exaggeration, contains a good deal of point. Some Johannesburg millionaires were going down to Cape Town, and on their way they invaded the refreshment-room at one of the stations, and bought up the whole of the tea-urn.   A lady came in, and not knowing this, asked the waiter for a cup.   "Excuse me, miss," said one of the co-owners, "but that tea is syndicated." An effective parody of a real and increasing evil, which is springing up everywhere, but which in South Africa exists in an accentuated form.

At last, however, the Cape colonists are awakening from their lethargy; they are beginning to understand that the wealth of their country is passing away to other lands; to perceive their danger and to struggle against it; and in all probability they will shake themselves free if we in England do not interfere on behalf of their opponents.   We must let them put things straight in their own way—intervention will only do harm, as intervention by the Home Government has always done harm in South African affairs.   It is the one thing that colonists cannot stand.   I remarked to Mr. Merriman one day, that, in justice to the Transvaal, Mr. Rhodes ought to have been detained in England, and tried at the same time as Dr. Jameson; not for vindictive reasons, but because if he had been convicted it would have been impossible for the Queen to accept him at any future time as Prime Minister of the Cape Colony.

Mr. Merriman flared up at once.   "I don't agree with you at all," he said.   "I am a strong enough opponent of Mr. Rhodes, but if we choose to elect the devil himself we are not going to have you say we shall not." The answer was typical of colonial feeling all over the world.

· It is quite possible that if Mr. Rhodes had stood his trial in England, and had been convicted and imprisoned as Dr. Jameson was, it would have produced a reaction in his favour, even amongst the Dutch. As it is, they feel that he has not only been screened from justice, but that he is being forced upon them by the Home Government, and that puts them into opposition at once.[1]

[1] With the aims of the Progressive party in the Cape most Englishmen must be in cordial sympathy: the strengthening of the tie with the mother-country, a reduced duty on food stuffs, an extended franchise, and a juster treatment of the natives. But all through his political career Mr. Rhodes has upheld the directly opposed views the elimination of the Imperial factor, a heavy duty on food stuffs, a restricted franchise, and more drastic native legislation. In 1896 he voted with the Dutch majority for an increased duty on wheat, grain, and flour; Mr. Merriman and Mr. Sauer, who are now branded as anti-Progressives, voting with the Progressive minority. The party names in the present election are altogether misleading. The struggle is not so much between the Progressives and the Bond as between the Rhodites and the anti-Rhodites. That this is the case is proved by the adhesion of the natives to the Bond.

CHAPTER XXII

THE less England interferes with the self-governing colonies in South Africa the better; but with regard to Rhodesia the case is entirely different. Through Mr. Rhodes it was originally affiliated to the Cape, but it still belongs to England, and it is too valuable for her to allow it to pass into the hands of the monopolists without an effort.

Unfortunately the same system of company control has been established there as in Kimberley, and unless it is speedily checked the country will never become the home of a freedom-loving race such as dwells in our other colonies.

The element of speculation that permeates everything forms a vast difference between the Chartered Company and the old East India Company, with which it is so often compared. I will give an example of what I mean. When I was in Umtali there was a persistent rumour that Mr. Rhodes, who was then staying in the Inyanga mountains, was seriously ill. It sent Chartered shares down at once, and I met an excited man who had come in from some distance away to wire instructions to Johannesburg to sell his shares at once. "I bought as many as I could," he said, "in anticipation of the boom in Bulawayo when the railway reaches there, but if Rhodes should die they will drop to Heaven knows what, and I can't risk it."

In every way this speculative uncertainty exerts an unwholesome influence.

The worst feature, however, of the Company's rule is the immense, and indeed the almost absolute control it exercises over every one who settles in the country. Not only does the Company claim fifty per cent. of the vendor's scrip in all gold-mining flotations, but before granting a prospecting licence it enacts an undertaking which makes subsequent freedom of action impossible. When he takes out a licence, a prospector has to sign the following declaration: "I, A. B., having taken out a prospecting licence from the British South Africa Company, do hereby agree to comply with the laws and regulations of the Company, to assist in the defence of its territories, and in the maintenance of public order when called upon to do so, and to obey without question all the decisions and directions of the Company's officers, subject to the forfeiture of such licence, and of any rights accruing therefrom: and I moreover hereby acknowledge the right of the Company to remove me from the sphere of its operations if I resist such decisions or disobey such directions." Comment on this extraordinary undertaking is hardly necessary. It is perfectly plain and unambiguous, and if people like to enter into a compact of such a nature they cannot complain; but it is not the way in which a free state can be created.

Under this undertaking any one who disapproved of the first Matabili war, and declined to take part in it (and I know of several who disapproved of it most strongly), were liable to forfeiture of their claims, and even to removal from Rhodesia.

It is this feeling of servitude that chafes so many of the settlers, and makes them secretly long for the hour when England shall take over the administration into her own hands. There are many men, also, who think that, even from the material point of view, it will be for the advantage of the country that she should do so; but it is only fair to state the opinion at which Sir Alfred Milner has arrived. When he was in Rhodesia last autumn, he said: "He was no flatterer of the Chartered Company, nor prepared to say everything they did was right. There were pages in its history which they and he would gladly see obliterated; but as regarded the development of the country, and its general economic policy, he thought it had a very high and honourable record. He would venture to say even greater progress had been made than if the country had been a Crown colony, and as an imperial representative he was glad to acknowledge this."

But this progress has been made at the cost of a great sum taken out of English pockets, and so far it

has been a feverish progress that may yet prove to
be ephemeral. It is not the steady progress of the
country itself. With all deference to Sir Alfred
Milner's great authority, what I saw of Rhodesia has
led me rather to concur with Olive Schreiner's opinion.
"If the Chartered Company were in ten or fifteen
years' time, or much sooner, to explode, and as a
company to loosen its control over the land and
people, it would yet be found that the whole real
wealth of the country was appropriated, and in the
hands of a few private individuals, forming syndicates
and trusts. . . . So, again, with regard to land tenure;
while in all progressive countries there is a tendency
to obtain and retain as large a part as possible of land,
mines, and great public works, as the property of, and
to be worked for the benefit of, the nation as a whole,
we in this country are for ever and completely alienat-
ing our public lands, our minerals, our precious stones,
and even our public works."

The main factor in the welfare of a country,
especially of a young country, is, as Olive Schreiner
says, that land should be cheap and easily obtainable.
Now, in Rhodesia almost the whole of the land has
been parted with to subsidiary companies, so that it is
difficult to obtain farms of any real value from the
Chartered Company direct; and however necessary the
subsidiary companies may be for the development of
a country like the Mozambique Company's territory,
which is incapable of white colonisation on a large

scale, they are certainly detrimental to the free development of a colony properly so-called, as Rhodesia will in time become.

Most of these companies are holding on in expectation of a boom, and will not part with any portion of their property except at extravagant rates. This wholesale alienation of the land is due to the manner in which the country was originally acquired. In order to induce men to take part in the expedition against Lobengula, they were promised gold claims and grants of land, which have proved to be a millstone round the neck of the Company, especially in the case of Matabililand, where pioneer rights were given to a force of over 300 men, consisting of fifteen gold claims and a farm of 3000 morgen (6000 acres), the Company merely reserving to itself the right, if a farm should be declared to be on a gold-bearing area, to resume possession on the payment of £3 a morgen (£9000) and whatever had been expended on improvements.

These grants were not weighted with any clause for beneficial occupation, like the Mashonaland farms, but were absolute grants, except for the payment of a small quit-rent. The men to whom they were given being for the most part in want of funds, were glad to dispose of them for a small sum, and they were rapidly bought up by land syndicates, which were thus enabled to acquire enormous tracts of country, which they hold without any obligation whatever to develop. One company, I was informed, holds ninety-two farms—*i.e.*

552,000 acres—for which it pays a total quit-rent of £46 a year. Moreover, concessions have been given to various favoured individuals, which have given rise to much discussion.

How little nations profit by the lessons of the past! Sir George Cathcart, writing in 1852, says: "It is much to be regretted that a general rule for the sale of Crown lands in the British colonies should have been applied to the exposed borders of this colony, affording opportunities to speculators to purchase the more valuable portions, which are kept for the purpose of profit at convenient opportunities, to the manifest danger of the country. Had the system laid down on the 15th of May 1844 for the sale of Crown lands been pursued for six months longer, the whole of the district would have been in the hands of capitalists, and probably remained untenanted for many years, and the abandonment of that part of the frontier must have been the result, unless the Crown repurchased at a fixed value, and occupied it on the system now pursued. As an instance, I may mention that one person (not a farmer) owns fifteen or eighteen miles of river frontage, which has remained unoccupied since purchase, thus excluding twenty farms with probably fifty defenders of the border." Exactly the same process has been going on in Rhodesia.

Mr. Charles Fulbert Bere, who before he went to Rhodesia had been in New Zealand, said in his evidence before the Bulawayo Chamber of Commerce:

"In Australia and New Zealand, a man who lands there is entitled to settle on easy terms. . . . Here they have given too much land away, and have not held sufficient for new arrivals, and the Government have left them at the mercy of possible land-grabbers."

We are continually being assured that the majority of the settlers do not desire to be placed under Imperial control, and I believe that is perfectly true. A great number of them are in difficulties, and are indebted to Mr. Rhodes for assistance; and they naturally advocate the cause of the man who has befriended them, and do not trouble themselves about the deeper questions involved. But though they are in the minority, there are not a few men who are looking forward to the day when they can feel once more that they are citizens of no mean country, and not lessees at will of a chartered company.

Still Mr. Rhodes' donations are so ample, and often so genuinely kind, that he will never be in want of supporters, sometimes more enthusiastic than discreet. A man came to me one day in Gwelo, and said that he could give me a lot of information about the natives, as he had been in the country ever since it was acquired. I thanked him, and asked what his view of the native question was. "If you want it short," he said, "they've been a lot too well treated—that's about all of it." "That's interesting and comprehensive," I replied, "but can't you give me some details?" He did so, but after a bit burst out with, "I see you don't agree with me." "No," I said, "I don't." "Well," he went on, "it's all very well for you people in England to criticise us when you don't know anything about the matter. Of course, we don't want to interfere with Lord Salisbury. As long as he lives he will be the Premier, but when he dies, Cecil Rhodes is going to be the next Prime Minister, and he'll settle this native question, because he understands all about it." This man was only one of many who have the same exalted opinion of Mr. Rhodes. Major Hurrell told me a pretty story, which he was kind enough to say I might repeat, explaining the personal magnetism that Mr. Rhodes exercises. Miss Rhodes said to him one day at Groot Schuur, "What a pity my brother should have to leave so lovely a place. Do you think he will ever come back to it?" "No, I don't think he will," Major Hurrell replied; "at least, not for any length of time. I think he is going to make his home with us in Rhodesia for some years yet." "Ah, well," said Miss Rhodes, "he is making homes for the little ones in England."

The sincere emotion with which Major Hurrell spoke showed how it is that Mr. Rhodes has obtained his enormous power; that it is due to his personality as much as to his wealth. The same feeling exists even in the Republics. One of the best known of Free State Dutchmen, when discussing the Raid, said to me, "We don't think Rhodes was influenced

U

by what are generally called sordid motives, but by
ambition. We were once close friends, and though
there is no hope that we shall ever be friends again
—the harm he has done is too great for that—we
do not impute to him unworthy motives in what he
did; not money motives." That a strong feeling of
personal regard for Mr. Rhodes exists all over South
Africa, and especially in Rhodesia, is undoubted. It
found a truer and more sincere utterance in the
address presented to Sir Alfred Milner by the people
of Umtali than in the speeches made at the railway
opening at Bulawayo. "We desire," they said, "to
call your excellency's attention to the fact that the
man whose conception the occupation of this vast territory was, and who led us successfully through years
of doubt and danger to a continually increasing prosperity, no longer holds any official position in its
government, and to assure your excellency of the
determination of the people of this country to stand
firmly by Mr. Rhodes, who has stood by us so well in
the dark days which are now happily passing away."

However opposed one may be to them in opinion,
one cannot but respect this feeling of the Umtali
people. Mr. Rhodes' indifference to hardships and
danger, his careless exposure of himself during the
rebellion, the reckless grandeur of his views, and the
expenditure of his private fortune in furtherance of
them, have won the fullest recognition even from those
who are most opposed to his methods. Nevertheless

the English Government ought not to take this feeling into account when dealing with the question of the revocation of the charter. What they have to consider are the broad principles of right and wrong; whether they have, or have not, been persistently violated? That is the question with which they have to deal, and no ebullition of sentiment should be permitted to obscure it.

The objection of the colonists to a Crown colony is reasonable enough. A governor, to all intents and purposes, would be as much of an autocrat as the directors of the Chartered Company; the people would be no better off, and would have no facilities for obtaining laws suitable for their special requirements. A Crown colony pure and simple is never developed as rapidly as a colony under responsible government, for the advice of the governor in all matters apparently trivial, but often of vital consequence to the comfort and advancement of the people, is almost invariably followed in Downing Street; whereas where there is a responsible government, self-interest prompts a rapidity of development to which a governor is not unfrequently utterly indifferent. Nevertheless, self-government is as yet out of the question; it would merely mean the handing over again of the country to Mr. Rhodes, and to the party he controls, and placing them in a far stronger position than before by giving to them the power of legislation; in the position, in fact, which up till now they have occupied in the Cape Colony. In a young State, where public opinion has not yet acquired strength, no form of government is so dangerous to liberty as that by responsible government. Sir Thomas More foresaw this clearly. "Therefore I must say, as I hope for mercy, I can have no other notion of all the other governments that I see or know than that they are a conspiracy of the rich, who, on the pretence of managing the public, only pursue their private ends and devise all the ways and means they can find out, first that they may, without danger, preserve all that they have so ill acquired, and then that they may engage the poor to toil and labour for them at as low rates as possible, and oppress them as much as they please. And if they can but prevail to get these contrivances established by the show of public authority, which is considered as the representative of the whole people, then they are accounted laws." What is wanted is not a Crown colony administered by a governor, but a colony like Natal until 1894, under a governor and a council, which shall be partly elective, and shall serve as a stepping-stone to complete self-government. But, as Mr. Orpen has wisely said, " If England prefers to rule directly let it do so deliberately and for ever, and not vacillate and starve or throw away Rhodesia as it did in other cases, notably Zululand." For every reason it is desirable to put an end to the present state of uncertainty, which is the cause of much discouragement and depression.

CHAPTER XXIII

PRESIDENT KRUGER has made a fatal mistake in not
continuing to act with the moderation he showed after
Dr. Jameson's surrender; a moderation which elicited
from Mr. Balfour the comment that he had shown
himself to possess . a generosity not the less to be
admired because coincident with the highest political
wisdom.   The severe measures adopted against the Reform prisoners; the importation of Judge Gregorowski
from the Free State; the vindictive recourse to the
obsolete Roman-Dutch law of treason, instead of to the
milder law of 1887; the harsh sentence of expulsion
against Mr. Lionel Phillips for a doubtful, and, at the
most, a trivial breach of his undertaking not to inter-
meddle in Transvaal politics; the absurd and odious
secrecy law; the refusal to grant the necessary economic reforms; the interference with the administration
of justice, and the treatment of Chief-Justice Kotze,
have produced the most unfavourable impression, not
only in England, but all over Europe.   These things,

and the corruption that is everywhere apparent, are ruining the prosperity of the country, and are causing so dangerous an irritation, that, if persisted in, nothing can prevent a revolution ; in which case it will be impossible to prevent assistance being given to the Uitlanders by their kinsmen in the English colonies. Such a revolution seems to be rapidly approaching, and if it is to be kept from assuming the aspect of a civil war, the English Government must put themselves right in the eyes of their Dutch subjects.   They must make them believe that any action they may have to take is not taken with the object of annexing the vast wealth of the Transvaal, but to restore harmony and peace to South Africa.   If they can bring about that belief they will insure their co-operation, and with their aid will be able to procure better government for Johannesburg by peaceable means ; but should they fail to do so, the first hostile step they take will produce an intense race agitation, which it will be impossible for them to control.

Mr. Hofmeyr, who is better qualified than any one else to speak on the matter, though he has asserted again and again the sincere if undemonstrative loyalty of those of his countrymen who are living under British rule, has no doubt as to what would occur in such a contingency. "Remember," he said not long ago, " those across the Vaal River are our kinsmen.   We are all related : all members of one great family.   Do not make any mistake.   The Vaal River and the Orange River are mere geographical expressions. There is a vast Dutch population from the farthest north of the Transvaal down to Cape Town. Over two-thirds of Cape Colony are Dutch, and of course we shall stand by one another in any event which threatens the independence which our brothers have fought for and won. Blood is thicker than water; their independence was secured by the blood of our common ancestors. Depend upon it, if once the spark of war is kindled, it will not stop where it begins. There will be a general conflagration from north to south. It will be absolutely impossible to restrain the Dutch. . . . You have not merely got to reckon with the small South African Republic in the case of war, but with all South Africa. Of course England would win in the end, but the struggle would be prolonged and bloody. The country would be desolated."

Not only would the Dutch be against us, unless we had placed our motives beyond suspicion, but not a few of British birth also.

Nor would the war be the easy matter some of the English papers seem to think. They are continually asserting that the Boers, now that the game has been destroyed, have lost their manhood and have forgotten how to shoot, but I heard from men who knew them well, that on the contrary they shoot better than ever. The same stories were rife at the time of the annexation. Anthony Trollope, writing in 1878, says: "The Boers are at present much abused for cowardice, and

stories without end are current in the country as to
the manner in which they have allowed themselves to
be scared by the slightest opposition. I fear that of
late there has been some truth in these stories, and
that the pluck shown by them when they made good
their hold upon the country has been greatly dimmed
by the quiet, uneventful tenor of their lives." Yet
within two years after this was written they had won
from us their independence.

The Boers do not care for fighting for the sake of
fighting. They have no professional-soldier element
amongst them as we have in England, and would
always rather avoid a conflict if possible, but if they
feel that their freedom or their land is threatened
they will fight to the death. President Steyn said to
me, "We don't want to fight, but you have taken the
Hinterland away from us. We have nowhere left now
to which we can trek, so if you attack us, we must die
where we stand." President Kruger has said much
the same thing. "If I see a lion," he once remarked—
"and the British Government is a lion—I try to get
out of his way; but if he attacks me, I will defend
myself though I have only a penknife in my hand,
and by the grace of God I will prevail." It is the
old Puritan spirit which will come to their aid as it
did before, if they feel they have God on their side;
if they do not, it will fail them just as it failed them
in the war against Secocoeni.

That England could subdue the Transvaal if she

chose is too apparent to be questioned. What she has to think of is whether her cause is just. Now the thing that above all others irritates the Transvaal Government is the claim to suzerainty, which Mr. Chamberlain has so persistently advanced. Does it really exist? and if so, does it exist in the form that he has claimed for it?

It is not, I think, generally recognised in England how strong a vein of national sentiment there is in the Boer character, or how galled they have been as a people by his assumption that the Transvaal is, in fact, a vassal State—an assumption which is generally accepted unquestioningly in England, in spite of the publicly expressed opinion of the Chief-Justices, both of the Transvaal and of the Orange Free State, that the suzerainty which was created by the Convention of 1881 no longer exists, having been expressly abrogated by the Convention of 1884.

The correspondence which took place at the time between the Transvaal Government and the Colonial Office has a most important bearing upon the contention of the Chief-Justices.

Lord Derby had requested the members of the Transvaal Deputation (S. J. P. Kruger, S. J. Du Toit, and N. J. Smit) to place before him in writing the objections they entertained to the existing Convention of 1881, and in their reply, dated 14th November 1883, this passage occurs:—

"(1) That the Pretoria Convention may not be

altered in some of its articles, but be replaced by a new agreement founded on the principles of International Law, and in genetical connection with the Sand River Treaty.

"(2) That in this new agreement every connection by which we are now bound to England should not be broken, but the relation of a dependency, *publici juris*, in which our country now stands to the British Crown, may be replaced by that of two contracting Powers."

Then they go on to say that there is "no objection to any later arrangements of commercial and other interests with her Majesty's Government, either in the Convention which may be arrived at now, or by a separate treaty." Acknowledging, however, the reasonableness of a distinct understanding upon a point too important to allow of any misunderstanding hereafter, the Deputation wish to explain that, admitting the proposed basis, there is no reason why the Government of the South African Republic should not stand in a friendly relation to her Majesty's Government, and why all points of common interest should not be arranged in a friendly manner, *as, for instance, mutual protection of commercial interests, a common native policy, and the like.* (The italics throughout are mine.)

"The Deputation would even go further, and declare what has already been repeatedly and openly declared by the Government and people of the South African Republic, that on their part there is no objection to give their favourable consideration to any scheme of confederation between the Colonies and States of South Africa, emanating from her Majesty's Government, and wherein the interests of the Imperial Government are duly recognised, *even in so far as a British Protectorate* might hereafter be required against any attempt on the part of transmarine Powers to take possession of South Africa by force of arms." (Nov. 23rd.)

This fully bears out the likelihood, that if the present vague and unsatisfactory Convention could be torn up and replaced by a definite and unambiguous treaty of amity and commerce, the Transvaal Government would not only be willing to give very extensive concessions to the Uitlander population, but would probably also join the South African Customs Union, and co-operate in any reasonable scheme of South African Confederation. President Kruger's proposal in 1883 comprised, in fact, all for which Mr. Rhodes and the progressive party say that they are now working.

In yet another letter, dated 5th February 1884, the Deputation say : " Would it not be possible to have the other articles of the new Convention—namely, those referring to the *abolition of the suzerainty*, and to the reduction to its legal proportions of the debt of the Republic, simultaneously drawn up and communicated to us." And Sir Hercules Robinson wrote on Nov. 23rd, 1883 : " If the suzerainty be *abolished*, I do not see that it matters the least whether the Transvaal burghers call themselves the South African Republic or the Transvaal State."

If these letters be read in conjunction with the fact that the word " suzerainty," which was contained in the Convention of 1881, is altogether omitted in that of 1884, is it not evident that it was omitted intentionally, because the understanding was that it should be, as the deputation say, abolished ? Lord Derby's final letter, dated 15th February 1884, confirms this view of the matter. " By the omission," he says, " of those articles of the Convention of Pretoria which assigned to her Majesty and to the British resident certain specific powers and functions connected with the internal government and the foreign relations of the Transvaal State, your Government will be left free to govern the country without interference, and to conduct its diplomatic intercourse and shape its foreign policy, subject only to the requirement embodied in the fourth article of the new draft, that any treaty with a foreign State shall not have effect without the approval of the Queen."

Mr. Chamberlain has all this correspondence before him, and it is difficult to understand how, in face of it, he can assume that the Transvaal is a vassal State. Why, the whole object of the Convention of 1884 was, as the Deputation said, to do away with the relation of a dependency, *publici juris*, in which the country then stood to the British Crown, and to replace it by that of two contracting Powers, with a restrictive clause, as against one of them, embodied in the contract.

His assertion is directly negatived by the historical

evidence as well as by the Convention itself, and the manner in which it has been made has aroused a very natural feeling of irritation. The one thing the Boers dislike is to be talked to in a superior and patronising fashion. A blunt man who treats them as equals they like, and they will not resent it even if he speaks to them in the most plain and unequivocal way; but it always angers them to be spoken to as though from another platform. The more one sees of them, the more convinced one becomes of the influence in their politics of the personal element.

The controversy has really resolved itself into a wrangle over words. The Boers are quite willing to acknowledge a suzerainty in its generally accepted sense of *paramountcy*. President Kruger said, " I accept suzerainty as explained by the general word; the definition being: suzerainty means, that the country has entire control as regards its own interior affairs, but that it cannot take action against or with an outside Power without the permission of the suzerain." But they object, and with reason, to its being construed into vassalage.

The attitude of the Transvaal Government in regard to the matter is a perfectly reasonable one. President Kruger, in his despatch dated March 1, 1896, claims: " First, withdrawal of London Convention of 1884, because in several respects it has virtually ceased to exist; because in other respects it has no more cause for existence; because it is injurious to the dignity of an independent republic; because the continual arguments on the question of suzerainty, which since the conclusion of London Convention of 1884 no longer exists, are used as a pretext—especially by a libellous Press—for inciting white and black against the Republic, and for bringing about misunderstanding between England and the South African Republic. In the discussion of the withdrawal of the London Convention of 1884, Article 4 should naturally not be kept back. He believes the British Government has decided to make no alteration in this article on false representation that the Government of South African Republic have sought the protection of other Powers. He says that there is nothing further from his thoughts than the protection of any foreign Power, which he will never seek. Neither he nor his people will tolerate an interference with their internal relations from any Power whatever, and he is willing to give the necessary assurances for this in order that her Majesty's Government need have no fear that her Majesty's interests in South Africa will be injured. Secondly, the substitution should be discussed of any treaties of peace, friendship, and commerce in lieu of London Convention of 1884 by which the existing privileges of England in the dominion of commerce and intercourse, and the interests of British subjects in the South African Republic, will be guaranteed on the footing of the most favoured nation, and herein he would be prepared to go to the utmost of what can reasonably be asked."

But though the Boers maintain that no suzerainty exists, there is reason to believe that they would be willing to acknowledge it if they were given a substantial return. The *Pretoria Press*—the Government official organ—on the 3rd February 1896 contained a proposal for the settlement of the existing difficulties, in which it was stated that the Transvaal Government would be willing to recognise the suzerainty to the fullest extent, provided that Great Britain gave it greater concrete effect by guaranteeing the permanent independence of the Transvaal against all comers, and the maintenance of Delagoa Bay as a neutral port; and it explained that by the latter proposal they did not mean that the Transvaal should have any control either of the port or the railway.

These alternatives are surely reasonable enough. Either conclude a definite treaty of amity and commerce as between independent contracting powers, or let there be an acknowledged suzerainty with the corresponding obligation of protection, and maintenance of the existing form of government.

The Boers are not actuated by hatred to England, but by fear for their independence: if that could be guaranteed they would be quite content, but at present they feel that it is insidiously threatened, and that the suzerainty is only used as a cover for an interference that shall ultimately lead to annexation.

Can they be blamed for thinking this, when they see the man who deliberately conspired against their

Government, and who makes no concealment even now of his hostility to it, protected from punishment, and assisted and applauded in every way by the English Government, and in a great measure by the English people. It is a truly regretable thing that Sir Alfred Milner's tour should have been utilised for a series of election speeches by English officials and members of Parliament on behalf of Mr. Rhodes. It at once drew forth vehement protests, not only from the Transvaal, but from Mr. Hofmeyr and from President Steyn; it has had the effect of crystallising the relative positions of the English and the Dutch, and has changed what ought to have been a purely local conflict into a national struggle. These speeches caused much anger in Dutch circles, an anger intelligible enough when the matter is regarded from the Dutch point of view. When one thinks of the terrible mischief caused by the Raid, and recollects that up to the present moment no attempt has been made to pay the indemnity; when one calls to mind that almost directly after these speeches were made an English member of Parliament told a Durban audience that the Transvaal was the only obstacle in South Africa to English progress, it is not difficult to understand that the Boers should believe that the British Government is an enemy against whom they must always be on their guard.

Mr. Chamberlain, who has a singularly clear perception of the right thing to do, has told us that "The question between Mr. Hofmeyr or President

Kruger, on the one side, and the personality of Mr. Rhodes on the other, is one of tremendous interest in South Africa, and we ought as far as possible to avoid showing any partisanship in these matters." Unfortunately that is precisely what we have not done. The Dutch all over Africa believe that England is trying to crush them out as a nation, and that belief naturally binds them together; for though the colonial Dutch are satisfied with our rule, they cannot help having a sympathy with their kinsmen in the Transvaal, and in the Orange Free State. In times of ferment, the tie of blood will always prove stronger than the artificial tie of political allegiance, and the art of governing a colony of mixed nationality consists in giving as few occasions as possible for the awakening of this latent feeling of brotherhood in the subject people with their free kinsmen outside the colonial border. As Mr. Merriman said in 1881, " Every shot fired in the Transvaal finds an echo in the Colony."

Unhappily it will take years for the existing state of tension to pass away; it is lamentable that it should ever have been evoked. I was told by one of the Free State burghers that he never went to bed without a rifle and a hundred cartridges by his side, to be ready to rise in a moment to repel invasion. He did this, he said, because the English troops had been sent to Ladysmith—a matter that President Steyn deemed so serious that he telegraphed to Sir Alfred Milner to ask what it meant, and was told in reply that it was merely for purposes of defence. This sounds ironical, but it really was not so, but only a plain statement of fact, for a general feeling of uneasiness prevailed at that time amongst the English both in Natal and in the eastern province. At King Williamstown I was told that they had welcomed the troops most thankfully. Before they came the town was quite defenceless, and the people feared that at any moment they might be raided from the Free State, or from Burghersdorp. In Natal the feeling was much the same. I met an old Scotchman there, who said that he and many others, like the Free State burgher, had his rifle and cartridges always at hand, and that they were longing to use them. "Do you think," he broke out indignantly, "that we are going to allow our fellow-countrymen in the Transvaal to be governed any longer by a handful of Boers?"

The necessity of holding people like these in control was in itself a justification for the sending out of the additional troops. Their presence did much to check the fiery spirits on both sides, and to prevent the collision which might at any time have occurred upon the borders of the Colony or of Natal.

It is much to be regretted that the struggle should have been degraded into a conflict of words, and that so free a use should have been made on both sides of vilification and abuse. President Kruger, even in the opinion of many of his own countrymen, has allowed his country to fall into a state of terrible misgovernment, but he is nevertheless one of the greatest and most heroic figures of the age, and the personal insults to which he has been subjected in the Press both in South Africa and in England make most unprejudiced Englishmen ashamed. The continual endeavours to distort harmless expressions into intentional disrespect to the Queen are contemptible and unworthy. He has always had the deepest respect for the Queen. He said emphatically one day to Mr. W. Y. Campbell, who has kindly given me permission to repeat his words: "The Queen is a good woman, a true Christian woman, and I have the Queen deep in the foundation of my heart." Mr. Campbell is the most strenuous and open opponent of President Kruger's oligarchical methods, but he places little blame upon President Kruger personally, believing that his errors in government are the creation of the English Colonial Office. It is an opinion largely held in Johannesburg. And the feeling against the great capitalists is equally strong. It is not they who deserve our sympathy. Most of them are birds of passage, and the industrial burdens, which are crushing out the poorer mines, are gradually throwing the whole wealth of the country into their hands. It is upon the working population—Afrikanders for the most part, born of the soil, yet treated as political helots—that President Kruger is inflicting such real and unnecessary suffering.

CHAPTER XXIV

Everywhere I went I found signs of the harm done by the Raid, and still more by the embittered wranglings that have followed it. Johannesburg is virtually the heart of South Africa. When she prospers all South Africa prospers with her, and when she suffers South Africa suffers likewise. In the Free State the earnings of the railways have diminished by a third; so, too, have those of the Natal and Delagoa lines. In June 1897, owing probably to the persistent rumours of war, the decrease of revenue on the Natal line was £20,019—a startling reduction. What so many men said to me seems pretty near the truth. We keep on disputing about our suzerainty, instead of trying to convince the Dutch that we intend to act fairly by them; and the result is that trade in Johannesburg is going steadily from bad to worse, and that trade in the Colony and Natal is following suit. Let it be admitted that there have been great faults on the

Transvaal side, suspicion has begotten unfriendliness; but the continual assertion of our suzerainty is hardly the best way to allay it, for suzerainty after all is a phrase which has no force unless it be used as the Dutch believe it to be used—as a menace. I heard it laid down in Johannesburg by a prominent Uitlander that the President of the Transvaal is but the servant of the Queen; that she has merely delegated her authority to him. It is too foolish an assertion to combat seriously, but it produces continual friction and anger.

It may be asked what all this has to do with Rhodesia and its Government. The bearing is very material, for the Chartered Company is the greatest stumbling-block in the way of a better understanding being arrived at with the Republics, both of whom look upon its continued existence as a threat to themselves, and as a danger to peace.

Only a month or two ago both the Republics declined absolutely to enter into an extradition treaty with Rhodesia; a measure that is urgently required. The Orange Free State had, on the 6th August 1895, actually concluded such a treaty with the B.S.A. Company, but after the Jameson Raid they withdrew from it. Yet, in the face of hostile actions such as these, Mr. Chamberlain felt himself justified in asserting that "if the majority of the people in South Africa are in favour of Mr. Rhodes, the whole of South Africa is in favour of the continuance of the Chartered Company as a company, until such time as Rhodesia can be made an independent and self-governing state." From this *whole* of South Africa the Dutch, a by no means inconsiderable element, must be altogether excluded, for there is every reason to believe that in this matter the colonial Dutch are of one mind with their Republican kinsfolk. They dislike the Chartered Company, but still more they fear it; the fear is unreasoning, perhaps, but it exists.

Nor can it be said to be altogether without cause. The hostility of the Chartered Company to the Transvaal is no new thing, and the Jameson Raid was but the climax to a series of unfriendly acts. I came upon an article in the *Financial Record* of Johannesburg, dated October 14, 1893, which is prophetic when read in the light of subsequent events: "But if within the space of twelve months from now, Mashonaland is filling up and is a prosperous colony free from the shadow of the black terror in perpetuity, it is legitimate to expect that Mr. Rhodes will look about him to discover, where next, like Jacob, it is his mission to wrestle with God; and that his eye will alight on his chosen servant Paul Kruger for the exercise of his giant strength. There are those who believe that Mr. Rhodes has only postponed a reckoning with the President of this Republic until Mashonaland no longer requires his energies, and when these two strong men at last stand face to face, the shock will be felt over the entire continent."

Can we wonder that one of the first things President Kruger asked for after the Raid was the revocation of the charter, "which, if it does not take place," says the despatch, " will continue a threatening danger to the peace of South African Republic, and thereby also to the whole of South Africa." And on the 13th January 1896 the following letter was sent to the High Commissioner from the acting State President of the Orange Free State: " I have been requested by the Volksraad to acquaint your Excellency with the following resolution: ' Volksraad desires to request the executive to enter into correspondence with his Excellency the High Commissioner, and to call his Excellency's attention to the fact that in the view of the Volksraad, the existence of governments, such as that of the British South Africa Company's, has proved to be, and will in the future continue to be, a great and threatening danger to the peace of the whole of South Africa; and that the Volksraad is of opinion that the peace and mutual confidence which should exist between the State and colonies, and which has now been so severely shaken, have little chance of being removed and preserved before that the charter of the said company is cancelled, and the Imperial Government, or that of the Cape Colony, shall take the direct responsibility of the government of the countries at present under the ruling of the British South Africa Company : further, that the Executive shall in the meantime endeavour to obtain a guarantee from the Imperial Government that the peace of South Africa will not again be disturbed from these quarters. Will your Excellency be kind enough to transmit the above to the Secretary of State for the Colonies?" This letter shows that the Republics were acting in agreement then, and there is nothing to indicate that they have changed their attitude since.

To continue the charter may be in the interests of certain great financial groups, but it will certainly prolong the strife that is doing so much harm, and will thereby cause more permanent injury to our empire than any temporary check that might be caused to the commercial development of Rhodesia by its conversion into a Crown colony. Nor is it by any means certain that such a check would result. There has been so much uncertainty about Rhodesia, so much heated discussion about the treatment of the natives and of the settlers, that many people have been deterred from going there who would go if they knew they would still be under British rule.

Now what are the provisions in the charter regarding revocation? It is worth while to look. The preamble is as follows:—

"That the petitioners believe that if the said concessions, agreements, grants, and treaties can be carried into effect, the condition of the natives inhabiting the said territories will be materially improved, and their civilisation advanced, and an organisation established which will lead to the suppression of the slave trade in the said territories, and to the opening up of the said territories to the immigration of Europeans, and to the lawful trade and commerce of our subjects, and of the natives.".

And Clause 35 runs thus: " And we do hereby lastly will, ordain, and declare, without prejudice to any power to repeal this our charter by law belonging to us, our heirs and successors, or to any of our court's ministers or officers, independently of this present declaration and reservation, that in case at any time it is made to appear to us in our Council that the Company has substantially failed to observe and conform to the provisions of this our charter ; or that the Company is not exercising its powers under the concessions and agreements, grants and treaties aforesaid, so as to advance the interests which the petitioners have represented to us to be likely to be advanced by the grant of this our charter, it shall be lawful for us, our heirs and successors, and we do hereby reserve and take to ourselves, our heirs and successors, the right and power by writing under the Great Seal of our United Kingdom to revoke this our charter, and to revoke and annul the privileges, powers, and rights hereby granted to the Company."

Whether the Company has substantially failed to observe and conform to the provisions of the charter is a matter of opinion. Personally, I think it has ; that it has not materially improved the condition of the natives inhabiting the said territories, but so far has considerably worsened it.

Moreover, they have broken a vital clause in the agreement entered into by them with the British Government after the first Matabili war, that "the armed forces of the Company shall not, without the permission of H.M. Government, act outside the limits defined in Clause 1 of the Memorandum."

Not so much to the Dutch as to ourselves is it due, therefore, that the charter should be revoked. That of the East India Company was taken away for less grave cause. Mr. Chamberlain's half measures will only lead to discontent: they will not satisfy the Dutch, who desire to deal with the British Government direct, and not with the Chartered Company, and they will assuredly be productive of trouble in Rhodesia itself. A dual control is not a good thing for any country; and if the High Commissioner should exercise an independent judgment, he is bound to come into conflict with the Company's officials on many questions. Indeed, he has done so already upon that of the exclusion of Hindu traders.

The *Bulawayo Chronicle* on the 2nd June of this year observed in the course of a leading article:—

"Further, the Government has been run as a triplicate entity—the Chartered Company, the High Commissioner, and the Secretary of State for the Colonies, not counting the Board of Directors, whose ideas often run counter to those of their administrator. Such a combination could not harmonise, and the wonder is that more blunders have not been made."

It is only fair to say that the article begins with the assertion that the Company's rule, faulty as it is, is nevertheless preferable to that of the Crown. "We may as well premise that we prefer the Chartered Company's government to that of direct Imperial control, as we believe that the former is more elastic, and therefore more suited to the requirements of a growing population. We can bend the sapling to our needs, but we cannot turn the rooted oaks of the Imperial system one way or the other." Later on, however, we find the explanation for the preference in this sentence: "Our native legislation is confined and cramped by Exeter Hall, through the Secretary of State for the Colonies."

If a dual or triplicate control is bad for the settlers, it is infinitely worse for the natives. This is what Mr. Carnegie says on that subject: "Ever since the late king's death the natives have been, as they say, 'longing for a fire at which to warm themselves'; in other words, they wanted a king, with whom they could be more in touch than they found themselves with the white Government. One abortive attempt was made to accomplish this, but failed. Later on the Government suggested appointing a native who should be the intermediary between the natives and the Government, but their nominee was unacceptable to the natives. Another and last attempt was made by the natives when this outbreak began. Thus, during all the last year, the natives were asking for some one to represent them to the Government—not that they were then wishing to rebel, but they wanted some one in whom they could trust, and who understood them, their ways, laws, and customs. As it was, first one man came, who told them he was their 'inkosi' (king); then another came with the same story; to-day they had one king, to-morrow he left and they had another. Sometimes there would be two or more claiming the same title over the same people. Between them it was not astonishing the native mind, accustomed to only one king, became somewhat confused as to who was their master, and how far each one's authority extended."

The man they now turn to is Mr. Rhodes. They see that the white men lean upon him, and obey him more readily than they will any one else; and he has a kindly way of talking to them in the homely parables that they themselves use, which brings them near to him. His attitude to the labour question, and his methods of annexation prove that he is in reality the most dangerous foe the native races have (Tengu Jabavu's adherence to the Bond shows that in the Cape they have discovered this), but in many ways he is exceedingly kind to them. After the rebellion, he spent £50,000 out of his own pocket in buying seed grain for the starving people. But his ambiguous position must be a perpetual bewilderment to them.

The natives are now our fellow-subjects as much as

our own kinsfolk who have settled in Rhodesia, and we are bound to see that justice is done to them as well as to the settlers. For that reason, if for no other, it would be infinitely better to convert the country at once into a Crown colony, with a Governor and Council, appointed partly by the Crown and partly elected by the people. They would certainly elect Mr. Rhodes as one of their representatives; and there need be no hardship to the Chartered Company's shareholders. The land, or so much of it as they have not already alienated, would still belong to them, and their half share in the minerals. They would be deprived of the revenue, but they would also be relieved of the cost of administration. According to the recently published report of the Chartered Company, it only comes to £380,000 a year, and the country is well worth the sacrifice. In years to come it will repay us for what we may expend over and over again, as an outlet for our population. More than that, it would be the first step towards the restoration of harmony in South Africa; it would make the Dutch feel that we do not shrink from our responsibilities; that we intend to enforce peace and good government in our own territories, but that we expect to see it enforced also in the Transvaal. We have no hesitation in compelling the people of India to pay £120,000 a year merely in maintaining the road to Chitral, or in spending £800,000 ourselves, wisely enough, on an Egyptian campaign: ought we, then, to hesitate about expending this £380,000 a year for what concerns us far more nearly?

It will come back to us, in time, in revenue; and it will yield us a yet richer return in honour.

The late Earl Grey, who from his position had an intimate knowledge of South African affairs, and who pondered deeply over them, used words so far back as 1880 which have acquired renewed weight from all that has since happened. "I have only to express my firm conviction," he wrote, "that if her Majesty's Ministers are not prepared to allow the present state of things in South Africa to continue, there are really but two courses open to them. The one would be to insist that increased authority should be placed in the hands of the Queen, in order that this part of her dominions may be firmly and impartially governed for the welfare of all classes of the population. The other would be to order the British flag to be struck, to bring home the Governor and her Majesty's troops from South Africa, and to inform its inhabitants that they must no longer consider themselves to be subjects of the Queen, or look to her for protection or assistance in settling their quarrels among themselves, and in managing their own affairs as may seem best to them. Between these two courses I am persuaded that it will be impossible to find any middle one that can long be adhered to. Of these, for the reasons I have given, I believe the first clearly to be the right one; the other I regard as altogether unworthy of a great Christian nation. Let us not disguise from ourselves that, by following it, we should give over for long years to anarchy and bloodshed what is now no inconsiderable part of the British Empire, unless, indeed, some other powerful and civilised nation should step in and assume the duty we had repudiated. We should also throw away a glorious opportunity of spreading Christianity and civilisation through a great part of the African continent. *And all this we should do from a mere selfish desire to escape an expense which, by wise measures, might be reduced to a mere trifle as compared to our resources.* By so acting the great British nation would be justly lowered in the estimation of mankind, and, what is infinitely worse, would, as I believe, become guilty of a grievous sin in the eyes of God." (*Nineteenth Century.*)

The one thing needful above all others for a young country is an upright and capable administration, and to obtain that not only money is necessary but status. Officials of a chartered company cannot feel the same pride in their work or in their position, cannot have the same high sense of responsibility that they would have if they were servants of the Crown. To establish such an administration would be a costly matter, but apart from all questions of obligation, the country is well worth the initial outlay.

But to take over and pay for the administration until it can pay for itself is a very different matter to the proposals of Mr. Rhodes and of the present Earl Grey, which have nowhere excited more hostile comment than in Rhodesia itself. The *Bulawayo Chronicle*, in the same article from which I have already quoted, strikes the following defiant note: "There is no gainsaying the fact that in future the aspirations of the settlers and the desires of the Chartered shareholders will not be the same, and a big choice will shortly have to be made by Mr. Rhodes; either he will have to be Rhodesian to the core, or he will have to be the managing director pure and simple. He has marvellous powers, we admit, but we do not perceive any method by which he can make the two lines of conduct agree. Without cause or warning we are informed that the expenses incurred in connection with this country are to be made a national debt on the country, that the price of self-government is to be, according to Mr. Rhodes, six millions, according to Earl Grey, ten millions. Half these expenses were incurred by the Chartered Company's servants, and were detrimental to the country, and since a master is responsible for the acts of his employee, the Chartered Company is distinctly responsible for the acts of Dr. Jameson. Without due notice we are threatened with a heavy customs tariff—a tariff not made in the interests of Rhodesia, but formed for the protection and benefit of another State. We do not expect to be free of taxation for ever and a day, but we do claim the Britisher's inherent right to be consulted before he is taxed."

There is a determined ring in this that makes one feel that if Rhodesia is turned into a Crown colony it will not be long before, like Natal, she will demand and obtain self-government.

Turn Rhodesia into a Crown colony: tear up the Convention of 1884; enter into a treaty of amity and commerce with the Transvaal in which, instead of the shadowy and fiercely disputed suzerainty over a vassal state, it shall be expressly provided, as President Kruger has himself suggested, that there shall be a confederation of the South African States under the protectorate of Great Britain—that is the net result of the views I heard expressed by the majority of those whom I met, who do not look upon South Africa as a battle-field for party politics, but to whom it is dear as the land of their birth, the land that they and their fathers have reclaimed from barbarism.

Only whatever we do let us do it with a free hand, and not half-heartedly. The tocsin of Imperial interests which has been clanged so assiduously during the last two years, has come in South Africa to mean the predominance of purely English interests, as opposed to those of the Dutch, who form three-fourths of our South African subjects. It has alienated them from us, and to regain their confidence we must make them understand that we do not regard their country merely as a source of dividends, or as a relief for our surplus population, but that we desire with their help to build up a great Afrikander nation, born of us indeed, but knit to us by ties of gratitude as well as of natural affection; that we do not desire to crush out their national sentiment, but rather to foster it until it gradually changes into a wider sentiment which shall embrace all the elements that constitute South Africa; that, in short, we do not look upon the Afrikander Bond as a traitorous organisation, but that we are in cordial sympathy with the object for which it was founded, as defined in its general constitution, that is to say, "the formation of a South African Nationality by means of union, and co-operation, as a preparation for the ultimate object,—a United South Africa."

That surely would be a more Imperial result than the forcible setting up of one race above another. But to carry it into effect neither Great Britain nor the Transvaal must allow any sentiment of national vanity to hinder the redress of an admitted wrong. They must remember that it is only right that makes might.

It is because Mr. Rhodes has habitually scoffed at and disregarded this fundamental principle that, in spite of his commanding genius, his lofty ambition, he has inflicted upon England such great and lasting injury. He has widened her territories, but he has immeasurably lessened the moral force which she has been wont to regard as her proudest attribute. The Raid is but a passing episode, and the effect produced by it will pass away, but when Mr. Rhodes' career comes under dispassionate review, this lowering of the moral temperature, not only of South Africa but of the whole empire, will assuredly be deemed the gravest of his faults.

But however fully we may recognise this, we must not let it blind us to the equally grave faults of the Transvaal Government, or to its deliberate and continued breaches of faith to the Uitlanders.

On August 8, 1881, when the Boers took over the administration of the country, they issued the following proclamation: "To all the inhabitants without exception we promise the protection of the law, and all the privileges attendant thereon.   To inhabitants who are not burghers, and do not wish to become such, we notify that they have the right to report themselves to the President as British subjects, according to Article 28 of the now settled Convention.   But be it known to all, that all ordinary rights of property, trade, and usage, will still be accorded to every one, burgher or not.   We repeat solemnly that our motto is 'Unity and Reconciliation.'"

How have they kept to the spirit of this proclamation?   In 1882 Mr. Kruger was elected President, and in the Volksraad session of the same year the first of the measures of exclusion was passed.   The franchise, which up till then—in accordance with Law No. 1 of 1876—was granted to every one holding property and residing in the State, or failing the property qualification, to any one who was qualified by one year's residence, was now repealed, and Law No. 7 of 1882 provided instead, that aliens could become naturalised and enfranchised after five years' residence, thus attaining the status of the oldest citizen.

In 1890 Law No. 4 was passed, creating the second Volksraad, and altering the Grondwet or Constitution accordingly. By this law full electoral privileges were only attainable after fourteen years' residence in the State, and the possession of the other qualifications of religion and property.

Law No. 3 of 1894 purports to supersede all other laws. Therein it is closely laid down that all persons born in the State, or who may have established their domicile there in 1876, are entitled to full political privileges. Those who have settled in the country since can become naturalised after a two years' residence, dating from the time at which their names were registered in the . field cornet's book. This naturalisation confers the privilege of voting for local officials, field cornets, landdrosts, and for members of the 2nd Raad. It is, however, stipulated that children born in the country shall take the status of their fathers. The naturalised subject, after having been qualified to vote in this manner, becomes eligible for a seat in the 2nd Volksraad, i.e. four years after the registration of his name in the field cornet's book. After he shall have been qualified to sit in the 2nd Volksraad for ten years he may obtain the full burgher rights or political privileges, provided the majority of burghers in his ward will signify in writing their desire

that he should obtain them, and provided the President
and executive shall see no objection to granting them.
It is thus clear that assuming the field cornet's records
be honestly and properly compiled, and be available
for reference (which they are not), the immigrant,
after fourteen years' probation, during which he shall
have given up his own country, has the privilege of
obtaining burgher rights, should he be willing and able
to induce the majority of a hostile clique to petition
in writing on his behalf, and should he then escape
the veto of the President and executive.

Besides these laws yet another precaution was
taken to keep all the power in the hands of the Boers.
The various towns which had formerly been entitled
to representation in Parliament were deprived of this
right, and have remained disfranchised ever since.   Is
it to be wondered at that Advocate Papenfus, in the
striking letter which he addressed lately to President
Steyn, should say : " I can safely assert that I have
failed to discover, during my residence here, how this
State can justify its claim to be called a Republic.
Leaving on one side, for the present, any mention of the
thousands of industrious citizens from over sea, who for
years have made it their home, how very few burghers
of the Free State (and those only for reasons which will
be apparent later on), and how very few others, comparatively speaking, of South African birth, who have
been peaceful and law-abiding citizens, of long and
honourable residence, have been politically enfran-

chised. I hold it to be the just right of every law-abiding individual, who has been resident for a reasonable number of years in any country which lays claim to be considered a civilised State, and who has a vested interest in that country, and who will swear allegiance to the government of that country, to claim and demand political enfranchisement. This is, in my humble opinion, the creed of true Republicanism, and this also is the basis of government and enfranchisement in the Orange Free State.

"But this is no Republic. Not only are thousands of law-abiding citizens at present without political privileges, but they are for ever debarred from obtaining them, and the barbarous spectacle is presented of a State claiming to be recognised and respected by the civilised world as a free people, and laying claim to a Republican form of government, excluding children born of the soil from citizenship."

That is a state of things which cannot continue. We must do right ourselves, not to conciliate the Boers, but because it is right; but they must understand clearly that we shall expect them to do what is right also, and that if they fail to do it we shall stand by the Uitlanders in the struggle that must come sooner or later. In all probability, if they see that we are in earnest, they will be only too willing to meet us half-way; for most of their mistakes have arisen through fear: a fear that it must be our first duty to allay. To use Mr. Chamberlain's words, "But as a

Dutch Government ourselves, as well as an English Government, it ought to be our object, in endeavouring to secure the redress of these grievances, to carry with us our Dutch fellow-subjects."

The prosperity of South Africa lies not in the hands of the ultra-English, or of the ultra-Dutch, but in those of the moderate men, whose one desire is reconciliation and peace.

Under the leadership of Mr. Rose-Innes, a man for whom all parties have the most cordial esteem, they are already strong in the Cape. They deprecate violence and race feeling, and will support progressive measures by whichever party they may be brought forward.

They, and the allied party in the Republics, are every day growing stronger, and, though in the heat of an election they may be swept aside, it is they who will weld the South African States into one country.

If that country were anywhere but in Africa, it would to a certainty strive to render itself independent of the mother-land: just as in families the children strive to become independent of their parents. It is a natural law which is at work in every colony, and as impossible to stem as Canute found it to stem the rising tide. No amount of imperialistic adjuration will influence it. But South Africa is not a pure colony. It occupies a middle position between a colony and a dependency. In a colony the original population is gradually replaced by the colonising element. This has been the case both in Australia and in America, where the aborigines have either become, or are rapidly becoming, extinct. In Africa, on the contrary, they are a persistent race, and, under the influence of peace, multiply more rapidly than the colonists. Moreover, in many places, especially in Central Africa, the climate is prohibitive of true colonisation, and in those places and in the native States which we have not yet handed over to the colonists, what we have to aim at is the creation, not of a colony, but of a native dependency, governed, like India, by British officials.

The existence of such a dependency in their midst would effectually preserve the connection of the South African States with the mother - country, and would prevent the undesirable intrusion of any of the other European nations. It is a dependency, moreover, that we are bound in honour to maintain, because the native chiefs invariably desire to place themselves directly under the protection of the Queen, and not under that of the various colonial governments. They have a feeling of *personal* loyalty to the Great Mother of them all, ardent and easily evoked, which properly controlled may well win for us in time the honourable possession of the entire continent. An African empire would be easier to govern than our Indian empire, because the natives of Africa have even less cohesion amongst themselves than the Indian races, and a more childlike faith in the wisdom and integrity of our rule.

It is a faith that we have too often betrayed, but which it is not yet too late to justify.

To shrink from native conquest is absurd. It is by conquest that all the native races hold the title to their land, the Matabili especially. They fully recognise its validity, and their own conquests are attended by abominable and unutterable cruelty.

Extend our sphere of influence, and if war be forced upon us, conquer, and then rule sternly, but with absolute justice: that is the rule a native reverences, the only kind of rule under which he will prosper. The dark regions which have been hidden for so long are rapidly unfolding before our view with all their boundless possibilities of wealth and power and prosperity. Our feet are on the threshold, and turn back now we cannot. But for the sake of our good name, because of their deteriorating effect upon our national character, we ought not to permit ourselves to adopt methods, and to commit deeds. which we expect from savages, but which are inconsistent with the character of a Christian people.

INDEX

Printed by BALLANTYNE, HANSON & Co.
Edinburgh & London